MW01229846

Steelside Queens…

Inside of the Trap

By

Lacy A. Pertee

This is a work of fiction. Any resemblance of any characters, names, or incidents are purely coincidental.

Copyright July 2020

This book is dedicated to Antonio Davenport

a.k.a

Moon

His energy will always be everlasting, even if his name isn't. A one of a kind builder and not a destroyer who loved and provided for all of his beloved family and friends alike.

R.I.P

I am also giving a special shout out to Raymond "Uncle Ray" Olivis, Truly a G's G. Without the presence of your life none of this story would have been possible. You are the #1 Comrade!!!

R.I.P

_____

Chapter 1   (July 2007)

Major Parker walked to his desk frustrated and exasperated by the reports in front of him. He is sure that this has to be a record number of officers fired in one month. Many incidents were isolated. In all, there were 16 officers fired. Most of them rookies on probation and hadn't been at the Baltimore City Detention Center for even a year. Those terminated included 14 female officers and two male officers. One of the women, Officer Bridgette Blackwell, turned out to be a runner. She just left her job and didn't return to the scene of the stash of tobacco found in the desk on her section.

Major Parker sat flabbergasted: **CONTRABAND!** The word stood in boldface print on 15 of the reports. Oh, for those who don't know what contraband is in a jail or prison environment, contraband is the things that are not allowed inside of the institution. Obvious contraband are cigarettes, drugs, alcohol, weapons, cell phones; as well as other vices. One of the officers caught gave an inmate a portable Play-Station. The detainees can be very influential and persuasive when it comes to getting an officer to violate the trust of the position. But as usual, they are almost always persuaded by the proverbial common denominator... MONEY! However, this new era of young female officers are becoming influenced by the minds, the money and the so-called gang culture of the men in their charge.

Major Parker stood prepared to address the 3to11 B shift after the roll call and before the assignment of their respective posts of the day. The 3 to 11 B-shift is the most violent and troublesome time in the jail. Thirteen of the sixteen officers fired for delivering contraband are B shift employees. Over 80% of them female. That's right! There are too many women in charge of the most violent men in Baltimore City. Some are the murderers that murdered for all and nothing. There are also several drug dealers that influence the guards and everyone else with cash. The best and worst:

schemers, scammers, manipulators, perverts, freaks, gang leaders, flunkies, and pretenders. In all, there are over three thousand of the accused wretched of Baltimore City's grassroots. The Major could not fathom what has become of his profession. He's been an employee of City Jail for over 30 years and because of such a troublesome time, he is certain that this will be his last year of working in this Godforsaken jail. There is just no way in hell can he take another complete year of this new breed. Discretion is not this generation's strongest point.

He walked into the room where the B shift supervisor, Lt. Gibson, began calling the roll and briefing the troops before taking their posts. Major Parker scanned the room before sitting. He couldn't help but to notice, once again, how young the women are sitting there in the Correctional Officer's uniform. Many of the women were youthful eighteen and twenty something year olds. *Naive.* They are at least green to the criminal minds of City Jail inmates. A lot of them look to be fresh out of high school and off of the Social Service's roll. No wonder the inmates are killing each other in the jail with real switchblades. Not homemade shivs or shanks. Switchblades! He thought to himself, *'How many of these young girls are related to these inmates?'* Although the administration had done its best to hire officers that lived in the surrounding counties, a lot of the young women lived in the city. The welfare to work program helped young females make the transition from sitting at home smoking weed, watching soap operas and yelling at babies into getting a G.E.D and then on to a job in Corrections and Safety. A lot of the women came to work straight from the hood and out of the projects. These are sisters, cousins, aunts, friends and baby mommas of the inmates. The entire jail has become an extension of the hood.

Lt. Gibson finished assigning posts and then turned the roll call over to Major Parker.

"Good evening, people," he began. "As you all know,

we now have a record number of officers who've not only lost their jobs, but in some cases, have been arrested. The trafficking of contraband into this institution *IS* not tolerated!" He said, raising his voice.

"The state of Maryland is preparing to send in covert agents as officers and inmates alike to combat the corruption that is ever so prevalent in this jail! For those of you that think we're playing games and decide that you want to continue smuggling contraband into this jail; or, you even know about stuff getting in, your head will roll like a wheel going down Greenmount Avenue, long and far! So, I suggest that if you are in violation of bringing contraband into the institution, or you are turning a blind eye with the knowledge of what's going on, let it end today! If it does not end, we will get you...

"I've never, in my thirty odd years of working for The Department of Corrections encountered so many derelict officers. Some of you are worse than the inmates! A lot of you young women just want to be down with a thug! Oh yeah, I know what's goin' on! Y'all gonna go down in prison right alongside of the thugs that you wanna be down with!" He said, sarcastically making an attempt to come across as hip. "They won't care one way or the other about your dumb assess losing your job just as long as they get you to do what they want you to do! Damn your job, your children, and your bills! I'm here to say; damn you, your children, your bills, or whatever if we catch you! Is that clearly understood?!" Major Parker's voice resonated within the silence of the meeting room. "...And you better hope that we don't lock your stupid ass up!"

"Yes, sir!" everyone replied in unison. He turned his back to the officers shaking his head from side to side as he angrily marched out of the roll call slamming the door. He left Lt. Gibson standing before the troops. The officers maintained the silence and began eyeing one another suspiciously.

"You are all dismissed to your posts," said Lt. Gibson. She stood at the head of the room alone in her thoughts. She remembered quite a few years back that Major Parker himself

4

was under investigation for bringing in drugs and food for a Baltimore Kingpin by the name of Rudy Wilson. Rudy and Major Parker were childhood friends. That controversy began in her first year as a City Jail officer and happened years before the state took over the jail. She thought to herself how he had some nerve to act like he is all upset and self-righteous. Although he is right about all of the young females from the projects and straight from high school. They were making it hard for her crew by being so damn dumb and careless. In every generation the new breed always make shit hot, but now it is ridiculous.

Lt. Gibson's thoughts were disturbed by her girlfriend and partner Lacy Landon. Officer Landon had been her best friend for the past ten years. That's when they were both COs without rank. Landon is still a CO II because she never wanted the responsibilities that come with rank. She makes just as much money, if not more, doing overtime. She also get annual raises the same as everyone else.

"Snap out of it, girl, and let's put our heads together. We got to figure out when we gonna get the rest of the stash in here. My car payment is coming up soon," Landon said in a whisper.

"Bitch, be calm. Ain't nobody tell you to go out and buy a brand new Acura any ol' way. You already got a Benz. You ain't having no problems with it, either. You're always spending money," she said, twisting her face and putting extra emphasis on her words to express the point being made about Landon's spending. "Besides, everything is gonna' be cool. Things gonna go right back to normal. In the meantime, we'll just have to chill and let these stupid young heifers, that don't have a brain, keep on getting jammed up. Our thing is going to be fine. It's just too bad that Bridgette got knocked," said Lt. Gibson.

"Yeah, it's messed up how that young dumb ass girl snitched on Bridgette. The dumb ass boyfriend ran his mouth about him and Bridgette's business to her dumb ass," said

Landon.

"I thought that BGF guys keep their business to themselves." Gibson expressed.

"Well, I guess they do, but you know how these niggas get weak and tell their girls everything," Landon said.

"Yeah, I'm hip. But, that shit is too close to us, and now Bridgette is going to have to find another job," said Gibson. "Well, she's smart. Thank goodness that she didn't go to her post when she was called and decided to head straight to the car. They forced her to resign instead of being terminated for job abandonment and giving her a contraband charge for all of the tobacco that they found in the desk on her post."

"I know. She said that she could have denied it and put up a fight, but fuck it... She said that this job is beginning to get to her anyway. She told me that she has a little money saved up from the past year of us doing our thing. She wants us to meet her after work at the Icon," said Landon.

"That's what's up. I'm there... I'll see you queens at break time," said the lieutenant.

"Gibson!" Landon called. "Girl, I need to borrow ten dollars for lunch. You got it?" Officer Landon asked her dearest friend. Lt. Gibson reached into her pocket and pulled out a ten dollar bill.

"Bitch, you need to learn how to save some money, I swear. You stay on some fly girl shit, with your Chanel #5 broke ass! Huzzy!" She scolded her girlfriend.

"Girl, please," Landon said, taking the money and not thinking twice about the insults. "You just do you and watch me do me," she responded and walked off to G-section, which is the post that she's assigned to. This is her regular section. She needed to talk to Uncle Twin, the leader of the BGF (Black Guerilla Family). They are the biggest and strongest among the prison families, or what civilians would call gangs. She and her crew had to chill out for a minute and the BGF would have to find other horses to bring in their contraband.

At least until the heat dies off. Nobody's horses were as serious and dependable as Lt. Gibson's and her "Queens". They were always on time and delivered in bulk. They charged fifty dollars to deliver each can of tobacco, a hundred for every ounce of weed, a hundred per cell phone, and fifty for each gram of heroin. There were special request for miscellaneous items such as cds, jewelry, air fresheners, blunts, cigarette lighters, etc. Those items were on a case by case basis. In a month's time, they would smuggle about 500 cans of tobacco, 25 pounds of weed, 50 cell phones and about 100 to 150 grams of heroin. After paying the potato chip delivery man to give the packages to the commissary officer, the women netted about 50 thousand dollars a month to be split five ways.

Besides, Lt. Doreatha Gibson and C.O. Lacy Landon, the crew consisted of Officers Belinda Berry, Officer Glorious Hope; who is a lesbian, and Officer Bridgette Blackwell; who is now jobless after walking off of the job. Information given to the administration by a jealous girlfriend of an inmate that she was bringing tobacco and drugs to done her in. Bridgette was tipped off to what was going down after stashing the goods on the tier she was assigned to. She went on her break while the major and two Baltimore City policemen were waiting for her to come back to her post. Needless to say, she left the jail, got into her car and waved goodbye to being a Correctional Officer. They couldn't charge her for a crime because they never caught her hand to hand with the goods. So, they forced her to resign for leaving her shift without notification.

Bridgette had a nice piece of money saved up because she sensed that the greed would catch up to her. After six years she didn't care much for her career choice any longer. The pay wasn't bad and her benefits were good but she began to hate the job and everything that came along with it.

Landon walked onto G-Section and began to take her inmate count. As she approached the front of Uncle Twin's cell, she stopped, looked at him, then she spoke. "I'm gonna hit your door when I finish my count. Come and see me at my desk before you run around on the tier, o.k.," she instructed him.

"Of course, I'll be right there… *Damn girl*! What's that scent you got on today?" Twin asked, admiring Landon's fragrance.

"It's J-Lo. You like it?" She blushed.

"Yes, in Beed," he replied. "Hurry up and hit my door!" Twin yelled from the bars of his cell when Landon walked away, continuing on with her count.
Just before she completed the count, an inmate in a cell by himself jumped up off of his bunk butterball naked and greased from head to toe with baby oil, black and shiny. Once Landon got to the front of his cell, he grabbed onto the bars and then posed for her. She'd become accustomed to such perversion. She looked him up and down.

"What 'choo gon' do wit' that little shit? Put your damn clothes on. I'm tired of you getting naked every time I come around for count. I got a trick for your ass tonight," she said, before walking off.

"You know you like it. I can see it in your eyes," Freaky Ty said, laughing. Years ago, when she started working in the jail, this kind of behavior shocked and frightened her. She almost quit right on the spot on many occasions. She couldn't believe that men could be so disrespectful and vulgar, and just downright nasty. It surprised her that some men could be capable of such an animalistic display of behavior. What made it so bad is that on the streets you could never imagine that a lot of these men would take part in that kind of debasement. They are neighbors, cousins, brothers, fathers and friends. Men that you see every day. The real freaky ones would wait for Officer Landon to come on the tier and masturbate as she walked by. In their demented

8

minds, they believed that this behavior endeared them to her. If not, why would she wear her pants so tight? What is the reason for the perfume? Her hair is always done up like she is going out. This becomes the thought process. Nevertheless, this is how she dressed in general, but you couldn't tell these freaks that she didn't come to work dressed for them. She made up her mind right then to have freaky Ty dealt with.

With her inmate count completed and before she sat at the desk to do her paperwork to record her status in the log book, she opened up Uncle Twin's cell. Like a dutiful soldier, he immediately followed the instruction to come see her.

"What's up, sugar?" Twin asked, smiling as always.

"Ain't too much. Blackwell won't be comin' back." Landon reported to him, sitting at her desk. Twin leaned over the desk so that no one could hear them talk. The voices echoed on the tier when very quiet, and in the jail people were nosey as hell and had bionic ears.

"The word is she got caught with a pound of weed and some phones," Twin said to confirm what the rumor mill reported.

"Heeellllll, no! These so-called men are worse than females, with their gossiping ways. They found some tobacco on her post that she was supposed to be dropping off to your comrade Jay. That nigga's girl blew her spot and ratted her out because she thought that she and Jay had some kind of a sexual relationship going on in here. She's a dumb bitch! Blackwell said his baby's momma was handling all of his money. How's he gonna help her dumb ass now? He's cut off, Twin." Landon said, agitated. Her decision was definite.

"Yes, that was some dumb shit to do. Blackwell didn't get locked-up, did she?" Twin asked with concern.

"No, she didn't. Somebody put her down before she went back to her post. Instead of going back, she just left the building and went home," Landon explained. "I'm surprised at Jay. He seems like a cool guy. Y'all need to straighten' him out for that one. He cost my girl her job and we gonna have to

9

shut down for a couple of weeks. Tell your comrades to keep their business to themselves. I mean, nobody should know anything about what each other do as it relates to getting anything from us... Damn! Niggas can run their mouths worse than bitches," Landon said.

"I'm sorry about Blackwell; and you're right about Jay being a stand up warrior that is firm with his spear. Maybe he shouldn't have said anything to his girl about the details of his business. I'm gonna send instructions that if anyone discuss any of our business concerning our horses with any civilians, they will be sanctioned severely. They can't even discuss business with one another concerning any business they have individually with the Queens as well. We'll have to give Jay a pass on this one because I don't believe that he thought his girl would do something stupid like that. He's coming up. He's one of my best seeds, but I will have a serious word with him. It looks like we'll have to suffer for a minute, huh?" Uncle Twin expressed.

"You got that, buddy," she said.

"Oh, well. I'm going to put Jama down with what's going on and give them their instructions." Uncle Twin said to Landon, using the swahilli term for family, referring to the men of the BGF. "Is there anything else that I can do for you, sugar? You know that I fall in love with you several times a day when you're near me," Twin said, in his slick voice.

"Uh, huh. I just bet you do, and as soon as you not near me, you fall in love with the next CO that you can get to put in work for you. How long you been here waitin' to get in court?" She asked.

"About 18 months," he answered.

"And how long you been on this tier?" She asked him.

"Oh, I would say a year or so," said Twin.

"Now, I have been working this section for over six months. Every time you get locked up the jail sluts fall for that slick shit you be talkin'. I ain't fall for it then and I damn sure ain't gonna start now. Besides that, even though your old ass is fine and sharp as hell, I don't need no man that stay in and out of jail, and I definitely don't mix business with pleasure, *Mr.* Uncle Twin," Landon informed him with a sassy tone.

"See, that's why I fucks wit' you, suga'. You get straight to the point, wit' yo' fine ass," Twin said. "Well, is there anything else that I can do for you before I run around the jail to do what I do?"

"I don't need anything right now but, I want something done about that nasty ass nigga Freaky Ty in cell 74. I'm sick and tired of him greasing up and holding his dick in his hand when I come around to count. He's gone too far! When he's out on the tier, he will stand at the grill from the time yall out for rec, until it's time to lock in, with a hole in his pocket and his hand moving inside of it. I promise you, if you take care of him, I'll throw in a bonus when the horses are let out of the gate." She promised.

"Say no more. It's done... Will there be anything else?" Twin asked.

"No. I guess that's it. You can go ahead and be the president of the jail," she said to him. Twin held the president of the Inmate Advisory Board post, which allowed him to roam free in and around the jail. His pass held his picture on it. Other board members had special passes, too. He maintained more access to places in the jail than most officers when he wasn't in his cell. He also held the strongest influence among the inmate population. He truly ran Baltimore City Jail.

"I'll see you at count time," he said to Landon.

"All right, sugar," she said to him, playfully.

Twin walked off and headed towards the long hallway that separated the north side of the detention center from the south side. He needed to holler at his young comrade Jay about his control; or, lack thereof, concerning his girl's mouth. They could not allow anything to jeopardize the best operation in the jail. There were other freelance horses, but none of them like the ones that they were plugged into.

The BGF protected these exclusive Queens on the

11

inmate side of the situation. These women provided goods for the Muslims, Crips, and the Bloods in the jail, also. The others had to pay a little more than what the BGF had to pay, so nobody could to fuck that up. Twin decided that the family would get two thousand dollars to CO Blackwell for losing her job. Jay would have to repay a thousand dollars back to the family's finances because, his girl caused it all.

Lt. Gibson and her team were assigned to the north side of the jail. She began to make her rounds and walk from tier to tier. This is the part of the job that she relished. She interacted with the inmates and officers alike. Most of the time the inmates would have a myriad of complaints or questions for her just to get some attention from a female. Although she'd gotten a little thick and places on her body were starting to succumb to the laws of gravity, she knew exactly what to wear that would put it all back into place to elicit comments from the sex starved inmates. The comments ranged from compliments to downright disrespectful insults. Most of the hurtful ones come without a face attached to it. There would be a loud voice in a crowd, or she would walk on a tier and the voice would be too far away to pinpoint. Sometimes the insults made her laugh, too. Then there were other times that the comments were so blatant and hurtful that if she couldn't identify the culprit of the insult, she would make the entire section suffer by taking the recreation for a day, a week, a month, or whatever time period came out of her mouth from that section. Her psychology is that the inmates will be mad at the person that done the name calling and disrespect. The men sometimes physically punished the person, or just gave him up. Sometimes it worked. She respected the really hard and witty men that were not scared to identify themselves, and didn't mind a good verbal combat from time to time. Lt. Gibson respected a man that said what he meant and meant what he said to her face, and not hide behind the crowd. Most of those confrontations ended with her developing a communication of mutual respect between her and the inmate. On occasions, it would lead to a relationship; and once the inmate got out, they could potentially get the coodie cat. However, she is very discreet and hate men that run their mouths. She always talk terrible and berate men that she think are weak. As far as the officers under her command are concerned, she's seen it all. Inmate officer fraternization at City Jail is the norm. Back in the day, it was a little more discreet and not as open. With the hiring of so many young women, it's like a soap opera. There are lots of relationships between inmates and officers, officers and officers, the inmate visitors and officers, male officers and inmates; also, female officers and female officers. Sex, money, drugs and mayhem is the order of operations on the streets and in the jail. It's all done so clandestine that you could be around it and never know that it's going on. Everything is a secret in the jail.

Lt. Gibson is a fighter. She never hesitate to step in and separate two combatants. She can rumble with the best of them. She's seen so much blood from inmate battles until it became a natural part of her reality; which is why she drinks on her way to work, at lunch break and the four nights a week that she meets her queens at the Icon Inn. That is her favorite place to unwind. It's located on Kresson Street, in Highlandtown.

Lt. Gibson is also like a big sister and mother figure to quite a few of the young female COs. A lot of them call her Ma. She saved a few of them from losing their jobs because she has befriended the right people throughout her career as a Correctional Officer.

She is very smart person, too. She uses her wits to choose the accomplices in her hustle very carefully. She's the leader of the best and most reliable horses in the jail. Blackwell is the closet that they've ever gotten to her crew, and they still don't know a thing. She ran her shit for six years and lives well from it, too. Landon is her voice with the inmates for business.

Gibson is very cunning and knows the way of the criminal mind so well that she uses the same tactics to get things done. However, she has a weakness for the muscular gang leaders that she befriends. Her problem is that she always take care of them but, become disappointed when they don't return the sentiments when they are released. Some guys sell her dreams of being with her. A lot of them are incapable of being tied down, and the streets are all that they know. Others are boys in men bodies. She grew to despise that type of a man. She didn't have a problem with putting that ass out of her house once she recognize that all they want is a free ride. Her heart has been torn apart enough.

Yes, in Beed! Doreatha Gibson really enjoys her job, and at 38 years old with no children, it is very fulfilling. Her job is her life. These are her children. Sometimes life away from the job gets lonesome. The violence on the job has transformed her into a person full of aggression but, at heart, she is still a woman. Her aggressive demeanor also comes from the fact that so many black men has disappointed her throughout the years. *Most* of the black men that she experience on a day to day basis are the criminal element. This standard of black man made her liken some of them to children that refuse to grow up. She can be condescending towards most of them because she feel that so many of them live life just to get over on somebody in one way or another. They play games while dealing drugs, looking for pleasure in material things, fighting like children, and using guns *waaaaay* too much and unnecessarily so. It takes an insecure and childlike mind to seek a weapon to face every disagreement and conflict, she thought, because most children lack the experience and maturity that it takes to think in terms of conflict resolution and problem solving. A man thinks and prepares himself for battle and defense. He lives to protect himself as well as his family against forces that would destroy him. Not destroy just to destroy. Although the black men excite her, as a collective, she's grown to be very disappointed

14

in them. She knows that Baltimore city spends $37 million a year in overtime for policeman to lock their asses up, while at the same time laying off teachers and closing schools, libraries, summer camps, and recreation centers. They help to aid in their collective demise. So, now her job is often that of a mother, a big sister, and in some instances a lover to the thousands of black men that have descended from the men and women brought into the city by way of ships docked at Baltimore's Inner Harbor and sold at the World's Famous Lexington Market. The job comes with some perks and some headaches, but it's still all good... Sometimes.

Lt. Gibson walked onto P and Q sections, which were the only dormitories inside of the main building of the jail. As soon as she walked through the grill and walked up the stairs to P section, the shit got real.

"Lt. Gibson, why they so late taking us out for rec?! Aren't we suppose to get yard today?!" An inmate yelled.

"Lt. Gibson, the CO won't let me use the phone! I don't know what his problem is!" Another inmate that stood next to the first inmate expressed. They were both trying to get her attention at the same time with their individual concerns. The children are restless and they want Mommy.

She sat down at the desk intentionally ignoring their pleas. She signed the log book and had a brief word with the officer working the section. He's African and a rookie. Africans are being hired as correctional officers just as much as the young females. You could rarely, if ever, get one of them to bend the rules. They are, for the most part, strictly by the book. They would turn in a co-worker with the same zeal as disciplining an inmate. Gibson made it her business to deal with them in a very strict professional manner. She stood and turned her attention to the inmates that continued to call out to her.

"Now, I'ma say this one time and one time only. I'm going to talk to you guys one at a time. The first one of you to interrupt my conversation with the other one, that's it, I'm leaving; you got that? Now, you go first," she said to the inmate that said he needed to see her about some clothes.

"Well, my name is Isaac James. I've been over here for ten days! My people came with my package and they wouldn't let me get it! My girl came with the children! Well, only one of them mine. Anyway, she can't keep bringing three children from west to east carrying my package, lieutenant! Can you see why they won't let me get my stuff?!" Isaac James complained.

Gibson picked up the telephone that was on the desk. She looked at the inmate that bragged to other inmates about how she is the one to see with a problem.

"Yo, I told you she good peoples. She gets on top o' shit." He said.

"What do you say your name is?" She asked.

"Come on, Lt. Gibson, you remember me. My name is Issac James. I was over here last year," he said. She vaguely remembered his face, but she didn't know him for sure. However, she relayed the information to the person on the other end of the phone and continued to look Issac dead in his face as the party on the other end of the phone explained to the lieutenant that Issac received two packages in the jail already. Her instincts were correct. He's lying.

"Boy, don't ever stop me for anything! If the whole jail is gonna rape you ten different ways in your ass, don't even ask me to put you on PC, 'cause I'mo' let em split yo' ass ten ways times ten! Get da hell away from this grill. You been here for over a month and you got two packages already.

"But, I thought when they move me to another section that the days start over," Isaac said, lying again. He knew that he couldn't get another package. He was lucky to get two.

"If you don't get away from this grill, I'ma blast you in the face with this pepper spray," she said, gritting between clenched teeth and holding her waist where the mace was attached to her utility belt.

"Damn, Lt. Gibson, you ain't gotta get all salty on

16

me," he said, walking away. "I told you, yo. She too damn smart sometimes… a fat bitch," he said in a low voice to a friend while walking away from where the conversation began. She made an attempt to respond, but she stopped just so his chump ass keeps on moving. She turned her attention to the next inmate complaining about recreation.

"What 'choo want!" She barked.

"I, I, I just want to know when our section is goin' in 'da yard?" He asked, a little hesitantly. After witnessing her exchange with the previous inmate, he didn't want to be the next target of her wrath.

"This section will be going into the courtyard immediately after the dinner meal. Do you have any problems with that?" She answered, directing her attention to him, as well as other inmates standing around listening for her answer.

"No, ma'am. I don't," said the second inmate, humbled.

"Now, what seems to be the problem with you, sir?" She asked in her most professional tone with a hint of sarcasm.

"Check this out, lieutenant. I asked this jungle boogie cat if I could use the phone before anybody else. He made a phone list and skipped all over me. I don't know who 'da hell he thinks he is, with his African ass. He knows that I asked him first," the inmate complained.

"Is this true, Officer Laryea?" The lieutenant asked her officer.

"Deez iz *not* true. I will not allow heem to Deesarespect me! He call me faggot. I'm not faggot! I don't deal in 'dat stuff! We don't have 'dat in my country! Girly boy. What dee fuck iz heez problem?" The officer explained, very upset. He batted his eyes making his point. This allowed Lt. Gibson to understand why the inmate called him a fag. His mannerisms were feminine to a young man who has been raised in a hard oppressive reality. In the young Blackman's reality he believes that every disagreement with another individual, or every confrontation with a person in authority

17

should be met with a hard manner or aggressive response to prove that he is a man in charge.

"Sir, did you call my officer out of his name?" She asked.

"Well, I wasn't talkin' to him. I was talkin' to my man right here," the inmate answered, nodding his head at a guy standing close by. "But, did you see how he did that shit with his eyes? Look like he likes that dick to me," said the inmate, as a matter of fact. Everyone within earshot that listened Gibson's exchange with the inmate began to laugh. She looked at the inmates and they stopped laughing just as quickly as they started. She hated nosey men. However, it took strength for her to resist the urge to laugh as well.

"Now, look. I'm not going to have you disrespect my officers. Open the grill, Mr. Laryea," instructed the lieutenant. He obeyed her command, and when he let the inmate out of the dormitory, the officer and inmate both eyed one another as though they would begin fighting on the spot. "You, come with me, sir," she said to the inmate. He followed her dutifully down the stairs and through the main grill of P section. They walked through yet another grill, down more stairs and then onto Q section. "What's your name?"

"My name is Elliot," he answered.

"Look, don't be giving my officers a hard way to go. They have a job to do and they don't need you making it any harder than it has to be. Now, go ahead over there and use *that* phone," she said, "I have to talk to Officer Hope, and when I've finished, you should be finishing your call, too."

"Thanks, lieutenant. I'mo take you out when I get uptown, for real," Elliot said, smiling on his way to the phone. Lt. Gibson thought Elliot to be sexy for real. He seems confident and hard. That is enough for her. She eyed him as he walked over to the phones before sitting at the desk to sign the log book.

"I've seen that look in your eyes befo', ho'," Officer Hope said to her friend.

18

"What're you talkin' 'bout, Hope?" Gibson asked.

"Don't play dumb. Plus, he younger than you, too, and he looks like he lift weights. You can fool some of the people most of the time, but I ain't no fool, bitch," said Hope. Hope is down with the queens. She knew Gibson well and could tell that she mentally molested the inmate that she brought to use the phone. Gibson looked at Elliot and then at Hope. She witnessed Gibson close her eyes and shiver as though a quick chill ran through her body.

"He is the truth! Momma need to see 'bout him!" Gibson announced in a hush to her friend.

"Woman, you are sick," said Hope. "What's goin' on with Blackwell?" She asked, quickly changing the subject with a more serious tone.

"She's fine. She told me that she has a nice piece of paper saved. She'll probably collect unemployment for a minute because, they couldn't say if or not she was connected to the shit. She also has money in her 401k, so, I guess that she'll be ok, until she can find a suitable job. She wants us to meet her at the Icon tonight," Gibson informed Hope.

"Blackwell's my girl. I feel a little bad for her, but I know she's strong. I guess I'll call Puddin' and tell her to meet me there," said Hope.

"I thought that the two of you were on the outs. Didn't you put her out?" Gibson asked. "Y'all are always fighting."

"I started to put her out, but, I just can't. I love her and I don't want to lose her, but she needs to understand that her laziness and partying is driving me crazy. I mean, she'll keep a job for a few months and then she'll get fired because she thinks the world is on her time and that the job needs her like she can't be replaced. I'm always picking up the pieces when she loses her jobs. Bills and everything fall on me. If it wasn't for Lamar, I would have put her ass out a long time ago. She lucky that I love her son like he is my own child. I'm getting tired of the bullshit. She about to trade our life of happiness for moments of partying," Hope confided. "The Icon is a good place for us to talk and air out our differences with one another."

"Then y'all gonna go home and have sex all night. That'll only last about a week or so, until the next time that she gets on your nerves or make you wanna whip her ass. Girl, I just think that you need a good piece of a real stiff dick in your life and some strong muscles to hold onto while you are cumming. You should try it sometimes," said Gibson.

"Go 'head, slut. I got my own dick and I ain't had a dick since a dick had me," Hope responded.

"That's why you need a piece and a taste to go along with it," Gibson said, while eyeing Elliot on the phone.

"Girl, you's a hoe... Anyway, they moved that guy Jay down here in dorm three," Hope informed Gibson, changing the conversation. Gibson immediately stood from the desk and walked to dorm three.

"Jayson Hill?!" She called out. Then she radioed for two escort officers from her two-way. Jay walked over to the front of dorm three.

"What's up, lieutenant?" He asked.

"I want you to pack your stuff. You'll be moving," she answered.

"I just moved over here today from the section. Why am I moving again?" Jay asked. "I'll tell you after you get packed," she said, walking back to the desk. Just then, Uncle Twin came down the stairs onto Q section.

"How are yall doing today?" Twin began.

"I'm cool. What's up with you?" Officer Hope responded. Lt. Gibson sat there stoically.

"So, what's going on, Lt. Gibson. I heard what happened to your home girl. I promise that I'll do everything in my power to make sure nothing like that ever happens again," said Twin, being careful to choose his words. He knew that the lieutenant *never* talked business, unless she initiated the conversation.

"Whatever, Twin," she responded. Twin walked away,

stopping briefly to talk with Elliot. They shook hands and began the discussion into their business. Twin walked over to dorm three and started talking to Jay. Jay explained the situation to Twin about moving to another section and not knowing what part of the jail that they were sending him to, or why. While listening to Jay, Uncle Twin noticed two escort officers talking to Lt. Gibson. Then she led the escorts to dorm three and then excused Twin from standing in front of the grille.

"Are you packed, Mr. Hill?" Gibson asked. Jay held up his belongings that were in a huge transparent trash bag to affirm that he was packed and ready to move. She opened the grille for him to come out of the dormitory. By this time, almost everyone in dorm two and three were watching the officers surround Jay. The inmates began cracking jokes on the officers and asking Jay what's going on and where is he moving to. "Put your hands behind your back," said Gibson.

"What?! I didn't do anything!" Jay yelled.

"We have to put you on administrative segregation for fraternizing with an officer," said Gibson. She made her mind up to put this guy on lock-up to pay for Bridgette losing her job. It wasn't totally his fault, but he is connected to it. Jay stood ready to go down fighting until Uncle Twin gave him a look that implied retreat. Then Twin began to make a plea to Gibson in defense of his comrade.

"Damn, Lt. Gibson. Jay is cool. He not causing any problems. Give him a break on my strength," Twin pleaded.

"The damage has already been done. For now, he has to go. I'll see what I can do about getting him off next week," she said. Twin knew that she lied to him and that she was on some payback shit. They'd known one another for years, and they both came up manipulating and taking charge in their respective positions. Not only did she have the upper hand being a lieutenant, she also is the true leader of their hustle. Although he could get her touched on the streets, he needed her. Plus, that wouldn't do anyone any good. He had to

21

concede and let her have her way.

Jay doesn't know that Gibson is the H.B.I.C. (HEAD BITCH IN CHARGE) of getting their goods into the jail. If he had known, maybe he wouldn't feel so bad about being moved. It would have been his sacrifice for bad business. The way it stood with him now, she is just another police. He relented and obeyed the lieutenant and allowed the two male officers to handcuff him peacefully. Twin picked up Jay's belongings in the bag and carried them along as the officers escorted Jay to T-section; which is the institutions filthy, dirty, stinking and tight ass lock-up tier. This is where you stay locked in all day and all night. You get a shower, maybe twice a week. To a gladiator, it's just another part of the jail. Jay is a gladiator. Uncle Twin will make sure that he has enough weed and tobacco to make his stay comfortable and pass the time away, but there is nothing that he can do to stop the move.

"Girl, you ain't right but, I understand. I guess you gotta make him pay, too," said Hope.

"You daaamn right! Maybe it'll help them sharpen their game. We makin' their stay here comfortable and financially rewarding to those who know what to do. Ain't no way in the world should a nigga fuck that up. Leave the jail business in the jail. His trifling ass girl probably laying another nigga as we speak," Gibson expressed with emotion. "Look, I'm going to finish making my rounds. I'll see you tonight, ok... Come on, Mr. Elliot. I hope you're finished," she said as Elliot said his goodbyes and got off of the phone smiling.

"Oh, your girl must've said the right things, huh?"

"That wasn't no girl! That was my momma. She my number one girl," said Elliot, walking up the stairs. Gibson looked back at Hope and winked her eye. Hope waved her hand to tell her go on. The hall officer opened the grille to let the both of them off of Q section and then opened the downstairs grill to let Elliot onto P section.

"Thanks a lot, Lt. Gibson. I mean that, for real," Elliot

expressed.

"Don't mention it. Stop giving the African such a hard time. And I hope that you know you owe me one. If you have a problem with any of my officers, just let me know, but don't be starting no shit, you hear me?"

"You got my word," he said.

"Are you with Twin and them?" She asked him.

"What choo' talkin' 'bout?" He responded.

"Don't play dumb. You know what I mean. You BGF?" she asked, putting her hands on her hip. Elliot looked at her up and down. She's not too bad. A little thick. Just like he likes his women. Her age made the catch a little challenging. Plus, she *is* a lieutenant! A good catch! He can sense that she is all on him.

"I'm *that*. You know; in the bush," he answered her. That's how Elliot identified his affiliation with BGF. He isn't supposed to tell her this, but a nigga will try to impress any female with whatever he can when he is in jail.

"Mmm, Mmm. I'll talk to you later, *Mr.* Elliot," she said, strutting with her sexy walk down the long hallway. Elliot continued to look at her walk away from him. She took a few steps and then looked behind her back to see if he continued checking out her goods. Elliot waved at her to acknowledge the fact. She threw her head up and waved goodbye from behind, and continued on with her sexy stroll, with nothing but ass moving and sashaying from side to side.

Twin helped Jay carry his property to lock up. Then he made his way around the jail to order all the comrades to never discuss their money business with anybody on the streets unless they are a direct party to the business taking place. They aren't to discuss the business with their wife, girl, mother, brother, sister, or cousin. They were also instructed not to discuss their business with each other; unless the business being discussed involved the other person. Comrades are not to know the specific business of another comrade as it concerns them making money in the jail with weed, tobacco, dope, or anything else that comes from the family unless the parties involved are helping one another. Everyone in BGF knew why.

Most of the comrades never knew that Officer Blackwell was a family horse until the shit hit the fan and the cavalry waited for her to return from her break so that they could take her down. That's just how covert the Steel-side Queens carried it with their hustle.

———————————————

Chapter 2

Belinda Berry walked into the Icon Inn with C.O. Paul Powers. The girls didn't call Delilah by her name. They simply called her Bee. She stood a tall redbone with long luscious legs. Bee, a borderline nymphomaniac, loved men. The only reason that she isn't considered a full fledge nympho is because she always get paid for giving up the koodycat. So, she's more of a hustler that loves to fuck. If your money is right while you are in the jail, and she liked you and what you had in your pants, you might get some of her koodycat. Bee use to be a stripper that previously worked at the Eldorado Club around the corner from their hangout spot, The Icon Inn.

The Icon is a bar and lounge that has a very modest clientele. Bee grew tired of stripping and one night, over five years ago, she met Lacy Landon and Lt. Doreatha Gibson in the Icon having a drink at the bar. Both women convinced

Bee to become a C.O. in the detention center. It was easy for her to join in on their hustle once she became employed and assigned to Gibson's team. The new career and extra money helped to take care of her four daughters. She's 28 years old, and her man habit hadn't changed. She loved the variety of men, but she don't need a man to help her raise her girls. Paul had been digging her and now he started to develop feelings for Bee. She began to see Paul exclusively because he was blowing her back out. She's still not ready for a commitment. He became determined to make her his woman. He's whipped!

"Hello, Bee, and how're you doing, Paul! What brings you here to our spot?" Bridgette asked Paul. He and Bee both sat on the stools to the right of her. Hope, Gibson, and Landon had yet to arrive.

"Well, I want to have a drink with Bee. I won't be here long. I just need a beer and I'll be on my way. I've been drafted to do a double tomorrow and I need all of the rest that I can get," he explained.

25

"I know that's right," she responded to Paul. Bridgette turned her attention to Bee. "What's up, girl?"

"Hey, girl! Come here and give me some love," Bee whined reaching over to Bridgette for an understanding hug. They both embraced briefly, and then sat back on their stools.

"I'm so sorry about what happened," Bee cried.

"It's no big deal. I've been stressed out anyway and I just had to leave. The job's getting to me," she responded. She gave Bee a look to let her know that she isn't going to discuss the business with Paul around. Bee returned with a gaze to let her know that she dare not say a word in front of him. Paul drank his beer without a clue to the body language being spoken. He also expressed sympathy concerning Bridgette losing her job.

The door to the bar opened and Hope's girlfriend Puddin', accompanied by two more girls, entered the lounge. Puddin' greeted Bridgette and Bee and then frowned into Paul's direction before throwing her hand up to speak. The three ladies headed to the booth in the back of the bar. One of them walked over to the jukebox and loaded it with dollar bills so that the music plays continuously. They all ordered drinks from Matt, who is the owner of the bar with his father-in-law and family. Matt also doubled as the bartender and security. He is a HUGE man!

Paul stood after finishing his beer and then planted a kiss on Bee's cheek before saying goodbye to Bridgette. He let Bridgette know that he'll miss working with her and put a twenty on the bar for his beer. Turning to leave, he waved goodbye to Puddin' and her girlfriends, who all seemed to turn their noses up at him. Paul thought to himself, *'Oh, they must be dykes'*, and then bumped into Hope on the way out of the door. Hope entered with Lt. Gibson. He spoke to the both of them leaving the Icon Inn. He looked behind his back before the door to the bar closed completely. He witnessed Hope walk to the girls sitting in the back booth, which confirmed his suspicion. All of Hope's co-workers know that she is gay.

'They taking over the city', he thought to himself.

Gibson walked towards her friends sitting at the bar and Hope greeted Puddin' with a kiss and then spoke to the two girls that sat there in the booth with Puddin'. Hope soon became agitated and expressed herself to her companion.

"Damn, baby, I just wanted *us* to spend time together tonight and talk to you over a few drinks. Why the fuck did you bring Yolanda and Rashon with you?" Hope became bothered by Puddin' and her tag-a-longs. Yolanda and Rashon remained quiet. They knew better than to make Hope mad. She will whip a bitch's ass and some niggas asses, too. But, she's a sucker for Puddin'.

"Come on, Glorious. Don't start the bullshit. You wanted me to meet you here, so I'm here. Won't you just be happy that I came, Damn!" Puddin' responded. Hope felt hurt, embarrassed, and angry by the way Puddin' talked to her in front of their friends. Puddin' sensed Hope's agitation, then she said, "You gonna be talking to your co-workers for a good minute, anyway. I don't want to be all up in y'all business. Rashon and Yolanda came to keep my company until y'all finish." That's a good one that she came up with and she knew it.

"I suppose you're right... here," Hope said, giving Puddin' a twenty, "Y'all go get some drinks."

"Is this it?!" Puddin' asked, taking the bill as though it was a piece of dirt and afraid that it would contaminate the rest of her hand. She expected more. Hope started to ease up, but with this display of ungratefulness from her girlfriend, she grew hurt and angry all over again. However, she didn't say a word. She looked at Puddin' and then at the two girls. With a slight feeling of embarrassment, she walked away and joined her co-workers sitting at the bar.

"What's up, huzzies?" Hope greeted her friends after she approached them. She took a stool at the bar next to Gibson. Bee and Bridgette returned the greetings.

"The bitch done made you mad again. She ain't gonna

27

be satisfied until you beat that ass... Oh, believe me, it's coming, soon" said Gibson, seeing through Hope's attempt to hide her feelings. Hope thought to herself that Gibson didn't miss a thing. She stays on point.

"Where's Landon?" Bridgette asked.

"Oh, she's comin'. She had to stay late and finish some paperwork on account of that freak ass nigga Tyrone Hill got stabbed terribly on her section. They poked his ass 11 times. Landon said he was screaming like a girl," Gibson reported to her friends and co-workers.

"Fuck that nasty ass nigga, Freaky Ty. He is a pervert, anyway. I would be frightened to death to have a freak ass nigga like him around my daughters. He's always flashing his dick at me and talkin' 'bout, '*You know you want it!*' All shiney and greased up... Did they scratch him or what?" Bee asked before taking a drink of vodka from her glass.

"Noooo, girl. They rushed that ass to John Hopkins's Hospital," Gibson informed them.

"He jerked off on me a few times, too," said Bridgette.

"I told that nigga several times that I don't like dick and that my dick is bigger than his. I even put it on and went to work just to flash on *his* ass," said Hope.

"You did what, girl?!" Bee asked, surprised and uncertain of what her girlfriend said.

"I sure did," Hope responded. The women began to laugh hysterically.

"What did he do, girl, when he saw it?" Gibson asked.

"He paused, looked at it really hard, and then said, '*Damn, bitch, that motherfucker is waaay bigger than mine! You gonna kill a bitch wit' that thing!*', I told him I already did, but that the dead bitch keep comin' back resurrected for some more. That stopped his ass from getting naked on me ever again," Hope said, hitting her drink. The other women were in stitches and having a laughing good time when Lacy Landon came into the bar. She walked towards the laughing crew, stopped, and then leaned back to assess the cackling wenches.

"What in 'da hell is so damn funny?" She asked. Lt. Gibson began to fill Lacy Landon in on what they found so hilarious, and in no time flat, Landon joined them in the amusement.

"Hope, you're crazy. They must don't know you ain't to be fucked with." Landon said, as a matter of fact. The laughter continued for a couple more minutes before one of them inquired about the results of the attack on Freaky Ty.

"He'll live, but he's in critical condition. Maybe he'll learn his lesson. I just got tired of his bullshit, so I asked Twin to do something about his nasty ass. He started creeping me out. I'll just have to pray and ask God to forgive me for putting Twin and them on him. I'm glad that he didn't die. I wouldn't be any good if that happens."

"That's your work, girl?" Gibson asked.

"Yeah. I'm afraid so." Landon said.

"I would have assigned you to work another section if I'd known he was getting to you like that," Gibson expressed concerned.

"Hell, no! Girl, I like my tier and the inmates on it. They already know how I run things. I just wanted him beat down and moved. I didn't believe that they'd do him like that. I should have known that he wouldn't go down easy. He really is an animal," she said, sounding surprised.

"That's exactly what I mean," interrupted Blackwell. "In a big way I am glad to walk away from that job. Although they probably would have fired my ass if they'd saw me touch that tobacco, I was kind of relieved, anyway. Just think, those guys in that jail are our men. When you look at it, we are a part of the very same system that puts them down, keeps them down, and beats them down." Bridgette said.

"Come on off of that save the niggas shit!" Hope expressed. "The niggas break law; and a lot of them are the same ones that go home and don't do shit for their family and then come straight back. They start doing the same bullshit that got them here in the first place."

"You are absolutely right; and a lot of them should be locked up for a lot of the shit that they do. But, none of you can deny that seeing all of those black men in jail while we are out here busting our asses to take care of our families is fucked up. It's like we should be home and our men be the breadwinners. On top of that, their evil deeds behind bars are out of this world. It makes them worse. Sort of animalistic. Those black men are angry. Angry at their failures. Their angry at us for always beating them down and not having their backs; angry at seeing us be the breadwinners, angry at being locked up for taking care of families that depend on them. Their angry at being around so many women day in and day out and not be able to feel our comfort, but always receive our harsh words: LOCK-IN! Whatchoo doing! LET ME SEE YOUR I.D.! NO! Keep the noise down! I'M WRITING YOU UP! Get outta my face! These are grown ass men that are talked down to by women. It fuels their frustrations. No wonder so many of them fight, get stabbed and try to kill one another. You don't hear about the murders inside of here on the news.

No wonder niggas like Freaky Ty are always being so nasty. He's rebelling against his powerlessness and inadequacies and basically seeking attention. He's lashing out at us for his lack of control. His dick in his hand is the only thing that he thinks that he can control without anyone taking it from him. And the rest of the black men are always clamoring for our attention. It's a job that we are placed in control over them. Look at us. None of us have a husband or a man of our own. We all have children; except for Gibson, and we don't need a man to take care of us financially, but there are so many ways that we do need our men to complete our families. What makes it so bad for us is that we have to see some good black men every day in the very worst of their existence.

"The job has changed me inside and it makes me

30

angry, bitter, and tough. Before this job, I never drank every night. Now, I need a drink every night to ease the pressures of the day that comes from being inside of one of the most concentrated den of corruption in Baltimore City. I'm going back to school to find another profession. I'm tired of nasty ass niggas like Freaky Ty and I'm tired of the bullshit we have to take just to provide for our children," Bridgette concluded. She swallowed her double shot, then ordered another.

"I have something for you, Bridgett... Twin asked me to give you these Green-Dot numbers. He said that each one of them holds five hundred," said Landon, handing her now ex co-worker a piece of paper with the MasterCard Green-dot numbers that the inmates used to make money by wiring money from one account to the other using their cellphones.

"He said to tell you that this is the least that they can do, and he wishes you the best for the future. They're all gonna' miss you." Landon said, handing Bridgette the Green-dots.

"You see, Twin got shit with him as deep as a cesspool, but he's a real man. That nigga knows how to play the hand that he's dealt. He takes care of his family and his people no matter space or place," Blackwell said.

"He's a manipulating motherfucker!" Gibson said, slurring in a loud voice.

"And what the hell do you call the shit that you do?" Blackwell asked her friend, the lieutenant.

"I look out for my peeps. You've been doing fine for yourself, haven't you? You ain't been complaining. You got a 70 thousand dollar Audi, bitch. Whatchoo mean!" Gibson snapped.

"Excuse me. My bad. I didn't mean it like that, but you got to admit that Twin looks out for his crew, too." Bridgette said.

"Yes, he does, but Twin can be really ruthless and cruddy with the violence," Gibson said. "Everybody else pays a greater penalty for some of his bullshit, while he goes

31

unscathed."

"Forget all of that shit! What we gonna do 'bout business? We need somebody to take Bridgette's place. We might as well give up on our hustle until we find somebody," said Landon.

"I've got an idea about who can take her place," interjected Bee.

"Who?" The four women spoke as one at the same time.

"Well, I was in the gym talking to that fine ass nigga, G-loc from over east. He's one of them Shotgun Crips. I've heard a lot about them from my home girls at The Eldorado," Bee explained, getting caught up into describing G-loc, while sucking her teeth. The women can clearly see that she likes G-loc.

"Girl, tell us who it is, wit' yo' hot ass!" Hope demanded.

"Oh, my bad," she said, and then continued. "Anyway, while we were talking, his comrade, Big Pimp came over to where we were at and handed G a half ounce of weed, a pack of Newports, and a cigarette lighter. I joked with him about locking his ass up, and then I asked him where he got the goods from. He told me that his baby momma gave it to him. He knew I didn't give a shit, but I still advised the guy Big Pimp not to tell people about his baby momma because of how nosey the inmates can be. Plus, they will tell on him and his baby momma in a heartbeat. He said that he knows better than to tell anybody anything. The only reason Pimp let me know, he said, is because I use to fuck with one of his homeboys up Poplar Grove and Lafayette, where the rolling 60 Crips. His baby momma is the short girl with the glasses that just started working," Bee said, hipping her crew.

"Who are you talkin' bout, Simms?" Landon asked.

"Yeah!" Bee answered. "I talked to her briefly. She seems pretty cool. I gave her a little bit of advice on how to deal with the inmates without saying anything that concerns her business with Big Pimp. I just basically let her know to be careful with the people that she might know from the street. She's not a simple minded young ass girl. She minds her business and she don't try hard to fit in with a lot of the C.O.'s."

"Candace Simms," Gibson said, pondering the information. "I talk to her a lot. She's one of the ones that call me Ma. I like her, too. She's pretty mature for her age. I was surprised to find out that she's only 19. Very mature for her age."

"Nineteen?! She's a damn baby! These niggas will try to eat her ass alive if they find out her business; and them hot ass Sergeants, lieutenants, and the other men will be trying hard to get in her panties. Oh, and I forgot; some of the female COs, too. You know they ain't shit, either. They always use their positions to impress the rookies so that they can fuck 'em and duck 'em," Landon reminded.

"Yup, girl, that's how they are," said Bee.

"You should know. They got yo' ass, too, when you started working here," Hope recalled.

"Correction! I got a few of their assess, cause ain't nary one of them get this pussy for under two hundred; and Major Parker paid five," Bee said, reminding her friends who they were talking to. "So, we got each other."

"You are such a trifling ho, girl," said Blackwell. They all chuckled and hit their drinks, relieved that Blackwell didn't become too upset about losing her job and still in a bantering mood. It's agreed that the lieutenant will talk to Simms and pull her in tight, so that she could take Blackwell's place. Actually, she would be taking Hope's place because, Hope is the last one on the totem pole. Hope can now move up a notch.

It's getting late and the ladies began to bring their conversations to a close. They all cried and expressed regret about Bridgette losing her job as they became well effected by the drinks. She adamantly let her friends know that she didn't care about the job, but not seeing them as much will kill her.

She promised to see them regularly at the Icon so that they could keep her up on that crazy ass jail. Steelside kept a lot of shit going on and some of the stories are such events to be shared. Bridgette let them know that she still had over $60 thousand saved and she planned to go back to school for cyber-security. The free time will give her a chance to finish getting college credits. She quit school several years ago to take care of her son after his father was murdered.

Everyone began getting out of their seats to say goodbye. Hope walked to the table where Puddin' and the girls were having a good time talking.

"Come on, yo. I'm ready to go," Hope said.

"Well, go 'head. I'll see you at 'da house. Rashon is gonna drop me off. Oh, and I need a few more dollars for something else to drink while I'm here," Puddin' said.

"Get it from Rashon," Hope suggested. Hope's feelings were affected by Puddin's decision not to leave the bar with her. She walked out of the bar and got into her car alone. She'd had enough of Puddin's shit.

The women continued to go to work for about two more weeks before they started putting the hustle back into effect. Gibson began talking to Simms a little more than usual. Sometimes, Simms would be a little reluctant to be around the lieutenant because, she felt that Gibson was playing her close to spy on her. Now she's afraid that Gibson grew a little suspicious of the stuff that she brought to Big Pimp. She chilled on bringing Pimp anything in the jail. She refused to lose her job so fast. She has two children, and now that Pimp is locked up, she has to take care of the children and the bills all alone.

Pimp got popped soon after she started working and her house came through for her in the Latrobe Courts Projects. Her sister stayed at her house to watch the children while she worked. The jail is in walking distance from Latrobe. She's not going to let anyone fuck that situation up for her.

Candace had her first child at fourteen but, the son that she and Pimp share is 2 years old. She planned to save money for a year, buy a car, and then use her income tax refund to move out of those godforsaken Latrobe Projects. Pimp is 23 and Candace just loves her man. He helped a lot when he was free on the streets, but he stays in and out of jail. She found it hard to depend on him for that reason alone. He takes care of his son and Candace's older daughter when he is free. For the most part, he's done his best to take care of them all. Her other baby's father is a deadbeat.

Red Mike is an East Baltimore Blood. He's known for getting money in the streets selling heroin. He also thinks that he's ghetto fabulous, but he don't do shit for his daughter or the other children that he fathered by other women. Only the son that he has from one of his children's mother. Every so often he will come around Candace and try to get some pussy. She stop giving in to him after she found out that she was pregnant by Pimp. Red Mike would give her a hundred dollars from time to time, but once the sex halted with him, he wouldn't give her a penny. Nothing!

Pimp couldn't stand Red Mike. For one, he is a Blood and Pimp also didn't like the fact that the nigga is in the streets getting money and won't do shit for his daughter. They exchanged angry glances with one another when in each other's company, but they didn't beef because of the children. They both recognize the mutual stalemate and respects Candace a lot for being such a good mother, but it won't take much for them to go at one another. Red Mike has a little heart, but his money and influence earns the streets' respect. The money made the streets fear what he can get done to a foe. Big Pimp goes hard and isn't afraid of a damn soul. He keeps a 9mm. and is also known to knock a motherfucker out with his fist, too.

After the day's roll call, Lt. Gibson asked CO Candace Simms to stay back after the others left to go to their assigned posts. She needed to have a word with her. Candace started getting a little nervous and thought for sure that she's getting ready to lose her job.

"Come on girl, I need you to walk with me to the medical unit," Gibson requested in a friendly tone that loosened Candace. The tension that she felt began to subside. While they were walking, Gibson began to get the ball rolling.

"Simms, do you know Aaron Richardson?"

"Lt. Gibson, he is my son's father," Candace answered with a hint of trepidation. All of the fears that she had about losing her job returned immediately.

"Oh, girl, don't be so uptight. Ain't nobody 'round. You can call me Ma," Gibson said to ease her fears.

"It's just that I didn't think anyone knew that Pimp is my baby daddy," she said.

"Well, you'd be surprised at what I know, who I know and how I know what goes on in this jail. This is Steelside and I am *The Queen Bitch*. Now, I'm gonna get straight to the point," said the lieutenant.

Once they reached the medical unit, they greeted the medical staff, then Gibson led Candace into one of the office cubicles. She took a seat behind a desk and Candace sat in a chair positioned beside her in a subordinate role, face to face, which is normally where an inmate would sit. They both leaned in close to one another, and that's when Gibson looked around before speaking again.

"My people and I are going to help you with getting things to your baby daddy a little easier. At the rate you're going, your young ass will get caught."

"But, I..."

"Pay attention and listen to me," Gibson said, cutting her short with a wave of the hand. "We will all take turns getting Pimp what he needs. Does he have a cell phone?"

"Yes," she answered.

"Good. The two of you must start setting up a Green-dot account, A.S.A. P." Gibson ordered.

"We already have a couple of them," Candace said,

36

once again, apprehensively.

"I knew my instincts were right. This is what I need you to do," Gibson said, handing Candace two phone numbers. "Call the second number when you've finished dealing with the first person that you call. After you've done everything, I want you to call me on my cell phone. You do have my number, don't you?" Gibson asked Candace, to be sure. It's mandatory to have her supervisor's number. She knew that she had the number.

"Do you mean the number that we have in case of an emergency for the job?" Simms asked.

"Yeah, that's the one," Gibson responded.

"Will I have to go anywhere? I don't have a car, but I do have money for a hack," Candace explained. The lieutenant saw this as a perfect opportunity to ingratiate herself to Simms and to also gain her confidence.

"Hmmm… Well, we'll have to straighten that out, pronto. Do you have a license?" Gibson asked.

"I just got my provisional license last month," she replied.

"When our shift is over tonight, you can take me home and keep my car. Better still, we can go to the Icon Inn for a couple of drinks, first. Do you drink?"

"I drink vodka and pineapple juice, all day long," Candace said, with a confident smile.

"Once we get settled in our business, I'll take you to my homeboy Obutunji. He owns a car lot. You are going to need a car, girl. He's gonna hook you up. The paperwork included… So, what's it gonna be, are you down?" Gibson asked.

"Ma, I'm wit' it," she answered.

"The only requirement from this point on is that you are not to discuss your business with anyone. Not your mother, father, sister, brother, and especially not Pimp," Gibson warned, making it a point to use her son's father's street name and stressing the seriousness of confidentiality. Simms looked at her and remained quiet, but twisted her neck and poked her head out to imitate the zippering of the lips that indicates silence.

"That's the business. When it comes to Pimp, you just tell him don't ask questions and keep his business to himself. Is he facing a lot of time?" Gibson asked.

"We don't know. They got him with 87 bags of crack. He's not on any probation, so he might be ok. He also got a gun charge, but they didn't get the gun off of him. The lawyer says he'll beat the gun charge, but the crack was in his pocket. The gun is why he doesn't have a bail or else I would have made sure that my man made bail," she explained.

"I see... Well, that's it, for now. I'll put you in the gymnasium with Officer Berry from this point on, cool?" Gibson said, letting her know that her post will change. "Just don't forget to meet me tonight when we get off, ok?" Gibson reminded.

The ladies continued to make small talk, but the deal is close to being sealed. Officer Candace Simms is now almost down with the queens. She can't figure out how this will go, but she could tell that money is the motivation. With all of the diamonds that the lieutenant wear and the way that she keeps her nails manicured, she looked the role of a Queen of some sorts. Candace can't believe that the lieutenant suggested that Candace drive her car. She drove a Forrest Green 650 convertible B.M.W, with customized B.M.W. rims. Candace always thought that her supervisor had it going on. She believed that her flash came from years of service to the public. Candace is only nineteen but being raised in the streets taught her that things that comes with a shroud of secrecy involved money or murder, or money and murder. There is nothing to indicate murder with the lieutenant. By the way she was instructed that they will take turns making sure that Pimp is all right suggested that this is undoubtedly about money.

Candace made her way to the gymnasium. Not one soul appeared inside. She walked into the door that led to the two full basketball courts. She looked into the office and didn't see anyone. She walked out of the office and saw CO Berry come from behind the gigantic 60 inch screen television that stood on the stage.

Bee didn't notice Simms at first. She continued to fasten her belt and make sure that her clothes were in place. Then Simms heard a door shut behind the television and soon witnessed the inmate that everyone called Uncle Twin appear. Candace knows that he has a lot of pull in the jail, but what she knew couldn't prepare her for the type of pull that she now discovered that he has. She's not dumb and she could tell that the pair just finished having some sort of sex. When Bee saw someone, she became startled. Then she realized that it was the rookie, that's when she felt relieved. Uncle Twin stopped in his tracks when he saw Simms, too. He quickly recovered and acted as though nothing's wrong. Then he made his way out of the gymnasium without a care in the world.

Candace heard about things like this going on; but, hearing gossip and rumors as opposed to knowing the truth are two different worlds. She began to wonder if it can be possible for her to give Pimp some koodycat. Just then, Bee disturbed her thoughts.

"What's up, Simms? I see you're in the gym with me today. Let me tell you something about the gym. We run this when we're here and the only rules that we have among the officers on this post is just like Las Vegas; what happens in the gym stays in the gym. You got that?" Bee asked the rookie.

"Got it like I got two babies," Candace re-affirmed. Her job started to become an adventure and she loved every minute of it.

Uncle Twin walked over to N-section and went to one of his comrade's cell. He had the tier officer open the cell door. He wanted to sit down for a minute because, the way he pounded Officer Berry over the table in that back room behind the stage had him tired. He's not as young as he used to be and on top of that, he wanted to take a blow of the raw dope that

39

he had folded in some paper on the inside of his sock. He knew that he had to give some to his comrade. He planned to smoke a couple of joints of weed, too.

There's cause for a celebration, anyway. Landon told him that it's back to business as usual by the end of the week. He already had connections with small time stuff: like making sure that he kept a couple of grams of smack for his personal, a little weed to smoke and some tobacco. Landon and Gibson represent the mother lode. They are *the* bread and butter!

"Hey, Ochie! We gonna be good this weekend, yo... Here," Twin announced, handing Ochie the dope in a small piece of magazine paper to take a toot from. Twin rolled the weed and continued with the news. "I want you to put that young nigga G-loc down with the business so that he can be ready. Tell him I said I ain't servin' him unless he got five hunned or better. I'ma stop pass Muk'min's cell before I leave. You know, the Muslims spend big, too. Then I got to go on the other side of the jail to see what's up with the Blood kids. The Blood kids be spending good money, also. I'll go over the Annex and the J.I. building tomorrow. Whatchoo' think?" Twin asked Ochie.

"Sounds like a plan to me, yo," Ochie responded. He is one of the older BGF members, along with Twin, that sniffed dope. A lot of the young members under thirty smoked weed, popped pills, and drank. Few snorted heroin. A lot of the older members loved the smack. Baltimore City. That's funny because, on the streets, these are some of the same older guys that the young comrades have little respect for. A lot of young comrades will look down on the older ones because they use heroin or smoke crack. In the jail the old heads are most of the move makers and leaders that the young comrades look to for strength, guidance, and motivation behind prison walls.

"Yeah, Ochie. I go to court in a few months and I want to give my lawyer a couple more stacks," Twin said, nodding with his eyes half closed in his drug induced stupor. He popped out of his nod, lit the weed and then continued. "We should be able to save up a nice piece of change this time. It's been almost a month and now that the heat is dying off, it's time for us to go hard again," he said, then pulled on the joint of weed. "You feel me?" He said letting the smoke out.

"I feel you, comrade. I got a fresh Green-dot just waiting to get rolling," said Ochie.

"Good, good... Let me get outta here, Ochie, and go handle my business, yo. I had to stop and take a break because Officer Berry put that good pussy on me. I needed to sit down and hit some blow," Twin said, shaking his head with the very recent memory of just having sex in the gym with Bee.

"She got that Commodores pussy, that *'Slippery When its Wet'*, Ochie. You got two fifty? I might can get you in it," Twin reminded Ochie of his promise.

"It's worth every bit of my two fifty. I got it. You said that you gonna look out for me, yo, with that redbone, Berry, comrade." Ochie reminded Twin.

"You might need three or four, Ochie. She's funny style. I'll see if I can pull it off for you for *that* price because, her price is really the four." Twin informed him.

"Oh, yeah? You know I'm going to prison. The last offer for me was twenty-five years. I think they gonna come down to fifteen and if they do that, I'm on it. That might be the last piece of pussy I'll get in years. See what's up with that, Twin. I'll pay four if I have to, yo," explained Ochie.

"All right, homeboy. The Twinster gonna see what he can do for you, comrade," he said, keeping Ochie's hopes alive. He never had any intentions of making the proposal to Officer Berry, but, it is good to have Ochie believe that he has something coming. Ochie kept business straight and never wanted to disappoint Twin, just hoping and praying that Twin could get CO Berry to sell him some pussy. That's his main motivation throughout his drab days of being in the jail.

Twin jumped to his feet and shook his comrade's hand.

41

They said their salutes and then Twin trotted along on his way.

      Gibson felt good about her plan and the new young member of the crew. Simms came across really cool. The only drawback that comes from bringing Simms to the fold is that her baby's father is in the jail. Some men can act like boys and are impatient. God forbid he's the kind that thinks he is her father, or the controlling type. Please don't let him be abusive. That's trouble waiting to happen. He would surely blow the spot! Most of the men in the jail lacked emotional maturity. A lot of them are raised without fathers and Gibson thought to herself that this is a big reason for most of the problems. For one, a lot of the men have deep rooted anger for the black man that left them, or the one that they never knew. So, it don't take much for them to turn around and hurt one another. Subconsciously, that kind of self-hate motivates the violence that they inflict on one another. Gibson believes that these fatherless men epitomize the ultimate self-hate. Also, they are passing it on to the coming generations. Simms did tell Gibson how good of a man her son's father is. Maybe he is different but, going back and forth to jail can still render her child somewhat fatherless and he too can grow to be bitter because it.

      "When will it all stop?! God knows we need it to end!" She yelled out to no one in particular and just to get relief from her thoughts. She made a mental note to check out this Big Pimp. With a handle like Big Pimp, he just has to be a character. For now, her self-interest comes first. P-section is the destination.

      Gibson came through the P-section grille, sat down at the desk and asked Officer Laryea for the log book. After the official business was over, it became time for the unofficial.

      "Laryea, can you let Elliott Walker out of the dorm for me?" Gibson ordered.

      "Sure, lewtenant," he said, walking to the dorm to let Elliott free.

"Mr. Walker, I need you to take a walk with me to the medical unit. You have to sign some papers," she said. Her comments were more command than instruction. Elliot didn't say a word. He followed her lead. She needed an excuse to get Elliot off of the tier without drawing suspicion.

Elliot dressed neat every day in the jail as though preparing to go somewhere like he is home and in the street. His clothes are of the latest fashion. Gibson can see that he can't possibly be a bum on the streets. However, the inmates can fool you. Often the men come to jail a wretch and leave shining. A lot of them return to the same trashy and drug addicted lifestyle. She prayed that he's not a junkie. He never talked that big dope boy shit to her like he has so much stuff going on uptown. However, the jury is still out on this one. He got game and she can tell that all of the guys in the jail respect him. He doesn't get locked up much, and if he do, he must have made bail every time because, she knows that she would have remembered this one if he had spent some months or better over Steelside. After about a month passed, she had to try him.

Gibson led Elliot to one of the cubicles in the medical department, where she often hold court. Once inside, she quickly handed him a cellular phone and stuck her long tongue down his throat. She caught him off guard but, he quickly recovered and let her have her way with him. He pulled her in close and palmed both of her ass cheeks while they kissed for a full minute. After the long kiss, the lieutenant grabbed Elliot's crotch to see if she aroused him. Elliot got rock hard. She looked outside of the cubicle to see if anyone else was around, and when she saw that the coast was clear, she unzipped his jeans and immediately went to work. She licked, sucked, and slurped his manhood like an Orange Cream Popsicle melting in the sun. Elliot began to explode so, she deep throated him and took one long and final suck. Once her mouth popped off of him, he popped off as well. With eyes bulging and wide, he watched his juices shoot all over the place. *'She is the truth,'* he thought. That had to be the fastest and best head that he'd had in his life. He can't believe what just happened. She zipped his pants up and patted his manhood with her hand.

"Maybe one day this can be mine. Do you think we can work on that, or let's just leave shit like it is and I won't bother you again?" She asked, simultaneously wiping his juices up with paper towels from the spots that they landed on in the cubicle.

"Damn, baby. You sure do drive a hard bargain... Let me think on that one for a while," he said, trying to catch his breath.

"Don't rush yourself. That phone is fully charged. I'll bring you a charger tomorrow. Make sure that you save enough juice to call me at 1:30 a.m. tonight, all right?" She whimpered. "Not a minute later," she said; then continued. "Mommy wants you to tuck her in after I get out of the bathtub, if you know what I mean. My number is in the phone and you are the only one that has *that* number, ok?" she continued.

"I got you boo... Boo, do you think that you can get me something to smoke?" Elliot asked. He figured that if she is going this far, all he can do is try. Hell, either she will or she won't bring him some cigarettes. That's just the start. He didn't realize that she controlled the controllers with the contraband.

"I'll try to do something for you in a couple of days. Don't worry about that. You just don't forget to call me," Gibson said. "Now come on, let's get out of here. We've been in this spot too damn long." Walking out of the cubicle and past the CO at the desk, she spoke in a loud voice, "Mr. Elliot, if you have any more problems and you can't get any help, you get your tier officer to call me, ok?!" She played it off perfectly.

"Yes, ma'am, Lt. Gibson. I sure will," Elliot responded, going along with the play she gave for the officer.

"Can you write Mr. Walker a pass to get back to his section, Officer Powers?" Gibson asked the duty officer, who just happened to be Bee's boy toy, CO Paul Powers.

"I sure will... Where do you sleep at," the officer asked Elliot, reaching for the pad that held the inmate passes. Lt. Gibson waved goodbye to Elliot and he returned the gesture. He retrieved his pass from the officer and walked unescorted to his section with a big dumb Kool-Aid smile on his face.

The work day seemed to fly by. Candace enjoyed working with Bee Berry. Bee let her know that if she had an inmate friend or family member in the jail that she needed to speak to, she could have him called into the gym and talk to him in private away from the many ears and eyes. Bee didn't want Candace to know that she knew that Pimp is her son's father and she knows him personally. Candace didn't hesitate to have Pimp called to the gym. After walking into the office, he winked at Bee and then hugged his girl. He appreciated the chance to be up on Candace in such an intimate way. Candace, surprised that the two of them knew one another, and just like a woman, became suspicious of the relationship. Pimp assured Candace that Bee is cool with him and used to talk to one of his friends back in the day. He also let her know how much Bee liked G-loc. Soon as he mentioned G, he walked into the office.

The two women kicked it with the inmates as though the four of them were on a double date instead of in the jail. When the COs made their lunch call for food from KFC, the women made sure that Pimp and G-loc ate with them; which meant that they didn't have to eat the horrible jail food. Pimp started pressing up on Candace about smuggling in weed for him. She advised him to be patient because it's being worked on. She didn't dare tell him that things are going on that will have him straight. For all that mattered, she didn't know how things would get done for him but, she knew that the plan is for it to happen.

Candace waited outside in front of the Baltimore City Detention Center, on Eager Street, for the lieutenant to arrive. All of the officers were either headed to their car, or someone picked them up after the shift. Once she appeared, they both talked and laughed while walking to the car during the nightly ritual of quitting time. The lieutenant's shining green car looked even sportier reflecting the light from the lamppost. Just before they approached the car, Gibson hit her button switch that opened the trunk. Once they got to the trunk, she looked around before grabbing the small bag that she had stashed.

"Here you go, girl. You drive," Gibson instructed, handing her car's remote to Candace. She started singing Mariah Carey's, *"We Belong Together"* in the quiet of the night, while getting into the Beemer. A cup remained in the cup holder and Gibson didn't waste time pouring the remaining third of a pint of vodka and added grapefruit juice to it, taking the bite off of the liquor. Candace starts the car and the Mariah Carey song that the lieutenant sang began coming out of the speakers with a symphonic boom from the high fidelity stereo. The seats hugged and adjusted to conform to Candace's back. She'd never driven a car like this. Red Mike had a Lexus LS 430 but, he would never let Candace drive his car. She couldn't believe that the lieutenant entrusted her to drive. Gibson hit her drink and then directed Candace to the Icon Inn.

Chapter 3

Candace rolled over from her slumber and grabbed her cell phone at 9 am. She was instructed by a smooth sounding guy named Jerry Tucker to meet him at the Reisterstown Road Plaza at 10:30. He let her know that he already knew what to look for to identify her. He would be identifying her by the car. So, the secret rendezvous would begin soon. Candace lazily willed herself out of bed. Heading towards the bathroom, she smiled thinking about the light fun she had with Lt. Gibson and their co-workers the night before at the Icon. It was a shock to see Officer Berry there. She let Candace know that it's all right to call her Bee. She said, that's what all of friends call her.

"That's how you can tell who I fuck with at that place. A lot of the bitches there are straight up bullshit fake bitches," she said.   Bee paid for Simms's two drinks. Candace didn't want to drink too much because, she would be driving the lieutenant's car. That didn't slow the rest of them down. CO Landon was there, also. The women called her L.L. or just plain L because, her name is Lacy Landon. Candace flat out liked her. She's always straight up. She appeared to be the leader of the pack. Any pack! Officer Hope was also present. Gibson let Candace know which girl that sat with Hope in the booth was Hope's girlfriend. Hope moved back and forth between the bar, where they all were sitting, and the booth, where her girlfriend sat with two more women. Candace remembered that Hope was on her heels when she first started working at the jail a few months ago. However, Candace made it plain that she is strictly dickly and didn't want another female laying up under her in bed. She loved holding onto muscles. She let Hope know that it didn't interest her to be with another woman and Hope never said another word out of the way to her again. Even at the Icon, Hope's words were minimal, until she and her girlfriend started arguing about something. The time drew close to 1 am when that started, which made everyone want to leave. Gibson grabbed Candace's arm and they both said their goodbyes. Candace had to take the lieutenant home.

The lieutenant lived in Essex and as Candace drove her home. She was careful not to drive the BMW too fast but, Gibson implored her to speed up. However, once she dropped Gibson off, she let loose in the sports car on open stretches of Eastern Blvd. She smiled in the bathroom mirror at the memory of being such a speed demon.

After showering and getting dressed, she played with the children, briefly, and then she let her sister know that she has some early business to take care of. Candace gave her sister twenty dollars for a bag of weed and some cigarettes to keep the children a little longer than usual. At first her sister complained about Candace keeping her from looking for a job, but that was all a front. The weed money quieted her. She saw that Candace dressed pretty sporty in a pink sweat-suit with pink sneakers. She looked out of the window to see Candace prepare to get into the BMW that some of the residents of Latrobe gawked at all morning while making comments about its possible driver.

"Bitch, whose car is that?!" Candace's sister yelled, like she gonna tell momma on her.

"Mind your business!" Candace responded.
"Bitch, you pushing that Beemer *iz* my bizness! Now, tell me, whose car iz it?"

"It belongs to a friend of mine," she answered.

"Must be some old head nigga from yo' job, cause ain't no other nigga I know gonna let you keep his whip like that overnight... Do he got any friends?!" She asked.

"Girl, shut up! You are too young for the guys on my job! You should take your ass back to school!" Candace scolded.

"Who's gonna keep these children while I'm in school?!" She asked, looking back in the house from the window at the two young children.

"I keep them in the daytime, anyway; and besides, I'll find somebody if you take your ass back to school. You let me worry about that. Just go to school!" Candace pleaded.

"All right, yo. I'm goin' back to school soon… Bring me something from the mall!" Her sister yelled again, before Candace's head disappeared out of sight, getting into the car. She heard her sister and had every intention of buying something for her and the children with the three hundred dollars that Gibson gave to her for expenses. Then she made her way to the plaza.

Candace followed instructions to the letter. She was told to park close to the mall's entrance and then call the number back once she arrived. Getting out of the car with her cell phone to her ear, she heard the song *"I'm the Man"* by Shawty Lo, coming from a guy walking towards her with his car keys in hand.

"Are you Simms?" Jerry asked Candace, holding his phone out.

"Yeah, that's me, but you can call me Candace," she answered, putting her phone away.

"Shorty, you fine as hell. Can I take you shopping?" Jerry asked, peering at her over his Cartier shades, with his chin to his neck.

"I don't except things from strangers," she said, playing defense.

"That's a lie because, I got something for you and we have to go shopping to get it," he responded, sounding more businesslike than before.

"Well, in that case, let's *do* this," she conceded, following his lead.

They both walked into the mall to the Lady Foot Locker. She looked at sneakers for the children while Jerry talked to the cashier. Candace requested her children's sizes in shoes from one of the shoe salesman, and then she walked to the counter, putting the sneakers on top.

"Don't worry about that, Candace. I'll pay for it," said

Jerry.

"Are you sure?" She asked. Jerry didn't say a word. He pulled a wad of hundred dollar bills out of his pocket and put two of them on the counter, making a motion with his head and eyes to indicate to Candace that whatever they met up for would be invested with her by the cashier.

"You keep the change and call me if you just need someone to talk to, Ma. I'm pretty sure we'll have an interesting conversation," Jerry said, walking out of the store. Candace blushed briefly from Jerry's flirting, then she looked to the cashier.

"Girl, he thinks he's the shit, but, he is cool," said the cashier.

"He seems to be," Candace responded.

"That'll be $131.29. Here is your change and your merchandise," said the cashier handing Candace two bags instead of only the one that held her children's shoes.

"Thank you," said Candace. She smiled at the cashier. Then she began to grab the bags. She continued on in the mall and saw a gaucho ensemble for her little sister at a women's boutique and she also purchased a pair of jeans. She looked at her watch walking into the parking lot. It read twelve p.m. Her next move is to call the other number that Gibson gave to her.

"Hello?" The female voice answered from the other end. The voice sounded familiar.

"I'm supposed to call you after I leave the plaza," said Candace.

"Simms, this Hope. Meet me on Lakewood and Monument Street," her co-worker instructed her on the other end.

"I'll be there in 15 minutes," she complied. Candace never looked into the bag, but she knows that Monument and Lakewood Street is a hot block in the city and that's where Red Mike, her daughter's father hang. She knew that whatever is in the bag couldn't be legal, but she decided to go along with the plan, act natural, and play it cool. Plus, she has to meet Hope. She didn't mind or feel uncomfortable about it. Hope seems cool enough. She didn't have anything against girls liking girls, but, as stated before, she loves boys.

While Candace sat at the light on Monument and Milton Streets, she called the number that led to Hope, once again. Hope lived on Lakewood St. Once Candace made the left turn onto Lakewood, she saw Red Mike's Lexus. She shook her head, parked, and then got out of the car. She spotted Hope coming out of her door dressed like Jim Jones. She wore the skull and bones belt buckle and all. She even wore a small but expensive necklace that had a smaller skull medallion with diamonds for the eyes hanging low around her neck. She rocked a men's diamond bracelet and a Jo Jo watch with diamonds flooding the bezel. Her jeans were hung low under her ass; and of course she showed off the boxer briefs. She rocked long braids in a design as well. Candace thought that she looks nice dressed in her clothes, outside of the uniforms that they all wore. Candace recognized that Hope is all Dom.

"What's up, yo?" Hope greeted.

"Ain't shit. Jerry gave me a bag. What's next?" Candace responded

"Get it and bring it into the house. Don't forget to shut my door behind you!" Hope yelled, walking to the house. Once Candace came inside, she handed Hope the bag. Hope tossed the bag onto the dining room table.

"Do you want some juice, water, or anything else to drink?" Hope offered.

"You can get me some juice," Candace accepted, then she took a seat. Hope disappeared into the kitchen to get them something to drink. Meanwhile, the short brown skinned girl that Hope argued with on the night before came down the stairs wrapped in a housecoat. She reached for a cigarette from the pack that sat on the table, and then spoke to Candace. Puddin' yawned after speaking, and you could tell that she'd just awakened a few short moments ago. She reached for the bag which held several smaller bags inside of it. She emptied the contents of the bag. Four blocks of compressed kush weed, two ounces of Kush haze, and a zip-lock sandwich bag filled across the bottom with beige powder she dumped onto the table. Puddin' reached into her pocket and pulled out a vanilla cigarillo and then proceeded to open one of the ounces of weed.

"WHAT IN THE WORLD ARE YOU DOING, BITCH!!!" Hope yelled, coming into the room from the kitchen with two glasses of grape juice in both of her hands. "Why are you goin' in them peoples' shit?!"

"Calm the fuck down! I just want to see how good the Kush is. You shouldn't have said nothing to me about it if you ain't gonna let me try it out," Puddin' explained, picking out a bud to roll up. Hope stopped and just stared at Puddin', obviously angry at her impatience and watching her fiend for the weed in front of Candace. She planned to smoke a blunt with Puddin' anyway, but she didn't have to be so fast in front of Candace with other people shit. "Do you smoke?" Puddin' asked Candace.

"Sometimes, but it's too early in the day for me and I don't smoke during the week," she explained.

"This weed is the truth! Look at them buds, boo!" Puddin' raised her voice to express herself about the weed, handing it to Hope before she rolling up. Hope turned her attention to Candace. She explained to her that she will be meeting Jerry two or three times a month from now on and that she will be paid by Landon right before the next pick up. She is to always bring the bag directly to her immediately after she gets it from Jerry. Reisterstown Road Plaza is not the only pick up spot. Hope also advised Candace to never give Jerry the pussy.

"Keep it business, but be nice," were Hope's exact words before winking.

Hope and Candace talked for a few minutes as Hope and Puddin' passed the weed choking between the both of them. Candace had to admit that the Kush smelled too good. What happened next was a total surprise. While Hope and Candace continued to make small talk, Puddin' opened one of the other ounces and scooped buds from it. Hope acted as though she ignored her girlfriend, when in truth, her blood began to boil. She did her best to hold her anger and ignored the act, but Puddin' tipped the scale by grabbing another unopened ounce of weed and began picking some more buds for herself. Hope's left arm looked as though she reached in her right pocket by the way that she dipped, but in truth she swung her arm from the east and landed a backhand pimp slap to the west coast of Puddin's face! She slapped her so hard that she toppled over sending the chair off of its legs and buds of weed flying into the air. Puddin' landed sprawled out onto the floor. Blood instantly appeared from Puddin's nose.

"I'm sorry, bae," said Hope, apologetically; reaching out to help her up, but Puddin' jerked away.

"Whatchoo hit me for! Bitch! Look whatchoo did to my nose!" She yelled. Candace did all that she could to keep from laughing.

"I guess it's time for me to leave," suggested Candace, before drinking a little more juice. "I have to get ready for work and then pick up Lt. Gibson." She stood up from the table just as Puddin' got up off of the floor. Puddin' headed for the stairs and Hope reached out to her, yet again.

"Get your fucking hands off of me!" Puddin' yelled, pushing Hope's hands away and stomping up the stairs, holding her bleeding nose.

"Come on, yo, I'll walk you to the car," said Hope.

"I'm very sorry you had to see me act a fool, but you just don't know," explained Hope, showing Candace the door.

"Don't worry, I understand. Plus, it's none of my business, yo," Candace responded.

As they approached the car someone yelled!

"Candace! I know 'dat ain't you! Come here, girl!" Red Mike hollered, rising from the steps and wiping at the seat of his pants. "Damn, you look good, baby momma," he said, giving her a hug. Mike looked at Hope and then back to Candace. "What up, Glo?" He said, speaking to Hope. Then he said to his baby's mother, "Yo, I know you ain't doing the girl thing, *is* you?" He looked confused.

"Boy, get outta here! If I am, it ain't none of your business," she answered, playfully punching him to make her point.

"Shit if it ain't! You *my* baby momma! I want to know what kind of example is being set for my daughter. No offense, Glo," he answered Candace before directing his last comment to Hope.

"Nigga, please! You ain't a bit more worried about who doin' what for your daughter as long as you ain't gotta do it. Besides, my girlfriends and I are doing a damn good job. We the mother and the father," Candace said, smiling at Hope and knowing that Red Mike will be confused trying to figure out if Candace is having lesbian affairs.

"Ain't this about a bitch? The whole Baltimore City is dykin' and gay! They 'don got my baby momma! I just don't know what I'm gonna do! What's wrong?! Do that lame ass nigga Pimp know you dyking?! Did 'da nigga make you want girls dealing with his lame ass?" Red Mike continued.

"Mike, I am not messing with girls and Pimp is locked up; and yes we *are* still together, so get that look out of your eyes!" She said, talking about the look that overcame him when she said that Pimp's locked up.

"Well, shiiit, Glo, my home girl and I know how she get down. She 'don bagged a few of my bitches," he said.
"I don't get down like that anymore, Mike. You know that I got a steady girl now," Hope responded, defending her honor.

"Well, whatever," Mike said, watching Candace hit the key switch to open the door of the BMW. "Damn, baby momma, I know you ain't get a City Jail job just to buy a B.M.W.?"

"Hell, no! This car belongs to my girlfriend at the job,"

she said to him. "I'll see you at work, Hope," she said, directing her attention to Hope and waving goodbye. Mike bent low to the driver's side window to talk to her before she pulled off.

"So, this is another one of your girlfriends' car? Candace, those bitches are just roping you in. Are you sure you ain't dippin' and dabblin' with the whole girl thing? I got a few girlfriends that get down. Maybe we can hook up sometime and go out for a while before Pimp gets home. Your ass is starting to spread out, too. All yall women asses start to spread out when yall start messing wit' them girls," he said, trying to sound seductive.

"Mike, I don't know what to say about you. Can you give me some money to go school shopping for your daughter? You know she starts school soon." She demanded. Mike pulled a knot of money out of his pocket and peeled off sixty dollars.

"Here, call me later tonight and then maybe we can hook up and I'll give you some more," he propositioned. She snatched the money in a hurry because, she didn't want to give him a chance to put it back into his pocket.

"No thanks. I guess I'll skip on that invitation, but thanks for the sixty dollars. That'll save me from having to spend my money on underclothes, socks and tights," she said sarcastically, starting the car. "See you," Candace said, holding her cheek out for him to plant a kiss on her face. Red Mike automatically obliged. Without hesitation, she drove off in the BMW, leaving Mike in the street facing Hope.

"Glo, is my baby momma dyking?" He asked.

"Mike, I've known you since we were in elementary school. Candace is cool as shit. I'm just getting to know her but, I don't believe she gets down like that. I can try her out if you want me to," Hope said jokingly. "She is *fat*!"

"Fuck-you-mean, no!" He answered. "I'll holler at you later," he said to Hope, walking up the street to where his boys were standing and continuing on with the business of running his dope shop. It impressed him how well Candace grew mentally. He remembered that she had to be just 19 going on 20, and for her age, she matured well from the little young virgin that he'd had when she was 14 and he was 19. He knew that she loved him back then, but he didn't want her to be his main girl at the time. He only wanted to pop the Berry. She wasn't a dumb ass little chicken-head anymore. She'd grown into becoming a real woman and it turned him on in a good way. He had a thought to sincerely get involved in his daughter's life and to offer Candace some genuine help by spending time with their child and taking her shopping. Especially now that Pimp isn't around. Candace had it going on and he didn't want her to get caught up with girls, although he didn't mind being with her and another female. That could come later.

Red Mike sat where he was at before seeing Candace. He took notice of yet another expensive car pull up by Hope's house. This car held a redbone with long legs. She had a body with curves, ass, and legs.

"Yo, Glo keeps 'da baddest bitches around. Plus, 'da hookas be having cheese, too," Mike said to his boys, who all agreed.

Bee stepped out of the car and sashayed her way to Hope's stoop. She could feel Mike and his workers' eyes on her. They were standing around and sitting on the steps with Red Mike watching, so she put an extra switch in her hip. She thought to herself that one of them had to be *"The Man"* on Lakewood. She knew they sold a lot of drugs down here. At times she missed the club and being around so many street hustlers that command respect and have a lot of money to throw away. Then she thought about the perverts and the trouble that some of the guys she admired caused that often lead to shootings. There were some homicides committed from incidents started in the club. The jealous boyfriends of some of the dancers were the worst.

"What's up, trick?!" Hope greeted, answering her

door. Bee could hear Puddin' ranting upstairs while coming into the house.

"Goddamn, Hope! Don't the two of you ever get tired of fighting? What's wrong now?!" Bee asked.

"Yo, she went in the Kush that Landon got for Twin so, I slapped the shit out of her, Bee! I didn't mean to hit her in front of Simms, yo. I don't want Simms to think that going in the shit is cool for business. I was gonna try some out anyway, but Puddin' just couldn't wait," Hope began pleaded to her friend. Bee didn't say a word. She took in what her friend and co-worker said to her and she thought that Hope should have slapped the shit out of Puddin's face a long time ago. Hope really loved Puddin', so she put up with a lot from her. She accept things from Puddin' that she never put up with from anyone else that she dated. Bee had a girlfriend before, but she never lived with another woman. She was mindful of not confusing her daughters by letting them see their mother in bed with another woman intimately all of the time. Her daughters have to make those kind of decisions without her influence. The experience allows her to understand her friend a little more by having been in a relationship with a woman. Hope was hurt by the fact that she'd slapped Puddin'. It showed on her face. She loved her girl. They'd been together for almost two years. Before committing herself to Puddin', Hope slept around with a lot of girls. She took pride in turning out women and girls that believed that they would never be with another woman. It was a game for her to conquer as many women as she could. She liked to give another woman the best sex that they'd ever had coming from a woman, and also to prove to her conquest that they didn't need a man to be pleasured. That was Hope's thinking until she met Puddin'. Most of the females that Hope dealt with were some beautiful dime pieces. Puddin' is an average looking girl and is very down to earth. They got along beautifully and became very close early on. Hope still flirted from time to time and would occasionally have sex with another girl. That would be once in a blue moon since she and Puddin' were together. After a while Hope's promiscuity stopped. Puddin' had a job and moved into Hope's house with her ten year old son Lamar. In the beginning Hope loved the idea of having a family until Puddin' lost her job. That's when a lot of her trifling ways started shining through. She'd gotten comfortable and lazy. Hope spoiled her to the point that she started taking advantage of the situation. Once discovered that Hope made money in the jail, she wanted to floss, party, and have fun all the time. Hope even took care of Lamar. She paid for all of his clothes and he has every PlayStation game imaginable. Lamar really loves Hope and she is worthy of the admiration that he has for her.

Puddin' came down the steps with a traveling bag full of clothes. "I'll be back to get the rest of my stuff later on in the week. I left a note for Lamar to come up to my mother's house when he gets out of school," Puddin' said, with a nasty attitude.

"Look, you're taking this a little too far. Take that shit back upstairs. I said that I am sorry, Puddin'," Hope pleaded yet again.   Bee began to roll up a bud of the weed that was on the table from the buds that flew out of Puddin's hand when Hope slapped her. Puddin' ignored the pleas coming from her companion.

"Here is your key," she said, holding it out to Hope. Hope looked at her and didn't say another word. She just stared at the key in Puddin's hand. Puddin' placed the key onto the table and then headed towards the door with the things that she packed.

"She'll be back," said Bee, after the door shut behind Puddin'.

"Shit, maybe I do need a break from her for a while. She's been stressing me out and I don't want to be beating on her. I'm not sending Lamar to anybody's house. He's gonna stay right here with me," said Hope.

"Damn,   this   Kush   sure   is   good!   Them

niggas...gonna...love this!" Bee said, coughing between words. "Go get your scale," she said to Hope.

"The bitch got one of my Green-Dot cards! It's like $1500 on the one that she took!" Hope yelled coming back with the scale. I should call and freeze the account," Hope said angrily. She put the scale on the table. Both women measured out an ounce each of the weed. They always took some of Uncle Twin's weed. Jerry had some of the best weed in the city. The Kush Haze is payment for the hit on Freaky Ty. *None* of that is for sale. The Kush Haze is all personal for Twin and the family. The women didn't dare touch the dope. They only weighed it.

Bee and Hope packaged the entire batch of weed after hitting it up for their personal stashes. It's now time for Bee to get to the tobacco store before sending the shipment into the jail. The lieutenant had a wholesale deal with a tobacco salesman in the Middlesex Shopping Center for one hundred cans of tobacco at $20 each. Twin pays for the cans at $50 apiece. He charges $150 to $200 a can. This is the wholesale price of a can of tobacco in the jail. A person can easily make $600 off of each can and still have a little something extra to smoke after cashing out.

The tobacco store is in Essex near Gibson's home. The lieutenant had it all set up. After getting the tobacco, Bee called Pudgy. Pudgy is the potato chip delivery man that delivers condiments to the jail. Pudgy gets $250 to put the goods in the boxes of potato chips that are delivered to the commissary.

Pudgy has been working at his job for 10 years. In fact, he and the lieutenant dated over six years ago. He is married but, back then their affair had gotten serious. The lieutenant wanted Pudgy to leave his family, but he just couldn't do it, although he really loved Gibson. The well-being of his family outweighed his feelings and desires. Lt. Gibson got him to bring contraband into the jail, at first, for free. As time moved on, he felt obligated to do so out of feelings of guilt at the way their relationship ended. Once he peeped that she was making a lot of money, he began charging her to bring in the goods. She didn't care because the money was there for him to get a cut. That's about the time when she and Landon started to organize the hustle. Mrs. Butler, the head of commissary, didn't mind playing her part for the extra cash. She would keep all of their goods in the commissary and get the lists from Landon or Lt. Gibson that let her know who gets what on the days that the sections of the recipients were to receive items from the store. So, it wasn't a problem for Uncle Twin to receive a huge shopping bag full of goods that contained pounds of weed, cans of tobacco, grams of dope, and/or cell phones. There were also times when Landon, Bee, Hope, and even once in a while, Lt. Gibson would come to the commissary and deliver certain items to certain customers themselves. Most officers got caught bringing stuff inside of the jail. Their biggest advantage is in the fact that the contraband will already be inside of the jail. Time and opportunity remained on their side for years.

This explains the gist of the operation. All of the players remained the same, with the exception of the main contact inside of the jail. That would be Uncle Twin, or whoever the top leader of the BGF is at the time. The leaders would always change because some would beat the charges that they were waiting to go to court for and go home. That's if things went well in court. If it didn't go so well, others would get time and transfer to one of the many Maryland penal institutions. The leader always took care of the family. Anything short of that could result in a greedy leader getting chopped up real good and made to be an example for the next man in line. Family first. For Gibson and her crew, their hustle is so automatic that it became like putting on the uniform. They maintained the most clandestine operation in the jail and arguably one of the best in the city. The reason for choosing the BGF for the hustle is simple; they are the oldest group, in terms of prison organizations, in the modern era within the state of Maryland's prisons.

When Gibson started out in her hustle, she only brought in weed, drugs, and liquor. However, when the cigarettes were removed from the jail and as cell phones began to be so common, the business of smuggling in contraband became much more lucrative. Collecting the money became easier as well. Before they started using the Green-Dot money cards, the inmates' contacts on the street would more often than not meet one of the women at the Icon Inn after the work shift. It's always risky dealing with people. Some of the inmates' people are assholes. A lot of them were the inmates' sisters, wives, girlfriends, mothers, home girls, and chicks on the side. Then there were the hustlers, who would sometimes know the women from being in the jail at one time or more themselves. People will always try to get over in some kind of way, but for the most part, the business stayed good. An occasional relationship would develop from the interaction with the women. Gibson didn't mind giving up a little nookie to one of the contacts that caught her with a few drinks up in her and while feeling frisky. It only happened a time or two, but she has been known to get her a jump off unashamed, and unabashedly. The Green-Dot cards eliminated all of that kind of contact with the exception of Jerry. Jerry is BGF and Jerry is one of the very smart hustlers in Baltimore that lives by discretion. He always see you before you see him. Coming and going. For instance; he sat in his car after his other business was completed and waited for Candace to leave the mall. The Green-Dot cards also ensured that the money will always be straight. Landon handled that part of the business. Twin gives her a list of numbers after he checks every one of them. The money attached to the numbers will in turn be loaded onto the various debit cards that the Steel-side Queens held. Pudgy and Mrs. Butler are the only ones paid with cash. Caution and care is very important. No one wants to lose the hustle. It became a lifestyle for the women. It is a lifestyle that gives them a bunch of perks. They are the shit in the jail and at the bar. However, times are changing and due to the lax on the hiring practices at the detention center, most of the young females aren't as cautious or as smart as the older ones. Most of the men in the city had criminal backgrounds, so they aren't eligible to become correctional officers. Not many white men want to be officers in Baltimore's jail; and historically, they wouldn't dare let their women work in a place like that en masse. No siree. That is just too many black men around to corrupt the whiteman's women. This left the young black women, with and without children, seeking a career away from their poor circumstances. They are available to become the zookeepers. The difference with this zoo is that the animals could think; and in fact, often outsmart the young women who would prefer to have a lot of these particular animals home in bed or at work for the cause of family. This zoo captures a cunning, clever, desperate and violent species that comes from the most abject and poorest of jungles. He is a Baltimore blackman.

After taking care of her part of the business, Bee called Landon to give her a heads up so that she can take the list of commissary recipients to Mrs. Butler. She then called the top queen to let her know that everything is all good and that she'd just finished the business with Pudgy.

"Damn! I'm sorry, Daddy… Go on and finish giving it to Mommy," Gibson panted to Elliot on the other end of the phone. She'd been disturbed from damn near rubbing the tip of her clitoris off while listening to Elliot talk to her nasty and fulfilling all kinds of sexual fantasies over the phone. She is glad to know that everything had been done, but she had to get Bee off of the phone.

"Oooooh! Oooooh! Oh yes! Oh yes, Daddy… Mommy's cumming… Mommy's cuuummmiiing, ooww!!!" Gibson screamed, after releasing a big one that left her satin sheets soaked with her sweat and juices.

Gibson and Elliot had been on the phone for over two

hours talking about what they were going to do to one another's body and simulating the sounds of lovemaking. If Elliot is as good as he talks, she couldn't wait long enough to bed him down and give him the goods. Maybe she can take him somewhere in the jail and catch a quickie. She'd already given him head a few times, but now she wanted to feel the pole move her soul.

"Elliot, momma's got to get up now, get cleaned and ready for work. I'll see you soon. I got something for you, too," Gibson said to her jailhouse boyfriend.

"All right, Momma. I'll see you when you get here. Don't forget my Swiss and Corned Beef on Rye, Baby," Elliot reminded.

"I won't... I'll talk to you when I get to work," she said, rushing to hang up the phone.

Gibson laid in her king sized bed sprawled out like a snow angel. Her thoughts were on Elliot coming home to her. She really liked him and now that she's getting older, she want a man of her own. Her heart is set on him being the right one for the future. A man would complete her life. He didn't have to be a breadwinner. She could handle that part. He did have to get a job. Maybe she could finance a legitimate business venture for him. She'd heard many inmates over the years express desires to open up their own business. Maybe Elliot is the ingenious type as well. With the way things are today, a man can do just as well if not better coming home from jail doing some kind of business instead of focusing solely on a job. Maybe he can sell clothes or move furniture and bulk goods to the dump. Maybe Elliot has some other skills. She will just have to find out. In the meantime, she had to get up out of the bed and begin her routine of the work day. Before getting up, she reached for her cell phone to check on the rookie queen.

"Candace?"

"Hey, Ma! Good afternoon," Candace said, glad to be hearing from the lieutenant. "I'll be there to pick you up before two o'clock."

"That's good time, girlfriend. How did everything go?" The lieutenant asked.

"Oh, everything went well. I kept my appointment, made a few rounds, and now I'm on my way to get dressed for work," Candace explained. Gibson liked how she relayed the events of her morning without going into details over the phone. Gibson knew at that moment that she is one of her queens.

"Were you ok with the appointment? I mean, like, is that an appointment that you think that you can keep regularly? If not, don't worry about it. Don't do anything that you're uncomfortable with," Gibson said, hoping that Simms will stay on board.

"Well, I'm fine and I know that everything's going to be all right, but I do have something to tell you when I see you," she answered. "It's nothing to be too alarmed about. It's just a concern that I have."

"Okay. I'm going to start getting dressed myself," Gibson said.

"That's what's up," Candace responded before she hung up her phone. She didn't want to approach the subject of Hope slapping the shit out of Puddin' over the phone. It's a hard decision to make about speaking with Gibson. She decided to wait until she pick the lieutenant up for work.

Gibson rolled her thick ass out of bed and turned her stereo on. Mary J. Blige's amazing voice moaned about how she'd been there and done that while promising never to get hurt again. She turned the volume up and began her routine of getting dressed. Mary spoke to her heart and mind concerning thoughts about Elliot. Time would tell if this relationship is just another passing fling or the one that she has been praying for. She already checked his rap sheet and besides an assault and robbery charge over 10 years ago, he had some minor drug charges. He also hadn't been arrested in 6 years. His bail is only fifty thousand dollars, which is the only thing that disturbed Gibson. Why wasn't it paid? In Baltimore, with two co-signers that have jobs and $500 bail can be posted for him. With fifteen $1500, which is three percent, a bondsman could pull him and he could just pay on the balance once he's free. Didn't he at least have fifteen hundred? Surely his hustle paid him that. He never bragged or pretend that he was making a lot of money, either. This is one of the reasons that she grew motivated to get to know him, intimately. He didn't bullshit her at all. Nevertheless, she could easily pay his bail, but that is a no-no. She didn't give any nigga the impression that she would ever be flat out weak for them. She decided to be patient and let the chips fall where they may. Besides, they hadn't known one another for two months yet, and Elliot being locked up gave her patience and control.

After dressing, Gibson put on her eyeliner and makeup, looked into the mirror, then backed away to take a view of her figure. She had a little pouch in front. *"Time to go easy on the fried foods,"* she thought. That's when she heard the familiar sound of her car horn outside of her townhouse. She hurried to water her plants, shower them with kisses, grab her bag and locked up after closing the door to her home.

Candace moved into the passenger seat while waiting for the lieutenant. Gibson jumped into the car and pushed the memory button so that her seat, steering wheel, and mirrors would adjust to her mode of comfort before speaking to Candace. Now they were off with the music jumping!

Gibson drove directly to her favorite liquor store and invited Simms to go in with her to purchase the daily dose of vodka and grapefruit juice. Candace seized the opportunity to inform the lieutenant of everything that happened earlier. She reluctantly reported the event that occurred between Hope and her girlfriend and made her promise not to mention it to Hope because she isn't the type to put peoples' business in the streets. Especially after being a guest in their home. Gibson looked concerned. She assured Simms that she wouldn't say a word but that Hope will more than likely tell her everything.

Once they were back in the car, Gibson informed Simms that she is officially in the family and that Bee, Hope, Landon, and herself, are her biggest allies concerning anything and everything.

"Welcome, Baby. From now on, you are a Queen and you will see it soon. Never hesitate to call any one of us for assistance on anything. We will even cut a nigga's balls off with you or for you. The choice is yours. You got that?" Gibson hoped that she would implant a sense of camaraderie in her young friend. Candace definitely felt accepted. The music went up and the Beemer went into gear, pushing them both back into the seat. Gibson hit her drink and sped off to Steel-side.

Chapter 4

"Elliot, you know that I love you. I've been bending over forwards and backwards all your life for you, boy. Now, you need to get your stuff together and leave that junk alone. You're over thirty years old, son. You shouldn't be livin' here with me any your aunt. You need to be responsible and get yo'self a good woman... What ever happened to 'dat gurl, Gina? You messed her over so bad. 'Dat woman cared about you a lot. You shoulda married 'dat gurl. 'Stead, you wanna stay in 'dem damn streets--Lord forgive me--hanging out wit' 'dem junk heads, noddin' around and carryins on. I'm just tired! I been tired of yo' shinanigans. I's talkin' to ya' brother 'da other day and he said I bet' not be foolin' wit' choo. He says I should let ya' rusty behind stay there and get clean 'til you go to court." Elliot's mother got cut short from her tirade with his interuption.

"He needs to mind his business, Ma," he protested. "He's always talkin' against me. Like, he thinks I'm the one that stole Aunt Shirley's money out of her pocketbook," Elliot complained.

"Well, you was 'da onlyest one in 'da house with her on that day. Who else coulda' done it, boy?" Elliott's mother asked him and responding to his ridiculous attempt to persuade her from believing that he stole Aunt Shirley's money.

"See, Ma, he got you faked out. See that Ma, you sound just like him. He's still mad because I kept his car for a few minutes too long," complained Elliott about his brother.

"He told me 'dat it was over two hours and somebody told him 'dey seent you with a bunch a people on Lanvale and Rutland chasin' 'dat stuff wit' 'dem junkies in his brand new car, Elliot," his mother said hysterically.

"Ma, I only went hacking for a few minutes. I wasn't coppin' no drugs, either," he explained, attempting to defend himself of the accusations. His mother had him dead to right.

"Hacking wit' 'dat boy's brand new Mercedes Benz?! Are you some kinda fool? You lucky he ain't kill yo' ass- excuse me lawd- yo' rusty behind! If'n you ain't park 'dat car in front of his house and put those keys in the mailbox and snuck on away, he probly would have. I can't stand to see the two of you fighting, but I woodn' ta minded it if'n he lumped 'dat head of your'n up sumthin good 'dat day! You must straighten yo'self up, Elliot!"

"I am, Ma... So, you not gonna pay my bail, Ma?" He asked, sounding like a little boy. "Come on, Ma. I've been here over a month now and been going to church every Sunday, and bible classes, too. I went to court and my next date is almost three months away. I'm already clean and I promise I won't mess with the drugs anymore. I'm finished, Ma," Elliot pleaded.

"And I'm finished, too. I'm just tied of yo' stuff, and I don't intend to waste another dime on bailin' yo' rusty behind out of jail again! Maybe 'dis time you'll get it together. I love you, son, but 'dat junk has got you losin' yo'self. Who are you?! You don't even know! Of course, I know 'dat stuff makes you feel good and it's hard to resist, but you have the constitution inside yo'self to set yo'self free of 'da devil's grip on yo' soul. I know 'dat it's not easy, but you are being a slave to sumthin' 'dat has no power over you unless'n you give it 'da power by puttin' it in you and givin' in to 'da weakest part of yo'self as a man. 'Da onlyest one any man or human bein' should be a servant to is a servant of 'da God 'dat created everything and gave man 'da power over all 'dat He created. Nothin' on 'dis here earth should be able to make a man a slave to it, when all of 'dis creation serves man. Until you all understand 'dat, Elliot, we'll continue to make ourselves slaves. Stop being a slave to 'dat junk. Make a decision to leave it alone. You've had your fun wit' it. It's time to change into a new man, Elliot. Give yo' self a chance. After you go to court in three months, I'll see about gettin' you out if'n 'dey don't let you go," Elliot's mother exhausted herself explaining her intentions.

"Ma, you ain't never left me in jail like this. You know these niggas are crazy! They just stabbed up a guy named Freaky Ty eleven times. He's in the hospital half dead," Elliot said to his mother, trying to make her believe that he is scared and possibly in danger, so that she would feel sorry and pay his bail. He didn't tell her that he and another comrade were responsible for the attack on Freaky Ty.

"Oh my God, son, 'dat's terrible! Well, you just stay out of 'dem fools' way and pray 'dat 'da Good Lord delivers you from all of 'dis here evil 'dat you are face'n. He'll do it fo' you, too, son. He's done it fo' you befo'. If Jesus puts it on my heart ta get you befo' yo' court date, I will. Just work on bein' a man, Elliot. Your mother loves you," she said.

"I love you too, Ma," Elliot responded with disappointment in his voice. "I'll call again soon... Ma, Tell Aunt Shirley I said, hello and that I love her."

"OK... Take care of yo' self, baby, and keep up wit' yo' prayers." They both said their goodbyes and ended the phone conversation.

Elliot put his cell phone away feeling dazed. He didn't want to stay locked up for another three months. He just knew that he would probably go home on his next court date with probation or something. He hadn't been locked up in a long time. That made him a prime candidate for probation and/or drug treatment in Baltimore City, for drug offenses. Now that it's final and he won't be making bail, he conceded to the reality that he's trapped in the jail for at least 90 more days. He thought about asking Lt. Gibson for bail money. She did say that she wanted them to be together. If he asked her for money, it might scare her away from him by thinking he is just another broke-ass-nigga looking for a dummy CO that he could work. Well, he is, but now that he is locked up and getting clean, he had plans on going uptown fresh and on his *A* game.

He can holler at Big Head Charlie now. Charlie always

told him if he stop getting high, he will hit him off lovely with a big boy package. Charlie knew that Elliot could hustle and get that money. He brought Charlie a lot of sales. He knew that Charlie's car and that big diamond bracelet he'd just bought came directly from the sales of Elliot's customers. If only he could make that money for himself, he would probably shoot past Big Head Charlie. Charlie came off the steps only three years ago and Elliot has been on his team ever since. Charlie is 20 years old and giving orders to Elliot. Elliot planned to run his own thing this time. Maybe this time away is just what he needed. He'd been chasing dope and coke for over six years straight, since the last time that he was arrested for two weeks.

'Momma just might be right about me staying in here for a minute,' he thought to himself.

He sat on his bunk and started reading a XXL magazine when he heard his name called for commissary. This confused him because, he didn't order anything from the store. He knew that he couldn't get anything because the money order that his mother sent him didn't arrive in time for him to put in a commissary slip. He walked to the desk and sure enough, there was a bag with his name and I.D. number written with a black marker on it.

"Sign your name here," said the tier officer, pointing to the receipt and the slot next to his name that needed his signature, confirming what he received. Elliot grabbed the pen from the desk and immediately signed for the goods.

"Aren't you going to look in there and check your stuff to see if you got everything," said the officer?

"Oh, yeah! You're right," he answered. He opened the bag quickly and looked inside of it before signing his name.

"All right, now! Don't be coming to me complaining, or talkin' 'bout, *'Ms. Braswell, they ain't put my noodles in there.'* I ain't gonna be trying to hear it! I saw how fast you looked in that bag. Yall always in a hurry to do absolutely nothing," She whined, mocking the complaining inmates, then she scolded them.

"Don't worry, boo, I'm good," Elliot said to the officer bringing the commissary to the inmates. He walked away from the desk with the bag. He wanted to hurry away before she could catch a possible mistake. He made his mind up to keep the stuff, knowing that he hadn't ordered anything. Just as soon as he got to his bunk, he looked around before opening the bag. As usual, there were about three people that looked away when he looked in their direction. People just can't help being so damn nosey. Once they got the message from his silent expression, he opened the bag. There were a couple of food items along with some potato chips inside. The bag also held a huge bag of menthol tobacco. Elliot's eyes widened. He closed the bag and put it in his tote box underneath his bunk, smiling. He took notice of the nosey stares, once again, but didn't say a word. One of his comrades came over to him and asked why he smiled so hard.

"It ain't nothing, comrade," he responded. He laid on his bunk with his legs stretched out and hands behind his head to relax. He thought about nothing but how good he intended to have it for the next 90 days over Steel-side since he had to stay and couldn't make bail. Head, brown (tobacco), plus Swiss and Corned beef sandwiches? A nigga' gonna be living like a king in the jail. Steel-side didn't look too bad at the moment.

Meanwhile, on the other side of the jail, an inmate by the name of Maximillian Muhammad was being let off of T section's lock up. He had been placed on administrative segregation without a formal written infraction because there weren't any witnesses to the mayhem that he wreaked on two members of the BGF. Max's incident began, it seems, when some BGF comrades attempted to rob two other inmates for their sneakers. Max tried to intervene, which caused one of the comrades to swing his knife at Max. That was all she wrote! Max, trained in hand to hand combat by the marines and adept in the martial arts as a practicing member of the Nation of Islam, didn't like the disadvantage of the inmates being attacked by the comrades. He gave the comrades a serious ass whipping that could have been worse. So, after the fracas was over, the two comrades were laying on the floor with several broken bones and Max was being restrained by three officers that claimed they never saw the attack, but apprehended Max because he was standing over the two victims. However, they both failed to say who attacked them. The duty lieutenant placed Max on lock-up and away from the population for his own safety and the safety of other inmates in the general prison population. After several letters to the security chief and various administrators, he is now coming off of lock-up, having convinced the proper commanders that he did not fear for his safety and desired to be back in the general population.

Also, on the very same day, Jay is finally being let off of the hammer by Lt. Gibson, after Uncle Twin continued to plead his case. She also believed that a month is just about enough time to make him pay for Blackwell losing her job. Jay found out that he'd been let off of lock up with the guy Max that beat his comrades. His knife is too sharp and he was now prepared to avenge the honor of his two comrades and represent for them. However, Uncle Twin sent word to all of the comrades that no one is to touch Max. These orders came from the street. Max is very prominent in the city among those who took on the cause of trying to change the conditions of black people at the grassroots in the city. He's a good soldier and one of Minister Carlos's best in the city of Baltimore. Jay didn't know any of this. In truth, he probably wouldn't care. All he knows is that this person violated the BGF! This is a very admirable trait within the organization. He displayed loyalty and upheld retributions towards all violators of the family. He is also one of the best warriors in BGF. They also advocate a positive and revolutionary change for black people, too, but in the jungles of prison corruption rules and righteous principles can get twisted by clever minds whose hearts are filled with greed and a psyche infused with self-hatred. These are some of the leaders that influence unsuspecting members and hide behind the collective whole. Jay is dedicated to the cause and only care about his BGF comrades. He doesn't realize that he is supposed to be a vanguard for every Blackman. Jay anticipated seeing this perceived enemy that battered his brothers.

Jay and Max were on opposite sides of the same section so, they never saw one another. However, word traveled that Max is supposed to be coming off of lock-up and into the general population. Their properties were brought to the section from storage and placed into the day room so that they could discard the jumpsuits of the segregated inmates and dress themselves with their personal. Their radios, commissary, food items, and other things that weren't allowed on lock-up are also with their property.

Max stood in the dayroom before collecting his stuff after a brief inventory. Jay walked in and his eyes locked onto Max as he continued to study this possible adversary. Max looked up from collecting his things and observed this brother whose eyes remained focused on him with such a fierce stare. Max looked away but continued to keep Jay in his peripheral sight. There is no question that the brother that entered the dayroom possessed the cockiness and demeanor of the Black Guerilla Family. Most of them walked around the jail putting their power on display. Max looked at it as insecurity.

"As-Salaam-Alaikum, brother," Max said to Jay. He offered his hand to Jay, who looked at Max's palm with a scowl and then back to Max's face. "Have it your way, but I'm not your enemy, brother. By the look on your face, you are your own enemy."

"Whatchoo mean by that, slim?" Jay asked, looking Max dead in his eyes, almost ready to attack.
"Well, first of all, Comrade George Jackson is the reason for BGF. He is the standard of a Blackman that we suppose to live by and he would've never condoned or even given his okay to

violate and abuse another Blackman for sneakers or anything else, unless that man is a rat or violated a principle like stealing, treason, or anything immoral towards another brother. That kind of materialism is what keeps us losing and stuck in non-progression. It just wouldn't have happened around Comrade George. I might not be a member of the BGF, but I reacted to the situation like Comrade George would have. That's the root of your animosity?

"Now I see why there was a point in comrade George Jackson's life when he contemplated joining with brothers in America as it concerned the revolution and our struggle during several years of his development. He believed that the brothers in Africa and Central and South America needed his services and that they had the true spirit of revolution because they weren't raised by and filled with the mind of their oppressors," Max explained, schooling Jay to things that he might not have known about Comrade George Jackson.

"Whatchoo' know about Comrade George? He ain't take no shit off of anybody and he hated all pigs. He was strong and he didn't care about this system because all it represents for us is oppression, slavery and death at the hands of fascist pig police that protect their oligarchs and feed off of the proletariat class. If you don't think like George, you ain't nothing. If you ain't BGF you don't count," Jay responded, continuing to express himself aggressively.

"You are right, brother. He did hate the capitalistic system of this government and the pig policemen who enforce the laws that are designed to protect the elite, while oppressing the ignorant and poor masses, who, in most cases, are the descendants of the poor slaves that built the United States and strengthen it as the leader of the so-called free world. That same mind of oppression is being emulated, in a very small way, by brothers such as yourself, who exploit and take advantage of brothers that are physically weaker or appear to be at a disadvantage. Why prey on another brother because they are alone against three, four, or more individuals that want to extort them for material and selfish reasons? Is that what you represent, brother? Is that what BGF consists of? George Jackson could see just how much a lot of his people, who were descendants of slaves, wanted to be like his slavemasters. We love to imitate power instead of learning, binding our causes and then grow into becoming powerful. Had George Jackson lived, he desired to go to Africa or Central and South America and link himself with revolutionary minds that weren't faked out by material greed and comforts for a very small portion of the people. His struggles were beyond the BGF. You are right. His revolution was for all of the indigenous and oppressed who were being dumped on by Capitalistic and Fascist powers... Here," Max said, reaching into his bag and handing Jay a book entitled, *"Blood In My Eyes"* by George Jackson. Jay isn't a dummy. He can understand why this brother is to go untouched. No one violates a member of BGF and is not dealt with severely. This brother is definitely the exception. He grabbed the book from Max and began looking it over. Then he went to hand it back. Max held his hand out in a manner that indicated he wanted Jay to read it.

"Brother, you go ahead and read that. It's a very interesting piece. Remember this: BGF, Crips, Bloods, Sunni Muslim, Nation of Islam, Ahmmaddiya Muslim, Shia Muslim, Baptist, A.M.E, Jehovah's Witnesses, Protestant, Catholic, Hebrew Israelites, etc, all of these are tribes that our people are a part of. It has been the aim of the enemy to keep us from feeling one another's pain, or thinking that the source of our pains and struggles are not the same. Tribes keep us fighting one another and not recognizing that we are all one suffering people. Our passions and desires to be better, to do better, and to have better are the same. My name is Brother Max, brother," he said, once again, extending his hand. This time Jay became compelled to grip it with a solid and firm hand shake. As they shook hands, Uncle Twin popped into the dayroom. He looked at the two men shaking hands and once they finished, he reached out for Jay's hand and pulled him in close for an embrace.

"What up, comrade? Hamjambo!" Twin greeted.

"Nothing, comrade. Cejambo," Jay respoded. "I'm glad to be off of the hammer. I ain't mad at the lieutenant. I guess she had to do what she had to do. It's about time her investigation is over," said Jay, not knowing that there never existed any investigation.

"I see that you met Brother Maximillian Muhammad. He's a sharp one. How's it going, Brother Max," Twin greeted him, extending his hand. Max received it and reciprocated the gesture. He knows Uncle Twin and what his position is with BGF. Twin is the kind of brother that held the minds of a true army in his hand. This fearless and small army could make a difference with black men. Not only in a physical war, but an army that can declare war against disunity, ignorance, and black on black violence. Also, and in the grand scheme of things, demonstrate that example for the youth of the city. In the minds of the BGF, Twin is a real revolutionist. In Max's mind, he is a purveyor of an unrighteous cause. His own. He is a greedy dope fiend that hides his weaknesses behind a generation of fearless warriors who are willing to fight for change instead of continuing on in the oppression of their own kind. If only they had somebody to give them the right and proper guidance.

Max has been in the jail for almost six months and he continued to be conscious of his surroundings. Twin once tried to recruit Max, but Max's allegiance is to Allah only and the true uplifting of a degenerate people. However, when dealing with people like Twin, he used diplomacy.

"What's good, Uncle Twin? As-Salaam-Alaikum!" Max greeted. He returned Twins handshake.

"Yeah, Wa-Alaikum-Salaam... You don't have to worry about the family in the jail, brother. They have instructions to give you a pass for harming the comrades. You know we don't usually let stuff like what you did slide, but I gave my word to Brother Carlos personally, that none of my comrades..." Uncle Twin paused in mid-sentence and went into a nod. After a few seconds, he popped out of his nod and said, "You cool, brother. You cool... Come on Jay. You're moving down on the section wit' me." He grabbed one of Jay's bags and walked out of the dayroom.

Max let Jay know that he will get the book from him later and that he hopes Jay gets something out of reading it. Jay's attitude changed and he smiled at Max. He promised to return the book just as soon as he finish reading it. Jay put the book in his other trash bag that held the rest of his property, lifted the bag over his shoulder and hurried to catch up to Uncle Twin.

The two comrades approached G-section and saw a few comrades hanging around on the tier. Jay began to smile at being around the familiar faces of the comrades that he knew on the tier. Entering into the section, he stopped at the officer's desk. Uncle Twin motioned for one of the comrades to take Jay's bags.

"I'mo put your stuff in your cell. Make sure that you come to my house as soon as you check in with Officer Landon," Twin instructed him. "Come on, Dime," Twin said to the brother that grabbed Jay's other bag. There were BGF brothers running around all over the section. Everybody came to greet Jay to the section. There were offers of food, tobacco, and weed. Jay accepted all offers. He is very glad to be off of the hammer. It wouldn't be so bad any other time because he would have had some weed and brown to smoke of his own. His girl Tiffany fucked that up for him by calling the jail to snitch on Blackwell. He'd been talking to Blackwell while Tiffany was on the phone. She'd gotten jealous because Blackwell flirted with Jay as a prank to get Tiffany angry. Tiffany was already mad at Jay because she found out that Jay and her best friend Sharonda had sex behind her back when he was free. She also found out that Jay was doing the girl Kenyatta. She couldn't stand that girl. She hated that freakball, skanky ass bitch, Kenyatta. Blackwell regretted her decision, but no use crying over the obvious. It lead to her losing her job.

Jay loved Tiffany. She mothered all of his children. They'd been together for over thirteen years. Their relationship began when they were in middle school. After being engaged for over three years, she grew tired of Jay continuously cheating around on her. Tiffany had all of his money and she always took care of him when he got locked up, like a mother would her son. She took care of all of the bills, the lawyers, the children, Jay's business affairs; and she made sure that his money was spent wisely. She shopped for his packages and collected his money from the homeboys that owed him. Jay's cheating made her sick and tired of him disrespecting her. Once she heard Blackwell on the other end of the phone, she went ballistics. She caused the entire jail to suffer. She was convinced that Blackwell and Jay were up to more than just business. Hopefully, everything is back to normal. It's now time for Jay to make more money. He's going to court in a couple of months and he didn't know if or not he would get prison time. At least he got Tiffany to calm down and forgive him. By the way that his comrades offered him weed and brown, he could tell that things just might be back to normal.

"Well, well, well. Mr. Jayson Hill, you are in cell 58, in the back of the tier," said Landon, coming down the stairs from the top tier. She discovered to herself that Jay is a cutie, but she would have to play hard with him for a while because of what happened to Blackwell. She knows who Jay is because of him being with Twin all of the time, but he never knew her relevance to the hustle.

"What up, Ms. Landon? That perfume you're wearing is the bomb. You know I been locked down for a minute and I might attack you," he said playfully. If looks could kill, Jay's neck laid streched on the chopping block and Landon looked to bring down the axe for the final blow. She stared at him like a principal would if one of her students got caught throwing eggs at her car. Remember, he caused her girl to lose her job. The harsh feelings festered.

"Whatever, boy. Now get away from my desk before I send you back where you just came from," she said, rolling her eyes. Landon had never talked to him like that before.

"What's wrong? What I do to you, Miss Landon?" He pleaded.

"You ain't do nothin'. Just get out of my face before I send you back to lock up, Jayson Hill." Jay shrugged his shoulders, did an about face turn and stepped onto the tier. Landon looked at him walking away. She likes Jay, a little. He is smart, strong, and don't take any shit from adversaries. He's well respected in the jail and Uncle Twin noticeably thought very high of him. Jay made it hard for Landon to stick to her rule about messing around with the inmates or co-workers. No one knew that she hadn't been with a man in over 2 years, with the exception of Gibson. She caught herself briefly fantasizing about Jay and quickly pushed the thoughts out of her head.

Uncle Twin had a young BGF brother assigned to stand post outside of his cell every time the doors open to let him know who came and went on or off the section.

"Hamjambo, comrade," Jay said to the bodyguard.

"Cejambo, Jay," said the young comrade, acknowledging Jay. They both shook hands and then Jay entered the small cell. Uncle Twin sat on his bunk rolling up weed.

"Here you go, yo. Sit down and light that up. I'm glad you off. You know you my seed and we got a few things to take care of today. It's a big day for us in the jail. It's the first time that we've been on since you went to the hammer, yo. Now it's time to get it in," Twin said to Jay. Jay sat on the toilet and began to light the joint that Twin gave to him. He had a small Bic lighter. There's no limit to the contraband that these guys have in possession. Jay hit the weed a couple of times before coughing uncontrollably.

"That's Kush Haze," Jay said, before he continued to cough up a lung.

"This is for you to get some bread with," Twin said, handing Jay an ounce of weed and a big bag of menthol tobacco. I need five back from that ounce and the same from the brown. Take these," Twin said handing Jay three fifties of Kush Haze. "That's for you comrade."

"Thanks, Unc! You are the truth! It's time for me to get it in, yo," Jay said, feeling excited and high from the weed. He only smoked twice since he'd been on lock up, and the weed was nowhere near as good as this.

"You still got your knife?" Twin asked him.

"Right here," said Jay, pulling his Sam Bowie knife out of the secret pocket that he made into all of his jeans.

"Did you pay your phone bill?"

"Come on, Unc. You know Tiff stay on top of her game. I would be lost without Shorty," Jay admitted.

"Yeah, I know... Jay, you gotta stop fucking so many bitches. Tiffany is a real nigga's dream. She down for her man's cause 1000%. She let me know that she is sorry for what she did, and I believe her. If she was anybody else but your children's mother, she might be severely touched for what she did. Never let your dirt contaminate your house. Stop fucking them bitches that live in your hood, yo." Twin admonished his soldier.

"You're right, Unc. Tiffany is a ride or die chick, and she be taking good care of my kids to the fullest. I just gotta marry her when I touch down," Jay expressed.

"Yeah, and if I beat this charge, I want a spot in the wedding," Twin said.

"Oh, you got that fo' sho', comrade." Jay said, showing the pearly whites.

"That's what's up... now come on. Let's get out of here and go take care of some bid'ness," said Twin, stopping to take a one on one from the folded piece of paper filled with some of the raw heroin that Jerry sent to him. The dope isn't a bomb; it's a missile!!! Twin closed the paper, put it in his sock, stood up and rapped, *"It's like a jungle sometimes, makes me wonder how I keep from going under,"* and then he exited his cell with Jay trailing behind him. It's now time for them to take care of supplying the jail.

Twin had his IAC president's pass and he gave Jay a folder with a lot of papers in it to make it look like Jay assisted him. At first Landon gave Jay a hard way to go about accompanying Twin to handle his business. Twin's antennas shot up right away. Jay had to plead with Landon to let him off of the tier. He explained that he's helping Twin with the inmate's affairs, which is really some bullshit he fed her. She finally relented and they both went on with the business.

"Damn, Jay! I ain't never see Landon act like that 'bout any nigga," Twin admitted more to himself than to Jay after observing the exchange between the pair.

"Whatchoo mean, Unc?" Jay asked.

"She gave you too much attention. She knows that I always go take care of my business.   Plus, I take who I want with me as long as it's just one person. I go by myself, most of the time. She knows that if somebody is with me, I need them." Twin struggled to make sense of her actions.

"Well, Unc, I don't know what's up with her, but she's been breakin' my balls since I stepped onto the tier. I thought that maybe the bitch is on the rag or something," Jay cracked.

"Now, that may be true, but it's more to it than that. She knew that you were coming on her tier. I personally made sure that you got down here on the section with me. She could have expressed her displeasure then, but she didn't protest one bit...I think she wanna give you some pussy, comrade," said Twin, like he really figured out the secret to world peace.

"Ha, ha, ha! *Helllll No*, Unc! Not Landon! She fine as all out, and I would love to book her, but everybody knows that Landon ain't to be fucked with like that. She cool and all, but she don't give *nobody* play. Not even the CO dudes, Unc," explained Jay.

"Well, I have never seen her act like a school girl with any nigga, and that's exactly what she was doing with you, yo." Twin schooled Jay.

"Are you for real, Unc? You think she likes the kid?" Jay inquired.

"I sure do, but Landon's a little off, yo, and if she does choose you, you gotta play your cards right or don't play them at all. She is serious company, yo," Twin said, warning Jay. He knows that his instincts are right. Why would she give them such a hard way to go when she know that Twin left off of the tier to go make money for them all? Landon use to tell Twin all of the time that she'll leave a nigga standing still at any time or any day, but *"don't nothin' move her but the money!"* He *knows* that she likes Jay. They continued talking and Uncle Twin teased Jay about it while making their rounds.

The Muslim brothers are first on the list. Uncle Twin and Jay went up to N section where the Imam Muk'min is housed. Twin walked to comrade Ochie's cell and sent Ochie to get Muk'min. Muk'min appeared with the big brother Nasir at his side. Nasir stood six feet, eight inches and weigh over 300 lbs. He wears a full beard perfectly rounded to his face and his hands are as big as baseball gloves. He remind you of Jonathan Ogden that played for the Baltimore Ravens. He never speaks a word and let the Imam do all of the talking, but everybody knows that Nasir will crush you. He's in the jail for two bodies that he's been fighting in the courts with for over three years.

Muk'min spent a thousand dollars just as he said he would. He wanted three phones and the rest in tobacco so that the Muslims could smoke and make some money for their own treasury. Even though smoking is forbidden to them, it is a creature comfort for the agony of detention. A few of them sniff dope and a lot of them smoke weed, too, but they have to get those vices on their own. Twin gave Ochie three grams and asked him to bring back $400 per gram. Ochie can make $700 to $800 a gram. He also gave him an ounce of loud. He wants $400 off of that, too. That's an easy eight to nine hundred dollar bag up. As usual, and before Twin and Jay depart from N section, Twin promised Ochie that he would check on getting officer   Berry to sell him some pussy. Twin loved Ochie. Their relationship as homeboys went back over 30 years.

After finishing up on N section, they made their way over to P and Q dormitories. There they saw Elliot in the hallway on P section. Elliot gave Twin a fifty dollar Green-dot card for his donation towards Jamma finances and told him that he would be sending him a bag of commissary for finances, also. He came up off of the tobacco that Gibson sent to him. Twin gave Elliot one of the grams to sell and took several orders for cans of tobacco and a couple of ounces of weed. Twin and Jay went on to collect well over another thousand dollars' worth of Green-dots from P and Q sections alone.

The next stop took them to J and K sections. That's where most of the Crips are located. When Twin and Jay walked to G-loc's cell, he and Big Pimp were already laid back blazing up weed. Candace and Gibson had a commissary bag sent to Pimp as soon as they got to work, along with Elliot's bag. They didn't mention anything to Twin about their own stash.

G-loc spent a couple hundred to keep business good and Twin gave him an extra courtesy fifty dollar bag of the Kush Haze. He liked G-loc. The both of them were some money getting young niggas in the jail. Twin, Jay, G-loc and Pimp sat in G-loc's cell for about forty five minutes smoking weed, talking on their cell phones, cracking jokes and kicking their bid. The four of them were acting as if they were on the streets. Actually, the only difference is that they couldn't drive their cars and they couldn't go to their own homes. In truth, some of the inmates could make their way better over Steelside than on the streets. One of the young Blood members told Uncle Twin that he saved up enough money to buy a big eighth of coke to start with on the block when he hit the streets from selling tobacco alone. He accomplished this in the five months that he'd been locked up.

Twin and Jay walked all over Baltimore City Jail wheeling and dealing. They went to the annex building and cleaned up in sales. They even made their way over to the J.I. building, which is an almost separate jail with over five hundred more inmates in residence. They now had a few thousand dollars in Green-dot numbers. Twin checked every last one of them. Once his cell phone went dead, it was time for him and Jay to call it a day. Twin counted four thousand dollars in numbers, and, as soon as he and Jay got back to G-section, he handed them to Officer Lacy Landon. No one saw it and no one knew. This would be the routine for the next ten days or so, until they ran dry and another move could be made. Now Landon could get the Jimmy Choo shoes that she'd been wanting. Her CLK also needed a tune up.

Max had to wait on T-section during most of the three to eleven shift until a bunk could be assigned to him. At first, he was classified to go back to the J.I. building where he spent most of his time waiting to go to trial. He wanted to return there because of the associates that he'd established with the officers and inmates alike. He'd grown accustomed to the familiar surroundings. The officers inside of the jail were a completely different set of COs than those that worked the J.I. annex building. He could make due wherever he had to be, but it became easier to settle in a familiar atmosphere.

Max received the news that he would not be going back to the J.I. building. It was decided for his safety and the safety of the two inmates that he'd been fighting. They both were still housed over J.I. He had to remain over Steel-side. Steel-side is notoriously more dangerous than the J.I. building, or any other jail in the state. In fact, it is one of the most dangerous prisons in the United States of America.

The traffic officer found Max a bed on Q-section,

which is the tier that Hope runs. Once Max got to the section, he was greeted by one of the prettiest faces that he'd ever seen in his life.

"My name is Officer Hope and I don't want a whole lot of bullshit on my section." Hope explained this to Max, in her straight to the point manner, when he arrived.

"Well, Officer Hope, my name is Maximillian Muhammad, but you can call me Max. You probably won't even notice that I'm around," he said. Max thought that Officer Hope is a very pretty woman. She had long cornrows in a very fanciful design and her skin glowed honey bun brown. She stood about five foot nine inches tall and she has long eyelashes that flutter over the prettiest brown eyes. Max immediately thought of the song by Mint Condition called *"Pretty Brown Eyes"*. She isn't too big, and although her uniform fits loose, he can tell that her clothes belie the curves of her body. She had a natural beauty. Max, overwhelmed by her, had to contain himself as a man should. However, her demeanor emitted masculinity. Max can't tell if she is a tomboy or a toyboy. She sounded rather aggressive in her tone of voice, but Max didn't care. Very few women moved him in the way that this one did. Even if she is a lesbian. He is a man and she is a woman. Max thought that she probably *is* a lesbian because in Baltimore a very large percentage of young women are finding comfort, solace, and security in their relationships with other women. He knows that it will be his mission to find out, one way or another, if she is a lesbian. Until then, it's best for him to remain nonchalant and incognito.

"I was told to put you in dorm #5 because, there are only eight beds in there. Somebody wants us to keep a close eye on you," Hope informed him. "Come on," she said, getting up from behind the desk, after sitting down to log him into the book. Before they could move, Lt. Gibson came through the grill and down the stairs onto the section. She wanted to meet this Maximillian Muhammad, whom her co-workers COs Elsey and Ricks spoke so highly of. They are women that fell in love with Max when he slept in the J.I. building. Elsey said that she almost came on herself watching Max take a knife from one of the gang members. The two guys were real trouble makers. The women officers also told Gibson how polite and intelligent he is. At first, they couldn't believe that he had a murder charge. After seeing him in action, they understood. He probably was provoked. In Baltimore City, a lot of the homicide victims initiated the cause of their own demise. Max is a very gentle person and he seems to be the last one to start trouble or even make a scene.

"Are you Maximillian Muhammad?!" Gibson asked him, excited.

"Yes, I am," Max answered. He could see the lieutenant bars on her uniform.

"Hope, I hear that this is one bad brutha. He'll fuck something up. You gotta watch him," she said, putting her friend on notice.

"So, you lied to me, Maximillian?" Hope asked.

"No, I didn't. I'm really laid back and I told you that you can call me Max," he said exasperated, unlike the whining men that the women so often encountered. Hope and Max's eyes connected briefly, staring at one another face to face before Hope instructed him to lock into his assigned dormitory. He stepped aside so that she could lead the way to dorm #5. Max studied the swagger in her walk. He just had to get to know Officer Hope.

"Do you work this section tomorrow?" Max asked.

"I sure do," she said, and then she walked away. While Gibson waited for her friend, she observed the exchange between the pair.

"He's the one, Hope," she said to her friend.

"What do you mean? You're a ho' if I ever knew one. I thought that you were on the guy Elliot," Hope said to Gibson.

"I don't mean for me! Girl, that's your piece right there! You better get a pickle or a beef sausage because, homeboy wants you. I see it in his eyes. You're gonna need some dick sucking lessons," said Gibson.

"You know I ain't for no niggas. I ain't had dick since dick had me. Now, stop playing, bitch. I ain't sucking his dick. But he is nice looking. Maybe he can suck mine." Hope said, laughing.

"Well, he's on you. Try it, you just might like it." Gibson said, winking at Hope.

Chapter 5

 "That's right, baby! Give it to me! Uuh, Uuh, Uuh! Oh Paul, give it to me! Do it feel good?" Bee asked, panting and breathing heavily in her moment of ecstasy.

 "Oh, yes! Yessss, baby! It feels sooooo good!" Paul responded and continued to thrust in and out of Bee's juicy tunnel. Her womb felt so warm to him and Bee knew how to contract her vaginal muscles. That made Paul go crazy! They were in a room at the Day's Inn Hotel for hours in downtown Baltimore, after taking in a night at the Comedy Factory. They'd been in every sexual position on the chart. Paul prepared to climax for the third time. Once he did, it felt as though he shot a blank. Bee drained the poor man so, he collapsed. He couldn't do anything else but lay on top of her with all of his body weight. Bee's eyes closed. She smiled and shivered thinking about how good Paul was just giving it to her. She laid beneath him on the king sized bed that they'd been rolling all over on.

 "Damn, Paul! That's the best sex ever! You really know how to hit it!" Bee said, her eyes still closed.

 "All of my love is for you, Bee. I don't want anybody else but you." Paul got himself together and leaned up on his elbows so that he could be face-to-face with Bee. He had that starry look in his eyes that she just cannot stand. She went on playing his game, returning his gaze. "Don't you know that I'll do whatever it takes to make you happy? I'm right here," said Paul. "Your hooks are in me and I'm caught on the line like a fish." Bee just laid there listening to the things that Paul pleaded to her.

 "Excuse me. Watch out so that I can use the bathroom," is all that she could say. Her voice now void of feelings and emotions. Paul got up quickly to retrieve the gift box that held the one carat diamond engagement ring from his pants. He discarded the box and then opened the case. He placed the ring on the nightstand of her side of the bed and turned the lamp to shine on it. He paid a pretty penny for the ring. It's just as opulent as the rings that she wore and he knew that she would love it.

Bee stayed in the bathroom for a good minute. Paul hadn't noticed it because he was tired and in the process of dozing off to sleep. When she reappeared, he smiled, but it quickly became replaced with a look of bewilderment. Bee began putting her clothes on. She saw the ring on the night stand but looked away from it. Hell, she couldn't miss it the way the nigga placed it under the damn light. She continued to search for her clothes that were strewn about the hotel room.

"What's wrong, Bee? Where are you going?" Paul asked confused. He jumped out of the bed just as naked as the day he was born. Bee stopped for a brief second to look at all of his mangoods that she decided to give up and walk away from. She knew that Paul had it going on. A tall handsome man that had dick for days, but she didn't want any parts of being in love. She loved men and couldn't be tied down to one nigga. It don't matter how good the dick is. Also, his paycheck just isn't long enough. She is an independent woman by every aspect of its terminology.

Bee is 28 yrs. old and is not planning to slow down until at least 40 and her daughters are older. Maybe then she could see herself with a man like Paul. Not now. Damn! Why did this nigga have to get his feelings all caught up into her like this? She is going to miss him blowing her back out, but the best thing for her to do is to cut it off right now.

"Paul, I'm not the woman for you. You are a good man, but I'm not ready to settle down, so let's just nip this in the bud," she said.

"What do you mean? I am prepared to spend the rest of my life with you. Isn't that what every woman wants in life?" He asked her, pleading with a Romeo and Juliet poetic voice. "I love you and I can't live my life without you." Paul put his boxers on, walked to the night stand to get the ring and grabbed Bee's hand, falling on one knee. "Will you marry me,

Belinda Berry?"

"Oh, Paul! Please, get up!" She said, pulling away from him. "You don't want to marry me. I have four children. My girls don't even know you that well. I got three baby daddies and my oldest daughter's father is doing 19 years with the feds. The other two niggas still come around from time to time and sometimes I have to fight with them about their children. I can't bring you home to my girls and in that situation. I just can't!"

"What do you mean? I will love them as much as I love you. I'll be a good step-father and I'll stay out of their father's way. Just teach me how to love you. I promise that I'll make you happy. I surrender my heart to you," he continued to wail while still on his knees. "We can give your daughters a little brother."

"Now, see, that's where you are wrong. Ain't nare another baby comin' out this pussy! No siree! Paul, I ain't havin' no mo' children! So you can just forget that!" Bee shouted. She began to get agitated by his clown ways. "Get the hell up off of your knees, man! Not only do I not want to marry you, I think that it's time that we not see each other for a while. You're too much for me to handle."

"What do you mean? Is there someone else?" He asked, with a gloss of tears ready to fall. "Don't I give you good lovin'? I thought that you love this." He said, nodding towards his penis. "Don't you want it for the rest of your life, baby? I will never go anywhere or think to leave you."

"JUST, STOP IT, NIGGA! PLEASE, STOP IT! I'm not getting married to anyone and that's that! Furthermore, don't call me again! Yes, you are one of the best lovers that I ever had and you do know how to treat a woman, but I got two daughters in private school and I pay daycare and a babysitter for the other two! I have my own home, my own car, and my own money in the bank! I have male friends that give me money, too! I don't need a nigga for nothing but to give me a wet ass! I'm going to miss you fucking my brains out, but it's

90

over and that's it!" Bee yelled. She grabbed her jacket after getting fully dressed during the heated exchange and walked over to the door. She went to open the door, but before she did, she turned around to look at Paul, who now sat on the edge of the bed with his head held low in such a pitiful state.

"I'm sorry and I hope that we can still be friends. Toughen up and just take it like a man. You'll see that this is best for us both," she said, opening the door to leave. She walked to the elevator and pushed the button. While waiting on the elevator, she thought about the great sex that she and Paul where having just less than an hour ago and for a brief instance, she thought about going back to the room to get her a goodbye piece, but then the bell rang to indicate that the elevator had arrived and broke her out of her spell. She stepped onto the elevator and pushed the button to the garage.

Paul sat on the bed twisted inside. He couldn't remember a time that he ever felt so rejected. He'd fallen in love with Bee. He thought that they had become closer. Shit, he wanted to marry her with four children. She should have leapt at the chance to have a husband like him. Didn't she know that a lot of women wanted to be with him? She should be so lucky to have him for the past six months. What is her problem?

Paul thought about all of the times that she paid for half of the dinner when they were out together. She just wanted to prove to him her independence. He didn't mind giving her money or buying her things. He even put in mad overtime just to spend all of the extra money with Bee. She never ever seemed to struggle and always looked good. He loved her style! She knew how to work her body and could handle every inch that he had. Most women couldn't do that. He thought that they were a match made in heaven.

Paul sat on the bed with his head in his hands and a knot inside of his throat and chest. He felt severely crushed. His thoughts raced over everything about their relationship. What about the times that she didn't answer her phone? He even thought about how she fraternized with the inmates. She never treat their nothing assess how they are supposed to be treated. Most of the drug dealing, dope sniffing, crack heads from Baltimore City are trash. So what he grew up in Randallstown and graduated from high school. Most of them city niggers don't even know what a high school is. Do she mess with one of them cruddy ass inmate niggas? Is it another one of their co-workers? He did hear rumors about Bee and Major Parker, but he just couldn't believe that. *'What would Bee want with his old ass anyway? How could she do this to me?'* Paul thought over and over again. He crawled onto the bed and cried himself to sleep and continued to clutch the ring that he'd spent an entire month's worth of pay to buy.

    Candace rented a car for the entire month. Once again, Lt. Gibson's connections got her a G-35 Infinity at a very cheap rate. She and the lieutenant put off getting Candace a car for a minute, but now the time arrived for her to buy her first one. She made a little over eight thousand dollars in the first month of hustling with the lieutenant and the girls. She became a regular patron at the Icon Inn, also. Her sometimey neighbors in the projects started speaking more, borrowing money, and always faked like they forgot to pay her back on the days that they agreed. Candace sensed the envy, but chose to keep her friends close; referring to the Queens, and enemies closer; referring to the low down crab bitches in the projects that drink all day, pop pills, smoke weed and hate on her for working towards a better life. If things continue on like this, Candace won't be living in Latrobe much longer. Lt. Gibson has a real estate agent that she deals with and already have him on the lookout for an affordable home in the Northwood area near Candace's parents. For now, the car has her focus.

    After taking her rental back, she and Gibson drove to Obutunyi's car lot, located on Joppa Road. He's one of the lieutenant's many friends. Obutunyi and Gibson met after she graduated high school and made an attempt at going to college. She needed money, so her friend's boyfriend knew of a guy from Nigeria that needed a wife to get him a green card so that the guy could stay in America. It was a business arrangement that turned into a lasting friendship. Obutunyi paid Gibson $10,000 cash and also gave her opportunities to make more money. During his early years in the states, he was a heroin dealer and once in a while, he needed someone to take a car out of town or to a certain location. Gibson was never enthusiastic about the trips, but she earned upwards of about $5,000 per trip. She only did it once in a while and continued on all the way up until she entered the academy to become a Correctional Officer. After that, she never wanted to take chances transporting large quantities of heroin again.

Obutunyi loved her straight forward and aggressive way; although, it would often initiate one of many arguments between the two. The women in his county are never that bold. They are not as disrespectful to the men as American women are. It became a problem with them early on, but after some time and as he got to know more of her, they would become lifelong friends. They were always combative with one another, but underneath it all was respect, admiration, and a lot of love. Obutunyi claimed that he didn't deal heroin anymore. He started with a used car lot that held fifteen to twenty cars, to having a fleet of new and used cars. Now he owns a myriad of new and used cars at two locations. One in east Baltimore County, on Joppa Rd. and the other on Liberty Rd. in west Baltimore County. Gibson didn't believe that his hands were totally clean. So what, as long as he didn't sell heroin anymore. She knew that he'd always have his hands in something. He stays out of town on business too much.

Gibson drove her car into the lot. She and Candace exited the B.M.W. "You go on ahead girl. Look around for a whip while I go talk to O," she said, walking towards the showroom. Candace felt like a little girl in a toy store with her pick of the Barbie collection that has all of the accessories.

She marveled at a navy blue Cadillac CTS, with its white leather interior. She put her face to the driver's window with hands over her eyes to peer inside of the car.

"Oh, shit! This car is *niiiice!*" She expressed to herself, excited. She peered into the window at the navigation screen, the wood grain that accented the boarder inside, and the white leather interior. She know that Pimp will love this one. The color is nice and she can see herself pushing the Hog, but she can't afford the $29,000 price tag. That's the sale price at that! She decided to walk around and look at more cars until she spotted a gold Nissan Altima. It's a '06 model, same as the Cadillac, but it's priced at $16,000; with the $4,000 that she has for the down payment, combined with her $36,000 a year, plus overtime job, she thinks she can afford this one. She continued to peruse the cars on the lot, and her mind was just about made up when Lt. Gibson came walking towards her with a tall dark skinned gentleman dressed in a very expensive suit.

"How do you do, young lady? My name is Obutunyi, but you can call me, O for short," he said. His African accent sounding quite thick.

"Pleased to meet you. I've heard some good things about you from my friend," Candace said with a smile. Lt. Gibson just loved her protégé Candace's style. She's very mature and perceptive for today's young women.

"I thought you say this is your god-daughter, Doreatha," Obutunyi said, continuing to shake Candace's hand.

"She is. I adopted her a few months ago," Gibson said.

"I hope she not like many of you friends that continue to be late on car note," he said without losing his smile.

"Look, don't start that shit, O! You're always gettin' slick out the side of your mouth. They pay you, don't they?" Gibson said. Obutunyi folded his arms and stared at Gibson menacingly, then decided to skip the subject.

"So, how may I help you? Do you plan on leaving here

in one of my many automobiles?" He asked, turning his attention to Candace while letting her hand go.

"Well," she reluctantly began to speak. "I really like that one over there. I believe it's more in my price range."

"Why, yes! The Nissan Altima is a very good car. That one has leather interior and also less than 10,000 miles on the odometer. I believe that I can set you up in it quick. Possibly taking a little off of the asking price, since you are Doreatha's godchild," he said, motioning them towards the car.

"That's the car you want?" Gibson asked, apparently agitated with a twisted face. "Bit... I mean, girl, you're a Queen. You don't want a car, you NEED a carriage. What about that pretty blue Caddy that you were checkin'?"

"Oh, no! I can never afford that one. I'm tryin' to move out of the projects. I can only afford $4000 towards the down payment, anyway." Candace said, not thinking about jumping out the window for the Cadillac. She only fantasized looking at it.

"Doretha, she likes the Altima and I'm willing to give her good deal. She first time buyer and...," Obutunyi got cut short in mid-sentence.

"Nigga, ain't nobody tryna' hear that shit. Simms, do you want to test drive the Caddy, or this young ass Altima?" Gibson asked her young friend boldly.

"Well, the Cadillac *is* expensive, but the Altima is..." Cut short, once again.

"O, get the keys to the 'Lac so that my goddaughter can check it out," Lt. Gibson turned to address him. Obutunyi retrieved his cell phone from his jacket pocket and called one of the salespersons inside of the showroom.

"Doreatha, I'm not giving another car away too cheap for any more of your friends. You must respect my bizness... Yes, Chuck, bring me the keys to the blue CTS and a tag." He ended the conversation with his employee and then turned his attention to the lieutenant. "She's only test driving it, but the Altima is hers," he said, protesting to Gibson.

95

"Whatever, nigga," Gibson replied.

"I am not nigga! I'm Nigerian! I know where I'm from! You people so hard headed!" Obutunyi professed, becoming unglued talking to the lieutenant. Chuck came out of the building and handed his boss the keys. He hit the keyless remote to open the doors. Chuck put the dealer's tag on the car. After Obutunyi started the car up, he moved out of the way so that Candace could drive. The console lights were something like a spaceship. Then the clarity of the stereo put Candice right in the club. The smell of new leather filled her nostrils as she adjusted the seat.

"Oh, wow!" She yelled. "I *really* like this one!" She programmed the stereo to 92 Q and a Ne-Yo tune began bumping. *"She makes the hair on the back of my neck stand up, with just one touch."* Candace rocked to the beat and the lieutenant entered the passenger's side.

"We be right back, O!" She yelled! Candace put the car in reverse and then drive onto Joppa Road. Obutunyi stood there with his hands crossed looking at Gibson and her young friend. He just shook his head back and forth. His dear friend set out to swindle him, once again.

Now, the Beamer performed fast and smooth. It's a sports car and handled like one. Although it's much more expensive than the Cadillac, nothing could prepare Candace for the glide of the ride experienced in the Caddy. It felt like she floated every time she hit the gas. She never imagined owning a car this nice. Gibson turned the music down.

"So, how do you like your ride?" She spoke.

"This Caddy is 'da shit… you gonna really work it out for me to get it?" Candace asked, still not believing that she can own the car.

"Do you think that you can pay $300 a month?" Gibson asked.

"Hell, yeah!" Candace yelled, excited.

"Well, it's yours. I probably have to suck his great big ass dick, but yeah, this is your car," Gibson said, exasperated.

"Oh? Never mind! I don't want you to do anything like that for me just to get this car!" Candace squealed.

"Well, then. He always makes me choke and gag. I'll let him know where to pick you up tonight so that you can do it... If you don't suck it right, you'll be stuck with that Altima," Gibson warned. Candace stared with her eyes ready to pop out of her head. She swerved to avoid hitting the car in front of her. Gibson couldn't control her laughter. "Look at your face! I am only joking. Ain't nobody sucking dick." Candace felt relieved. The lieutenant is very cunning. It's hard to tell what is real or fake with her, but Candace loves the way she rolls.

"Ma, you crazy," Candace said. "So, you like my new whip?"

"Girl, I love it. Wait till Hope, Bee, and LL see you pushing this. Them heifers gonna hate," Gibson predicted.

Candace drove back to the dealership. Lt. Gibson went in to talk to Obutunyi. They both came out arguing back and forth walking to Lt. Gibson's car. She reached into the car to get Candace's Gucci bag, and then they both walked towards her sitting inside of the Cadillac. The lieutenant handed Candace her bag and told her that she'll see her at work. She looked at Candace and gave her a wink before sashaying towards the BMW. Obutunyi began talking to Candace like she is his high school teenaged daughter.

"I will see you one week from today with a down payment of $3500. Your payments will be $289. If you late one day, I will take car, young lady. Do you hear?" He admonished.

"Yeesss!" Candace said, like a little girl.

"I will not be playing with you... Now take this car and get out of here," he said in a fatherly tone. He backed away smiling so that she could relax before taking the car.
Candace got her T.I. cd out of her purse, popped it into the player, and there it is. The beat kicked in and T.I. began.

"Big shit poppin' and lil' shit stopping!" She headed

home to Latrobe to get ready for work. She got the Caddy! She couldn't wait to get to work and show Pimp pictures of the car on her cell phone. She still held the $4,000 in her bag.

Candace parked her brand new car on the street in front of Abbott Court where she lived. There are three homes that share the same stoop and Candace lives in the middle apartment between two so-called best friends: Shania and Kierra. The two of them are friends every other week. One week they are fighting, arguing, and then not talking to one another. The next week they are smoking weed together, sitting on the steps being nosey, gossiping with one another, or flirting with the drug dealers in their court. It don't take much for them to become at odds with one another. One might get mad because the other one smokes most of the weed. One of their children might have hit one of the other's child. One of them might have told the other one's business to someone else in the projects. They have even gotten jealous of one another when one gets more attention than the other one from a man. There are also rumors that they slept with each other, but no one knows for sure. What they always get along about is hating on Candace. It doesn't matter how nice she is to them, or how well that she looks out for them. Their hearts are full of envy for Candice on the tag team tip.

They both lived in Latrobe for a couple of years before Candace moved in. Candace comes around and in a few short months she has a job at the jail. Just lately, they see driving all kinds of fancy cars and she's been keeping herself and her children fresher than usual. That being nice shit that Candice does makes Shania and Kierra feel that it's all an act and the bitch thinks that she is a better than the both of them. That is so far from the truth. Candace is a genuinely cool person. They hate on Candace because they hate themselves most of all. She represents what they want, but are just too lazy, selfish and mis-educated about life and love for self to want more or know any better.

Candace got out of the car and took the few short steps

to her house. Shania and Kierra were sitting outside.

"Hi Candace... Damn girl, you sure been pushin' some serious whips! I need to get a job at 'da jail, too," said Shania, sarcastically. "Whatchoo doin' over there girl? I aint gon' put your business in 'da street. I got a home girl 'dat be selling pussy in 'da jail. She gets paid, too."

"Hell no, girl! Are you crazy? For your information, the Beamer belongs to my boss and the Infinity was a rental, but this one is mine." Candace finally let herself brag a little. She knew that they were hating.

Shania did all of the talking. Kierra didn't say anything but that the car is nice. She owed Candace twenty dollars and hoped that Candace forgot about it or just wouldn't mention it. She surely didn't have it. She remained quiet.

"Mmm, hmm, it's pretty," Shania said, sucking her teeth and turning her attention back to Kierra to talk about somebody in the projects's business.

A lot of poor black women in Baltimore are mis-educated, financially inept, oversexed and emotionally scarred. Candace went into her apartment thinking that it won't be soon enough before she get her and the children away from Latrobe. Walking up her stairs, she could hear the two of them backbiting. However, she's just too happy to let them steal her joy.

She couldn't wait to get to work so that she could tell Pimp everything. She started to call him on his cell phone but, she wanted to tell him face-to-face. She wished that this would be the day that she can give Pimp some sex. They were very close to doing it once before, but Candace got cold feet. She felt like she was disrespecting herself. She did give Pimp hand jobs several times and he definitely got the head a couple of times. She's so happy with the way things are going for them that she's not willing to take the chance of messing everything up and losing her job. They are both making and saving money. Now her attention is on moving into a house soon. This is just what they needed. Pimp can get a job when he comes home and they will be a family like how she was raised with her mother, father, sisters and brothers. There shouldn't be any reason for him to go back to hustling in the streets. She hated it most when she heard gunshots, or somebody got killed and not finding out exactly who it is until Pimp came home nice and calm as if anything ever happened. That's her greatest fear because he never backs down from anyone. Sometimes black men never realize that walking away can save a lot of people that love them a lot of pain, grief, and turmoil. If many of the brothers could do it all over, most of them would have chosen to walk away, not beef, and live. Maybe not for themselves, but for their children, women, and others that love them. Candace is determined to build a foundation for the family when he Pimp comes home because, she is ready to stick by him until the last day of their lives. That's real love.

Candace prepared herself for work and when she stepped out of her door, Shania and Kierra were both sitting on the steps smoking a blunt with one of the guys in the neighborhood. She remembered that she used to do the same. She thought that she'd never give up weed. She gave it up long enough to get her a job and beyond. Now she smokes weed occasionally without feeling like she need to smoke every day. She is careful not to pick up the habit again.

It seems like such a long time ago, when in truth, it was less than a year ago. She got into her new car feeling giddy about the good things that are happening in her life. She also thought about Lt. Gibson and the girls, as well as the things that they are doing to make money. She said a small prayer and thanked God. She started the car and once again, T.I. blasted through the Bose speakers. Candace drove out into Madison Street to take the very short drive to the jail and show off her car.

While driving down Eager Street amidst the cars and small crowds of co-workers that were in the process of changing shifts, she noticed the stares that made her feel like all eyes are on her. She parked the car and tried her best to hide the excitement going on inside without cracking a smile. That is until she spotted Landon, Hope, and Bee standing together in front of the outside gate that lead to the entrance of City Jail. Lt. Gibson's car was parked, but she didn't see her anywhere. Candace figured that she's already inside of the prison.

"Awww, shit! That's what I'm talkin' bout, bitch! You got a blue Cadillac, huh? Let me find out you Crippin', bitch," said Bee, jokingly. The two of them had become extremely close since they'd been working in the gymnasium together. Candace winked at her.

"Keep that on the low, ho." Candace whispered so that only they could hear, after walking up into the midst of the women.

"That's nice! Oh, you really fuckin' with us now," said Landon.

"That's a pretty color, Simms," Hope added. They all began to walk inside of the jail. The officers all carried transparent handbags and were briefly waved over with a metal detector's wand before completely entering. The women walked together to roll call laughing and joking. Candace felt a true sense of camaraderie and closeness among them. Gibson waved to her crew also before getting everyone's attention to brief them all and assign the teams to their post.

The four women continued walking together after roll call. As they were leaving the briefing room, Bee stopped to speak to Paul Powers. He looked at the women, rolled his eyes at Bee, and walked off to his post.

"Daaaamn, yo! What up with that?" Hope asked Bee.

"He started talkin' that love jones shit like he was tryna' wife me. Don't he know he ain't got no business tryna' wife a ho? So, I dumped his ass. If he can't dick me down without catching feelings, then I don't need him. I left his ass at the hotel with the ring in his hand. My pussy ached horribly after that, too. I had to hurry home to get that one up out of me. Whewwww! I'm gonna miss that thing," Bee expressed, sadly.

"Bitch, yo' ho ass is just too much," said Landon.

"Well, a girl's got to do what a girl's got to do. Niggas do it all the time. I'm just flipping the script," Bee confessed without remorse.

"So, now your hot ass is gonna go mess with G-loc up in that gym all day, huh?" Hope wondered?

"Well?" Bee responded.

"You's a trick," Landon said.

"You damn right! G-Loc got three hundred for me, too. Simms and her baby daddy gonna watch my back. Ain't that right, huzzy?" Bee turned her attention to Candace.

"Shiiiit! You gonna watch *my* back today. I ain't had none since Pimp been locked up. I'm tryna go myself, trick," Candace replied.

"Oh, shit! Bitch get a new car and a new attitude to go with it. You been around Gibson too damn much," said Hope, in her serious way. They all laughed, agreeing.

"Hey, Candace! Candace! I mean, Ms. Simms!" A voice yelled as the women started up the stairs, going past C section, where the recently booked inmates entered, commonly known as recieving. Candace looked over her shoulders in the direction of the voice and she couldn't believe her eyes. She located the voice and the face.

"What's poppin', Ms. Simms?" Red Mike had a smile on his face that Candace wasn't feeling.

"Oh, shit! What are *you* doin' over here?" She asked him. "Yall go ahead, Bee. I'll be right behind you." Candace instructed her partner for the day.

"Who's he? His face looks familiar," Bee said.

"Girl, that's Red Mike! What've you done?" Hope asked her homeboy, looking in his direction. "You see him on my block, Bee. He's the one with the red Lexus."

102

"Oh, that's right!" Bee remembered.

"I got jammed up in a house raid," Red Mike revealed to Hope.

"I have to go now. I'll holler at you later," Hope said to him, now rushing to her post. Bee and Landon also moved quickly to their posts as well. Candace hesitated a few more minutes so that she and Mike could talk privately.

Landon, Hope, and Bee walked up the stairs and went through the second floor grill, which lead to the E-section's medical unit, where inmates with medical needs are housed. F & G Sections were on that side of the jail, too. There's also a long corridor that connects the north side of the detention center to the south side. Hope and Bee said their goodbyes before walking to the south side. Hope walked her way to the Q-section dormitories and Bee walked to the gymnasium post where she works at with Candace.

Landon, while on the other side of the jail, walked past F section and onto G section. She put her jacket onto the chair and sat down at the desk to get her paperwork together for the count. After the count, she had about an hour of free time so, she decided that she would walk down to the medical unit and holler at her co-worker, Consuela, and wait for Gibson so that the both of them can discuss business.

Landon stood up from the desk to take the count of inmates. Approaching Jay's cell in the back of the tier, her heart began beating fast like it always does when she is near him. She spied him doing push-ups in his cell with his shirt off. She came to a complete stop to look at the muscles in his back. Packed tight with every definition of every muscle in Jay's medium built frame showing, she stood there stuck.

"Where's your cell buddy?" Landon asked Jay, marking on her count sheet.

"Oh, he went to court today. I think he went uptown because he was scheduled to be in the courtroom early this morning. He should have been back by now. He said that he would probably be going uptown today, anyway," said Jay, getting up to face Landon. She who stood in front of him separated by the cell bars. She wanted to reach out and grab his chest. Jay noticed her eyes freeze on his body, then followed her gaze downward.

"Can you hit my door after you let Uncle Twin out of his cell?" Jay asked, startling Landon and snapping her out of her daze.

"I don't know. Let me think about it," she responded as she began walking away and continuing on with her count. She embarrassed herself.

"Hey, Honey! I know what that scent is. You ain't had that one on in a looong time. That's Chanel No. 5, am I correct?" Uncle Twin asked when she stopped in front of his cell.

"It sure is," she answered.

"I'mo be on my A game when I get uptown from fucking with you, boo," Twin said, handing her several green-dot numbers through the bars. "They are all good," he said in a low voice, making reference to the numbers. That meant that he checked them all out. "Don't forget to…"

"I know. I'mo hit your door just as soon as I finish the count," she said.

"I need for you to hit Jay's door, too. I got a new case law to pass out to the population that has something to do with search and seizure and I need him to help me," he said.

"Whateva, nigga. I'mo hit your cells. Just be a little patient," she said.

Landon finished her count, put her paperwork together, and then hit the radio to report confirmation of the count. After that, she hit Uncle Twin and Jay's cell doors. Twin came out of his cell and walked down to Jay's cell.

"You ready, comrade? This is the perfect time. Just do exactly what we talked about and I guarantee you it'll work. I got your back, aiight," Twin assured him.

"Let's make it happen," said Jay. Twin walked down the tier to talk to Landon. He informed her that Jay has something in the cell that belongs to his cell buddy and he don't know what to do with it; so, she needs to check it out.

"Damn, I just got to work and yall worryin' a sista' already," she said to Twin before walking down the tier to Jay's cell. Approaching the cell door, Jay grabbed her wrist firmly, but not rough. Then he proceeded to pull her into the cell. Uncle Twin witnessed Landon disappear into Jay's cell and that's when he looked out into the hall that lead to the sections. The coast was clear for Jay to do his thing. Jay looked into Landon's eyes and gently placed her onto his shirtless body. Her face briefly touched his chest before he put his hand under her chin to guide his mouth to hers. He began kissing her gently, and within seconds, his kisses became very passionate and full of desperation. The kisses moved to her neck so, he started taking gentle bites. He did all of this while unfastening her pats. Landon pushed away, but something inside of her wanted this soooo bad. This is Jay! This is the same man that she took home and fantasized about being with. She had to stop him because this puts her job at stake but, she can't resist. She felt his hand touching between her legs. He forced his way without violating her virtue. His hand met a stream of wetness. Once Jay felt that she'd become soaking wet, he grew even more excited. He pulled her pants down to her ankles and Landon began to assist him by kissing him hungrily and stepping onto her pants to get them completely off. She kicked them to the side and Jay picked her up and gently laid her down onto his three foot by seven foot bunk. He put his hand under Landon's uniform and softly squeezed her breast as he seductively tugged onto her nipples, which were erect and getting stiffer. He opened her legs and in one motion, after seeing her protruding clitoris, he went down face first with his tongue going to work. The moaning came softly, and then a little louder. Both cells on either side of Jay knew the plan but, they were surprised and excited themselves. They couldn't believe that hard ass ball busting Landon would give up the good. They heard her whimpering like a needy virgin.

105

Landon used one hand to guide Jay's head and the other one went into her mouth, biting down on her fingers to keep from screaming. Jay got up from in between Landon's legs and replaced his lips and tongue with his thick dick. She held onto his neck with both hands as he pushed in and out, in and out, in and out! She released his arm just fast enough to put the sheet over her mouth and face to muffle the squeals of pleasure and ecstasy that were sure to escape. Jay buried his face into Landon's uniform blouse to cover that ultimate noise that comes exclusively from a man as soon as he releases. Especially when it's good! And just like that, it was over.

After every drop of Jay went inside, Landon pushed him off of her and immediately jumped up to grab her uniform pants. Jay handed her a clean washcloth that she quickly snatched from him without making eye contact. He pulled up his pants and wiped the sweat off of his face and chest with a towel. He knows that he won't have a problem getting a shower every day now. With her permission.

"Go ahead and take your time to get yourself together. I'll make sure everything is cool and signal you when the coast is clear. If I get loud, that means that someone is coming. Just fix yourself up," whispered Jay.

"How does my hair look, boy? Did you mess it up?" She worried, hitting at him embarrassed and playful.

"No, it's not bad at all... Here," Jay said, handing Landon his mirror, a brush, and a small comb before grabbing a shirt and leaving Landon in the cell to freshen up. His next door neighbor had his hand out between the bars so that Jay could slap him five with approval before he headed up to the front of the tier to report what he'd done with Landon to Uncle Twin. Uncle Twin stood about twenty yards in front of him with a big ass gold toothed smile on his face. Jay gave him a handshake and they embraced.

"I told you, comrade." Twin gloated.

On her way to the gym Candace's feelings and

emotions went bananas. Both of her children's fathers are in the jail at the same time. It weighed heavy on her heart. There are a lot of guys in the jail who have children by the same woman. Some of the men are enemies of one another, friends, and some don't even know one another. However, the women aren't COS or employees. Some employees did have children's fathers locked up but, two baby daddies? This can prove to be a lot for her to handle. On top of that, they both hold positions in rival organizations, and a very small disagreement can have them trying to kill one another in the jail. Red Mike is arrogant and Pimp knows that behind Mike's money and influence over his set, he is a man with the heart of a coward. Pimp doesn't respect any man that can have sex with a woman without using protection, knowingly make a baby, and not be concerned about with whom or how his child is being raised. He loves Candace's daughter. Maybe not as much as he loves his own child, Little Pimp, but more than enough to take care of her like she is his child. Candace is praying for them to not meet up and clash. This put a damper on her joyous day.

After Candace reached the gym, Bee couldn't wait to show her the room behind the big screen television on the stage. Bee let her know that she could bend over and let Pimp hit it from the back, or get him to sit in the chair. She can ride it like a pony. Candace cracked up listening to Bee's instructions because Bee is just too damn bold. But Candace also took mental notes. It did lighten her mood.

"Look, they are going to be up here in the gym for an hour. You get fifteen minutes to do your thing. We don't want the inmates to get suspicious so, wait until I put the movie on. Tell Pimp to go in the room as soon as his section comes into the gym. That way, nobody will see the two of you go into the room together. Then, you come out first. When I see Pimp come out of the room, that's when I'm going in to let G-Loc hit this and get that money. So, make sure that when you see me disappear, get up on the stage and watch my back, you got me?" Bee instructed.

"Yeah, I got you," Candace responded. "Bee, I'm a little nervous. Are you sure we ain't gonna get caught?"

"Girl, please! I've been getting it in for the whole six years that I've worked here. Now come on so that we can get cuz and them up in this gym," Bee said.

Everything went as smooth as Bee said it would go. Candace was able to take one shoe off and one leg out of her uniform pants to slide up and down on Pimp as he sat in the chair, kissing her man. It took Pimp a little less than five minutes to bust off in her. He became nervous as well. Candace, now no longer afraid, felt totally in control. She assured Pimp that they would do it again soon. It would be longer next time. She gave him a bag with a meal that she cooked. Then she left out of the room with instructions for Pimp when to follow. Bee followed suit and the plan went fine, with one exception. While Bee crept into the room that Candace and Pimp exited to do whatever she planned to do for G-Loc's three hundred dollar Green-Dot, Paul Powers came into the gymnasium from the other end. Candace started to go to the room to warn Bee, but got stuck standing by the stage with Pimp because Powers could see her from where he stood. As soon as she decided to move, Bee came out of the door, but didn't see Paul Powers. She quickly fixed her clothes. Paul spotted Bee and began to walk in the direction of the stage. Bee looked at Candace smiling until Candace's eyes directed Bee to look in Paul's direction. Bee spotted Paul walking towards her. Paul then saw an inmate come out of the very same room after her. Paul stopped in mid stride. He looked at G-Loc with nothing but anger and fury beginning to burn inside of him. He turned his attention back to Bee, who stared back at Paul to see what he would do next. She prayed for him not to blow the spot and turn the situation into an emotional storm. Bee could see the hurt, pain, and despair in Paul's eyes. She turned her gaze to look away from him. All of this went on amidst a sea of two hundred inmates in there for recreation and oblivious to what is taking place.

Several inmates were attending to their own vices of selling and buying drugs, tobacco, and making deals. Some plotted violence. Others walked, talked, and lied about uptown, who got locked up, who got shot, who got killed, and who were on their way over to Steel-side from Central Bookings. There were small gatherings of men who were BGF, BLOODS, CRIPS, Muslims, and plain old homeboys from the same neighborhoods. Some homeboys who hadn't seen one another in years were reunited as well. At the same time, Paul's world crumbled and he began to believe that he finally lost the woman that he truly loved to a nothing ass criminal gang banging inmate. He turned towards the very same door that he'd just unknowingly entered into his gloom. He decided then and there that the bitch Bee has to pay!

Chapter 6

Tonight all of the Queens wanted to drink, listen to music, and talk shit to one another. A lot has happened in their personal lives, along with the everyday stress of working in the jail. The obvious occasion for them meeting at the Icon is Candace copping her Caddy. She fell right in with her co-workers, who had become much more than that. The Icon is the spot for stress relief. They all kicked their Nike boots off, sat at the bar, and got their drink on.

Lt. Gibson explained to the girls the look on Candace's face when she informed her that she would have to give Obutunyi some head. The other three women could identify with the situation because she played the same practical joke on every one of them. Hope experienced the scene herself. Hope has a custom built black Dodge Super Magnum. Hope recalled the time that Gibson convinced her that she had to give up some coochie for the Magnum. She explained to Candace that she got quiet while driving the car and admiring its handle.

"Girl, I wanted that motherfucking car so bad that all I could say to Gibson, with the saddest ass voice is, damn, lieut, I ain't had dick since dick had me." They all laughed.

"Is that the only line you know, bitch?" Bee asked Hope.

"Heeellll yeah! At the time, I couldn't think of nothing else to say because I wanted my car and the thought of that nigga getting in my tight ass pussy, with his African ass, could have been a reality... Shiiiiit!" Hope said, before taking a gulp of her ice cold Corona, with a twist of lemon.

"Well, I thought we were gonna have an accident on Joppa Rd. today when I told Simms what she had to do. She almost ran into another car trying to switch lanes," Gibson reported. The laughter started again.

"Thanks, Ma! Yall shoulda seen the look on my two neighbor's faces when I drove into the projects. Especially when I informed them that the car belongs to me," said Candace. "The hoes got quiet. One of 'da bitches didn't say too much anyway because she owes me some money."

"What did Pimp say when you told him about the car?" Hope asked.

"Oh, I almost forgot. After I gave my baby some of his coochie..." She got cut short.

"Aww shit! No you didn't girl?!" Gibson asked, surprised. She couldn't believe it.

"I sure did! Didn't I, Bee?!" Candace slurred, bragging and prodding Bee for confirmation.

"Yeah, she got her feet wet. I mean, her womb," Bee confirmed.

"Well, all right!" Gibson yelled, giving Candace a hi-five.

"Well, what did Pimp say?" Hope asked again.

"Oh, he's just lovin' how we comin' up, although he's really concerned about me. He tells me to be careful all the time," she answered. "I sent pictures of the car to his cell phone."

"Just like a nigga. Like a woman can't get their grind on and make shit happen on the hustling tip, too. Selling pussy is the oldest hustle in the world. Men didn't invent that shit. There are a lot less women locked-up for hustlin' and getting money," said Bee.

"What did he say about Red Mike being in the jail?" Hope asked. Candace took a swig of her drink and put the glass down. Slumping her head with her arms on the bar as though an invisible weight had been placed on both of her shoulders.

"I didn't say anything to him about Mike being in the jail yet. He probably already knows," she sighed, lifting her head.

"Well, how do they feel about one another?" Gibson asked, as the conversation turned serious for the concern of her young friend's wellbeing. She can tell that Candace is worried.

"Pimp isn't insecure about me. He knows that he is my man and that I don't fuck with Mike's dead beat ass. It's really Mike that I worry about. He thinks that he is the shit that don't stink. In all actual reality, he is some *real* shit. He think it's all about him and he don't care who he uses or manipulates. He'll get a hundred niggas to kill each other and fifty more will go to jail while he's all up in some hotel room with a chickenhead freak, or in a mall trying to stay fly fifty miles away from the action when it's going down. He's already bragging that he doesn't have a bail and that he'll be good when he goes to court because he's paying somebody to take the charges. He said that the house raided isn't in his name anyway. I just hope that Mike doesn't try to front on Pimp in the jail, or maybe say something about me and him that Pimp will get mad about. All I need is for my children's fathers to be in the jail fighting one another," Candace sighed.

"Yeah, that nigga Mike is a show-off. Plus, he doesn't know what to say out of his mouth most of the time. I hope that they don't get into it for your sake," said Hope.

"Do you want me to send one of their asses over to the J.I building?" Gibson asked.

"That's not such a bad idea. Pimp ain't going anywhere. First, let me see how things go before I interfere. But, before I see them clash, I'll get you to move Mike. Pimp got to hit this again!" Candace slurred, now really feeling the effects of her drinks.

"I think that there is some kind of a big ass plan or a conspiracy. I mean people say it all of the time. That shit got to be looked at for real. Here I am a single mother, no doubt, with two children whose fathers are in jail. Both of them are unemployed and I'm the one with the job. When they are free the first thing they'll look to do, more than not, is go and get some more of that shit to sell. Pimp will do it to get money and help me provide for my daughter and his son to preserve whatever structure of a family that he has, according to his knowledge. He didn't have such a good example. His father was in prison for most of his life. Pimp also likes to dress nice and be with his crew and do the things that men do after paying bills and seeing to it that we have at least a sense of good food, clothing, and shelter. Mike, on the other hand, loves to look good, call shots, and count money to place himself above everybody around him. He rates his manhood on how much money he's got and how many shots he can call because of it. Yet and still, he is a man, and why shouldn't he live beyond a slave ass job that drains his energy for a car with payments and live at home with his mother or a female until he can afford to scrounge up a savings from job raises just to make bigger bills? There's nothing wrong with a man that wants what he wants. It's also honorable and admirable to be a leader, but why should a lot of *our* men have to lead us like this?

"I thank y'all for helping me out. Lord knows that I do, but most white women don't have to think about what they'll have to do when or if their man or their child's father leave out of the house and as soon as he takes too long to return or answer his cell phone if he is somewhere dead or locked up. It's all so crazy! Something just ain't right about how poor black people live in Baltimore, and I don't believe we put ourselves in this situation and I'm not playing the victim. I believe that we are guided, nudged, mis-educated and tricked into living into some of these deplorable situations," Candace concluded, ordering herself another shot after killing the previous one.

"Hey! Hey! What are you so quiet for?" Gibson asked, turning her attention to Landon, who stared straight ahead while playing in her drink with the stirrer. Her mind filled with visions of what occurred earlier that compelled her to give in to her fantasy. It was so real and she lived it over, and over, and over again in her head ever since it happened. She wanted to be back in the jail and in Jay's cell giving him more of herself.

"Do you hear me, LL?!" Gibson shouted.

"Oh! My bad," Landon said, breaking the silence of her thoughts. She did hear a little of what Candace said, so she commented on that. "Simms, it's a terrible shame of what you have to go through. It's hard for me to get close to the kind of men that I really want to be with since my son's father was killed, and probably for the very same reasons you spoke on. They will tell you," Landon pointed at her girlfriends, "I don't keep men too long. For one, sex has not been very important to me. It's overrated. I believe in commitment and companionship and I love a fearless, smart, intelligent, and strong man. My son's father was all of those things but, the streets snuffed him right out. That was over fourteen years ago and it's not getting any better out there. It's fucked up that a lot of the best of our men can't seem to find their way out of a maze of dead end situations and we have to baby sit all of those able body sexy ass men, girl," she said, closing her eyes and envisioning Jay sexing her.

"I've always thought like we all have been tricked and that somebody is royally fucking us over, too. But what can you do? The bills still have to be paid and you got to take advantage of everything and every opportunity that the white man gives you as a black woman. We still all gotta eat and most of us got mouths to feed. I, for one, like to look good doing it."

"Me, too!" Bee blurted out in a voice that hinted that she had a few strong drinks too many. "I don't need a nigga to do shit for me but give me some money, a wet ass, and then get ta' steppin'. I tell my daughters now, while they are young, to depend on themselves and their own ability. I tell them to not allow themselves to be controlled by any nigga and don't go chasin' behind no nigga. I tell them if they are smart they'll learn that they can have a man eating out the palm of their hand. It could be one or it could be many, but they should also never depend on a man to make them happy or feel complete. Not these hustling ass niggas because, they are here today and gone tomorrow, in most cases. I've got a daughter whose father is in the feds. He left me $50,000, and all of my children's fathers have been in and out of jail. They do great when they are on the street, but that shit don't last. So, coming from where we come from, you gotta get it in and get what you can. Simms, you don't need a man for shit!"

"Bee, you see, that's where you're wrong because, I want a man! I want my man! I want Pimp to be the leader of our family. I want much more for him to want to feel like he got to just '*do what I gotta do*'," Candace said, mimicking Pimp and all of the hustlers from the hood. "Somebody somewhere has manipulated our men into believing that street money and surviving through poverty in the streets and by way of street life is the only answer, when in reality, it's the *trap* that seems to catch them all the time."

"Max did say to me that the man is the natural head of the family and that the family is the collective body of our people. He also said that if you can kill the head of our people the collective body will inevitably die. So, if you kill the black male: politically, mentally, morally, socially, and academically, by wiping him out of the family structure physically: that is by prison or death, then you are destined to extinguish the black race; or at least maintain that class in perpetual servitude. Oh, and making a black man believe that he's made it beyond the majority of his kind is also a form of mental death," said Hope. Gibson almost choked on her drink. Landon sat there stunned with her mouth wide open and amazed. Bee looked around as though she knows that what she just heard did not just come from Hope's mouth. No one responded and the silence made Hope look up to see everyone staring at her.

"What?" She asked, laughing at the looks of surprise.

"Glorious Hope, is that you in there?" Gibson asked, getting all in Hope's face and looking into her eyes.

"Can somebody put my friend back into her body? Matt, give me a double, quick! Did yall hear what the hell

Hope just said? Did she say what the fuck I just heard her say?" Bee asked in serious disbelief.

"Since when in the hell have you started listening to a man about anything, 'Miss Lock Their Jailbird Asses Up and Throw Away the Keys?! Ain't you the one who say that's more pussy for you? When did you start caring about niggas; and who the fuck is this Max person?" Landon asked.

"Well, I'll be damn! L.L., he's some fine ass Muslim brother that moved onto her section," Gibson informed Landon. "And when I say fine, I mean fine. Plus, I saw him all on her stud ass, yall!" Gibson reported.

"No, but seriously. I ain't never talked to anyone that makes a lot of sense about everything. That nigga knows a lot and he makes you feel what he's saying to you. Like, what Simms's talkin' about. Max said that everybody is always talking about the strong black woman and how we are strong this and we been through that, but black women aren't only born to be hard workers, over stressed, widowed, children raising, children killed and aborted; whores, bitches, men babysitters and objects of a blackman's filth. When he said that I started to listen. I even made him the hall man so that he can talk to me without everybody all up in our conversation. You know how some inmates can be nosey as shit. But, Max doesn't mind because, he'll talk to anybody that will listen. He's really into making people think," Hope explained.

"Well, all that shit that you said that he said is exactly what I be feeling too often than not, Hope," Candace agreed.

"My girl is gonna get it, my girl is gonna get it. She's gonna get that thing, thing; she's gonna get that thing, thing!" Gibson began singing and dancing in her chair, directing her song to Hope.

"Bitch, please! It ain't goin' down like that. You making a big deal out of a friendly conversation," said Hope.

While the girls continued to tease Hope about her new found friend, Puddin' walked into the bar followed by Yolonda and Rashon.

116

"Glo!" Puddin' called out. Hope turned to see her girlfriend.

"There's my baby right there," she said to her co-workers, smiling as she got off of the barstool with her Corona in hand to meet Puddin'. She missed Puddin' a lot and hadn't seen much of her since the day that she left. Lamar continued to stay with Hope on the weekdays for school, but every weekend he was at his grandmother's house to spend time with his mother. Lamar never told Hope that his mother didn't spend that much time with him and when he does stay at his grandmother's house, Puddin' is not there, most of the time. Lamar loved his mother and like Hope he always hide his mother's negative behavior and downplay her faults. Hope loves Lamar just as much so, she takes great care of him and provide for him as if he's her own child.

"Hey, baby!" Hope called to Puddin' while putting her arm around neck with the hand that held the beer. She quickly kissed her lips and then she spoke to Rashon and Yolanda. They both hugged her and commented about not seeing her. Hope, now tipsy from the few Corona's made a mental note of Puddin's hair being in a bum ass pony tail and not done like she always keep it when she stays at the house. In truth, everything about Puddin' looks worn and stale as though she slept in her clothes. Puddin' being with Rashon and Yolanda didn't put her in the best of light, either. All they do is hang out, get high, and party. They are made for one another. Puddin' fell right in line with them. Hope decided to look past her thoughts and enjoy Puddin's company. Maybe this will be the night that they make amends and Puddin' comes home. Hope joined the three women and they all sat at a booth in the back. Hope treated the three to drinks.

Next, Paul Powers entered the Icon Inn looking for his beloved Delilah, with a hope that she consider making an effort to ease the pain in his aching heart. He needs to see her and he want to be with her. He decided to overlook what he witnessed earlier in the gymnasium. Maybe she isn't having

117

an affair with the inmate that followed her out of the stage room in the gymnasium and it's all in his mind. It tears him apart not to be with her. He spotted Bee sitting at the bar with her crew and decided reluctantly to walk over to them.

"Excuse me, Bee? May I have a word with you in private, please?" He asked after speaking to everyone. Bee looked up and cocked her head to the side. She let out a huge breath of exasperation. She did not want to be dealing with Paul right now.

"Uuuhhh! Come on," she said, getting up from her stool and grabbing his hand to lead him to another booth for privacy. Paul mistook this as a sign of affection. Once they were seated, everything that Paul had on his mind to say to Bee got lost with his nervousness and anxiety.

"Damn, L, that nigga just don't want to give it up, does he?" Gibson complained, looking at the couple and then turning her attention to her drink.

"Well, if he knows like I do, he might as well do like Keisha Cole says and let it go. Look at his sad ass," said Landon. The three women observed Paul plead to their girlfriend who sat there half ignoring him. In unison, they turned to face the bar and began to laugh.

"Awww, he looks so sad, poor boy," Candace teased as though she felt sorry for him. A part of her did because she was there for the entire episode.

"More like a pathetic puppy," said Gibson, with no feeling for him. They laughed again while getting Matt's attention so that they could order another round of drinks. Paul made small talk telling Bee how much he misses her. Then he asked her do she miss him.

"Come on, now! Don't start it!" She barked and then rolled her eyes. Bee couldn't believe that this man didn't get the message. He turned her completely off. Earlier that day she thought about maybe getting with him in a month or so to get her a shot of that muscle one more time but, he killed any desire that she would ever have for him again by hunting her down; with his weak ass. Paul began to think that maybe he's being a little too soft. Maybe Bee wants him to be more aggressive like her thug friend in the jail. He has to straighten his back and demand that she realize they are going to be together; and that's that. He knows that he is harder than that jail ass nigga that he saw her with. This is where his mistake began.

"Who in the fuck was that in the gym with you today coming out of the stage room?" He asked her sounding tough with eyes bugging.

"What?!" Bee twisted her face confused at Paul's attempt to question her.

"Man, don't be questioning me! Just who do *you* think you are?!" She kept her voice low, but she got angry.

"Come on! We're getting the fuck up out of here!" Paul demanded, standing and grabbing Bee's arm to pull her out of the seat towards him and the door. In the motion that jerked her to her feet, she slapped him with the momentum of her body coming up. The slap could be heard over the talking and the music. Paul already had Bee by one arm. He grabbed the wrist of the other one when she tried to slap him again. Everyone heard the slap and it registered to the Queens that Bee needed them. Gibson moved the quickest with Landon a half of a step behind. They couldn't get to that nigga's ass fast enough! Gibson went straight for Paul's neck, seeing that he stood vulnerable as his hands were preoccupied with holding Bee. Gibson began to tighten her grip around his throat. Landon kicked him in the nuts so hard that he turned Bee loose and grabbed at his aching jewels while being choked at the same time. That's when the Corona bottle came crashing over his head. Gibson had to let him go because of the small shards of glass that she felt sting her face along with a mist of beer from Hope's bottle splashing onto her. Paul fell limp and began melting to the barroom floor. Candace and Bee didn't hesitate to kick and stomp Paul's head, face, and ribs. All he could do to protect himself is ball up and beg for mercy.

119

Gibson, Landon, and Hope followed suit and joined in to rain kicks and blows to every available portion of his body. They were beating the shit out of Paul! Matt headed towards the melee yelling.

"Heeeey! What the fuck is yall doing to my spot?" He yelled again once he saw one of the women throw a chair down onto Paul. Junior, Matt's father-in-law, stopped Matt for a couple of seconds to look at the women work Paul over before they moved in to diffuse the ruckus. Junior witnessed the entire incident from the start when Paul first grabbed Bee. Matt and Junior never have good feelings for men that will put his hands on a woman to hurt her. That is for weak suckers.

"THAT'S ENOUGH!" Matt yelled. "You bitches are gonna kill him! Ain't no bodies dropping in this bar! Take that shit outside!" Matt and Junior, along with another male patron, were able to get the women to stop beating on Paul as he laid motionless and defenseless.

Someone called an ambulance, but before they made it to the bar, Paul regained consciousness and willed his bloody and battered body out of the door and into his car. Somehow he drove himself away. The women gave each other hi-fives. They continually asked Bee if she's all right.

After they all calmed and returned to the seats at the bar, and Hope returned to the booth where Puddin', Rashon, and Yolanda laughed and joked about Paul getting beat up, they ordered their last round.

"After this one, I'm gone. Elliot's been calling me and I told him that I would be home around two," said Gibson.

"I want to drive the children to school in my new car, too," added Candace.

They were all winding down and letting exhaustion settle into their alcoholic bodies from such a long and eventful day that capped off with them having to give a nigga a beat down. Approaching the booth, Yolanda asked Hope if she'd take them to her house while Rashon went to buy drinks for them. Hope obliged and the four women said their goodbyes to Hope's co-workers once Rashon returned with bags in hand.

Yolanda lived in The Douglass Homes Projects in East Baltimore, which isn't too far from Hope's house on Lakewood. They all got into Hope's car feeling the effects of the alcohol. The women were loud listening to the music and talking about how Paul got his ass whipped. Hope explained to the trio what lead to the beef between Bee and Paul. She explained that Bee had him pussy whipped and wouldn't marry him. Hope had witnessed a few of Bee's pussy whipped victims, but this is the first one to get so out of control and put his hands on Bee.

The crew went back and forth male bashing and saying that he got what he deserved for putting his hands on Bee and also how weak most men are. This was the content of their very loud laughter and conversation right up until Hope made the left turn from Orleans Street onto Caroline Street and to the destination.

"Thanks a lot, Glo. I swear I didn't feel like waiting outside in the cold night to catch a hack," said Yolanda as the car stopped in front of the walkway that led to May Court where she lived. "Are you comin' in, Glo?" Yolanda asked.

"No, girl. I'm tired as hell. I'm going to take a bath and get into bed," she answered.

"Well, thanks again, and it's good to see you. I hope that it don't be a long time before I see you again. You know that you can come in for a while and rest on the couch if you want to. We're gonna play spades and listen to some music. You are more than welcomed," Yolanda said, opening her door behind Puddin'. Rashon slid over to exit the car on the same side.

"Are you comin' in Puddin'?" Rashon asked, getting out of the car.

"Yeah, I'll be there in a minute," said Puddin'. Hope's head snapped to face Puddin'.

"Oh, you're not going home with me tonight?" Hope

asked.

"Whatchoo mean, Glo?" Puddin' responded.

"You know what I mean," Hope said, visibly angered that Puddin' chose to stay out late in the projects at this hour of the morning instead of going to their comfortable home where her son slept.

"Well, I'm having fun and I'm not ready to go in the house or go to bed," Puddin' explained.

"What in the… " Hope started to bark, but then she calmed down before continuing her statement. "I just thought that you came to be with me tonight. I miss you, baby."

"I did want to see you, too. That's why I came to the bar. I miss you, but I'm not ready to go to your house just yet. Why don't you come in for a while?" Puddin' asked Hope.

"No, because I'm tired and I want to go home to my own house and lay in my own bed. You know I don't like hanging in that dirty ass house," Hope said.

"It's not dirty like that because I cleaned up earlier today," Puddin' said.

"Oh yeah?! Ain't that a bitch? What all three of yall fucking now or something?" Hope charged, letting her anger return. "Fuck all that. Are you going with me or are you staying down here in these nothing ass projects?"

"Shit! If you want me to go with you, come on then," Puddin' said with an attitude. Hope paused to analyze the entire situation and decided that she didn't want to force Puddin' to come with her if she's not willing on her own. She began to despise Puddin' in the moment for her lack of wanting to accomplish anything in life. Hope grew frustrated with loving Puddin'. "I just took a pill about an hour ago and you know that I can't go to sleep once I start rollin', Glo."

Hope stared at Puddin' and didn't say a word. "What?" Puddin' responded to Hope's look.

"Go ahead with your friends, boo. Maybe we'll hook up some other time," she said after her brief silence. She resigned herself to understanding that the woman that she loves can't love her back in the same way because, she's clueless when it comes to loving herself. Puddin' is a pleasure seeker, masking her pain of ignorance and low self-worth with drugs, sex, and partying. This is the story of the many unfulfilled. They all thrive together finding jokes and laughter in everyone else's shortcomings and failures. They never know what it takes to win from working a good plan so, they feel unworthy and worthless.

"Give me a call tomorrow and then maybe we can hook up this weekend and take Lamar somewhere together," Hope suggested.

"That sounds good... Glo, I need my hair done. Can you give me a few dollars to get it done, please?" Puddin' asked.

'This bitch got some nerve! That's all she wanted anyway,' Hope believed. "How much do you need?" Hope asked her.

"Well, I want to get some micros so that I won't have to keep getting it done, and if you can give me a couple extra dollars I'll give it back to you the very first chance I get." Puddin' waited for Hope's response. Hope started to give Puddin' one of her Green-Dot cards but, she remembered that Puddin' took one the day that she left the house. She reached into her pocket and pulled out some bills. She counted two hundred dollars for Puddin's hair and fifty dollars for Puddin' to spend. She put the remaining seventy dollars back in her pocket.

"Here," said Hope, handing the money to her.

"Thanks," she answered. Puddin' started to protest but, she thought better. Hope knew that she needs more than fifty dollars to spend. Maybe she could buy the hair and pay somebody to do it. That will put a few extra dollars in her pocket to buy something to wear for Sunday night at the Towers Lounge on York Rd. That's *"Ladies Only"* night. Soon as she put the money in her pocket and before she could say good-bye, somebody let loose about eight gunshots into

123

the night.

"Girl, what the fu... Go ahead and get outta here, Glo! I'ma run to Yolanda's! The shots came from the other side!" Puddin' said with excitement. She opened the passenger door ducking low to let the door cover her. "I'ma call you tomorrow... Glo, I love you," Puddin' said, running into the court before disappearing. Glo can't help but to think that this bitch has to be insane!

Hope put the car into drive and made a u-turn onto Caroline Street to head in the direction of Monument Street and the short mile or so that leads to where she lives. As soon as she completed the turn a dark figure appeared of a person running from the opposite court and over to the other side of the street where Yolanda's house is located. She could see the person clutching a large caliber automatic handgun. He continued to run over to Yolanda's side of the street into another court. Hope shook her head and once she approached the intersection of Caroline and Orleans Streets, the light turned red. However, there weren't any cars in sight in either direction. So Hope went straight on through the red light to get as much distance as quick as she could away from Douglass Projects.

Continuing northbound onto Caroline Street, she stopped at the light on Madison and saw a speeding blue Cadillac flying westward down Madison. It's Simms on her way home from the bar. Hope smiled thinking about her co-worker and new member of the crew. She's a young woman that has her head on straight. Her family is her priority and she works to do all that she can to make a better life for them. Her man included. Hope found herself wishing the best for her and her man. Maybe he will come home and appreciate the foundation that his woman is building and choose to suspend the livelihood of the streets for a job and a better structure for his family.

Family is the key to turning things around for young

black people. A renewed sense of putting family first by protecting, providing, and guiding the family towards the love of self, and to begin appreciating the dynamic struggle that has them positioned to become the leaders and innovators for a better future, instead of sliding lower into the bowels of American society is needed. Simms is only nineteen years old with a sense of duty and purpose. Puddin', on the other hand, is lost inside of her ignorance and pain. She is unwilling to fight through a struggle that will only lead to discovering new and better things about herself.

Hope entered her door with all of this on her mind. Max had her thinking a lot about the position that young people are in as it concerns the streets. He also stresses black male and female relationships. Hope was turned off by such talk at first. Listening to Max makes her understand the importance of family and then she began to realize that the breakup of the family structure, in addition to the outrageously unhealthy relationships of black men and women, is the biggest reason why so much distrust and death prevails among black people in American society.

Hope turned the television off in the living room. She didn't bother to wake James, who watches Lamar until she comes home from work. He's eighteen and this is his senior year at Patterson Park High School. He's Hope's next door neighbor and is like a little brother to Hope. She decided to let him sleep until morning. She went up the stairs and looked into Lamar's room. She stood there watching him by the light of his television as he slept. She thought about the man running with the smoking gun a few feet away from her just moments ago. A feeling of dread overcame her thinking someone had been killed and left to die in the dark of night while the attacker escapes detection and gets away with murder. There is no doubt that the shooter and his possible victim or victims are young black men. She dropped to her knees and prayed to God with a tearful eye that the young black beautiful man-child that she's looking over will never become that dark figure running away in the cover of night, or a victim of such callousness. She also begged her creator to keep Lamar away from that place of the faceless sea of black men that remains in her charge day in and day out in the jail. Their eyes possess pain, hurt, rage, hopelessness, fear, and hate; inextricably mixed with contentment. That's scary! It's as if they are in a land of the living dead. There's also a feeling of strength in those men with a disconnection to real power. She got up from her knees and turned Lamar's television off.

After showering, Hope walked into her bedroom. Letting her towel drop, she paused to look into the mirror at her very curvaceous body that stood on a five foot, nine inch frame. She pranced and turned admiring her beautiful body. Her flat stomach as well as her hips and ass are slender. She wears loose clothing so that they don't accentuate her body's dimensions. Sometimes it is hard. Especially with the style of clothing that's changing into more of a form fit. She began to feel very sexual and started thinking about Puddin' and how she wished that she would have at least come home to make love to her. Hope thought about how she use to have girls literally eating out of her hands. She is a King Bitch and can make a woman beg for her services of pleasure. She began to laugh coyly and rub her hands over her breast. When she did that, thoughts of Maximilian Muhammad entered her mind. This surprised her! She never cared for men in that way. She was never raped or abused physically like a lot of her lesbian friends and lovers that make them discount men as lovers. She's just turned on sexually by females. This is not to say that every so often she will admire the physical anatomy of a well put together man and wonder what it would be like to have sex with him. She never gave in to such thoughts because, to her, nothing can compare to the shared feelings and pleasures of a woman's body and touch. It's just sooo sensual to her. However, Max stays in her head when she touch her body. She closed her eyes and began to imagine that it could be him putting the lotion on her. She immediately

126

snapped out of it and ran to her dresser to retrieve a set of pajamas to jump into. Without hesitation, she turned out the light and crawled into bed, pulling the covers all the way up to her neck. She continued to fight within herself, pushing thoughts of Max out of her mind every time that they popped up. She rocked in her bed until she fell sound asleep.

Gibson talked to Elliot on the phone the entire time that it took for her to drive from Highlandtown to her townhouse in Essex. The vodka and grapefruit juice had her toasted and she needed him to keep her alert while she drove. The main topic of conversation was about her and her girlfriends beating up Powers in the bar. They both laughed hysterically about the incident. Gibson's amusement became affected by her being drunk and Elliot laughter. He continued to ask for details of the incident to keep her aware while she drove and because he couldn't stand that CO nigga Powers. It's all funny to Elliot. He pictured the battle while he and the comrades in his dorm congregated in the shower to listen to Gibson on speaker while smoking weed. They huddle up just about every night to get high and talk all night long until sleep overtakes them. This is their escape.

Nowadays, Elliot always provides weed and tobacco to smoke, along with a couple of others who has ways of getting their vices, too. Uncle Twin would also give Elliot some smack. They kept their dealings with the smack very low key because, Elliot didn't want it to get out to Gibson that he snorts dope. A lot of the guys could tell that he got high off of more than just the weed, but they would never confront him about it because he got them high regularly. They wasn't going to fuck that up. They talked among each other all of the time about how high Elliot would be and blaming it on the weed. He would smoke a lot of weed to justify being so high, but the freeloaders knew better. He and Uncle Twin had too much sneaky business together and everybody knows how Uncle Twin gets down.

Lt. Gibson and Elliot grew pretty close over the past couple of months. Not a day went pass that they didn't talk to one another. Gibson even got acquainted with his mother. Elliot loves his mother a lot and she made sure he had nice clothes to wear and money for commissary until Elliott let his mother know that she can keep her money because his new girl makes sure that he gets along just fine. He will be going to court soon and his lawyer assured him that he should go home. His mother warned Elliot not to mess over Gibson and that he had to come home and do right. She advised him that this has to be Jesus's way of showing him that he needs to change his life. Elliot agreed and promised himself that he won't use drugs once he comes home. However, he continues to have grand ideas about getting money with Big Head Charlie.

Gibson began to prepare for Elliot to come home. She went shopping to buy clothes for him and took them to her house. She networked with friends for job tips and openings to ease his transition. She even planned to buy him a car after his first week home. She's going to take a thousand to Obutunyi and get a nice used car for him to get around with until he can do better for himself. She has it all planned out. Until then, she continued to sneak him around in the jail to get a quick lick or a piece. She even gave him some coodicat in the elevator where the food carts are carried from floor to floor. She makes sure that he never runs out of tobacco and got him weed as much as she could. It will only be a few weeks before his court date and Gibson continues to be excited about it. She believed that he could be the one for her. He's strong and attentive and doesn't put people in his business. More importantly, and by all indications, he's a single and free man without a baby momma or a wife.

Paul Powers didn't go to work for some time. He took personal leave days and then a little of his vacation time. When he finally reported to the jail, it was on the eleven to seven late night shift. He only saw Bee briefly in passing at work, but from time to time he would follow her in the mornings before she went to work herself, determined to catch her doing something that he could hold over her head or destroy her with. He bought an old 1989 Maxima to use for spying. He discovered that she has a lot more male friends. He took pictures of her meeting with the major. Twice he saw her meet with an Utz potato chip truck driver, but he didn't know what to make of the meetings. She'd open her trunk and give him a couple of medium sized boxes. They would laugh and joke with one another and then be on their way. He's the only male that she didn't spend more than fifteen minutes with. Paul decided that he should look more into the truck driver's identity. He kept his 357 Magnum with him when he went out to spy on Bee. If he could catch her in a secluded area, he thought that he might even blow her brains out for humiliating him in front of all those people. It's a thin line between love and hate. Bee crossed that line and as soon as the moment presented it to bring her down, it will be by his hands. The only question in his mind is if he will bring her down in life or in death.

Chapter 7

These days Landon couldn't wait to get to work. Seeing Jay is all she thought about. She started taking chances with him by having sex in the shower after count and a lot of times during the count. That's the way that it started; in Jay's cell. They began talking on the phone all of the time. Jay convinced Landon that his children's mother isn't anything to him because of what she did to get Blackwell fired. By this time, Jay found out that Landon is one of the big connections to the hustle. He still didn't know everyone involved. He just knew about her. Uncle Twin revealed it to him and after some time, she informed him a little more. She continued to keep her co-workers' roles confidential, but she wanted Jay to know that she's running things as well. Jay never connected her to Blackwell.

Everyone on the section knew that Landon and Jay were having sex in the shower. The comrades kept it to themselves and those who weren't BGF wouldn't dare let themselves get caught talking about Jay's business with the CO. For a while their relationship remained confined to G-section, then among certain comrades throughout the jail. Landon picked up on how different the inmates reacted to her. She got a lot more respect and when telling someone to do something no one hesitated or took their time to get it done. Protests were minimal. Her tier was always one of the cleanest sections in the jail. Nowadays it is the cleanest and most organized. She has the section with the least amount of violence, which allows her to let inmates do whatever they want to do. The only time that she had problems is when certain captains or other brass came around unannounced and would smell weed or tobacco. However, she continued to get high praises. Now when she walks through the jail or happen to work overtime on another section the inmates speak to her politely. When an occasional loud mouth disrespectful inmate is at odds with her, a word from a knowing source changes that attitude and she get apologies or disgruntled retreats with knowing glances.

Landon ate up all of the attention. She feels like she has juice. The one time that she decides to get with an inmate, after all of these years, she picked the perfect one. He's a BGF member, he's ten years younger than she is; he's very mature, intelligent and commands a lot of respect among the men. She's becoming obsessed with Jay and he loves it! She's definitely one of the finest women in the jail and she has some money. Jay can tell that Landon is stuck on him hard. Uncle Twin constantly warned him about getting too close to her. Getting some pussy in the jail is one thing, but to start playing a woman like Landon can lead to catastrophic results. For instance, she'll shut down and won't say anything to him when he's on the phone with Tiffany. She has a problem with him talking to her for long periods of time. Her reasoning is that if she is only his children's mother and he cut her off for what she did, then why spend such a long time on the phone with her. It's bad enough that she comes to see him every visiting day with his sons. Jay couldn't call Tiffany or talk to her during Landon's shift anymore unless he's somewhere else on another section in the jail with Uncle Twin. He'll call Tiffany before Landon gets to work or as soon as her shift ends and just before she gets home. By that time he tells Tiffany that he's tired and is going to sleep. Some nights he'll talk a little longer if Landon is out or at the Icon with her co-workers, but she always call him as soon as she leaves the bar. Dealing with Landon is like playing a game to Jay and makes him feel like there isn't any woman that he can't have.

Uncle Twin observed the relationship between Landon and his young comrade. He recognized the potential problem and can tell that it's growing out of control. They are very discreet when it comes to having sex. Landon's job isn't in jeopardy on that concern. However, she began to get jealous of everyone that he gives attention to. She questions Jay about spending too much time with Twin. While she's at work she doesn't want him out of her sight. She also goes crazy when another female CO comes around and Jay would do so little as speak to them. She quickly cops an attitude and get on her police shit, then lock the tier down early, or get aggressive and smart with the other inmates until Jay gives her the necessary attention that calms her. Twin really likes Landon but, it isn't his place to tell her to ease up. He also don't want Jay to think that he's hating on him, either. He thought about getting Gibson to approach Landon, but he also didn't want to put Landon's personal business out. He knows that they are best friends and it is very unusual for Landon to be in this sort of a relationship. He don't know if Lt. Gibson is hip to what's going on. He believes that Officer Berry would have mentioned it to him by now because she always talk about the Queens in general conversations with him. She tells him which CO's are having sex in the jail to justify her own promiscuity. On top of that, he didn't say anything to the lieutenant because he couldn't tell what type of response that he'd get from Gibson. Sometimes she can be very difficult to talk to. What he doesn't know is that Landon's behavior changed among her friends, as well, and Gibson already heard about Landon and Jay.

This is the day that Gibson decided to approach her friend, but, first, she wants to observe Landon on the tier around her young lover before saying a word. She just couldn't believe what she'd been hearing from Elliot. It made her very angry that Landon hadn't said one word about the affair. She needs to know if it is true. More than likely it is the truth by the way that her girl has been distracted lately.

Gibson made all of her rounds before ending up onto G-Section. She wanted the inmates to be in the day room or on the tier moving about. Even if the section is still locked down, the tier workers would be out and about roaming around as long as it isn't count time. As calculated, when Gibson entered the doorway that lead to the section, Landon sat at her desk and sure enough, Jay sat in the chair next to the desk facing her. Jay spotted the lieutenant and mean mugged her before promptly getting up and excusing himself to walk off down the tier. He was still angry about Gibson putting him on lock-up. Gibson waited a few moments until Jay got down the tier before uttering a word.

"What up, huzzy?" She began. "I see your boyfriend is still mad at me for putting him on lock-up."

"What do you mean, my boyfriend?! You must be out of your mind! You know that I don't fuck wit' these niggas like that!" Landon barked in defense.

"Damn, girl! Slow down! Shit! I'm only messing with you... Look at his sexy ass," she said. "Call him back. I want to have some fun with him for a minute. I'm bored and I ain't got anything better to do."

"Girl, you crazy. I ain't gonna do that. Leave that man alone, with your hot ass. Don't you already have a nigga in the jail? You know shit like that causes problems," said Landon.

"Since when did you start trippin' about me teasing niggas? Girl, you better call his ass for me... Then again, I'll get him myself," Gibson said, walking onto the tier. Jay sat on a crate inside of his cell on the phone. He didn't hear Gibson coming. No one did because she held her keys. Before Jay knew it, she stood in front of his cell looking at him hold a conversation with one of his comrades about Landon being wrapped around his finger.

'So it is true,' Gibson discovered. Jay looks up and is astonished that the lieutenant stood in front of him. He completely forgot about the conversation that he was having about Landon. He became more concerned that she caught him with the phone. With eyes wide, he didn't know what to say or do, knowing that this bitch can put his ass back on the hammer in a heartbeat. He froze for a brief moment and then disconnected the call.

"I caught you, didn't I?" She said. She decided not to play the hard role. It didn't matter, anyway. She's not sweating the cell phone. She came for a different reason. "Ha, ha, ha! Look at your scared ass. Ol' tough ass BGF Jay. Ain't nobody worryin' about you or that phone. It's probably a thousand of them in the jail. I just want to see how well you're making out. Ain't no sense of you holding a grudge. I was just doing my job. You understand, don't you?"

"Yeah, I guess I do," he said, mad at the inmates on the tier and himself for slipping by letting her walk up on him. He eased up a little, then she continued.

"You be more careful around here with that phone. You are lucky that it's me that caught you. You know some of the brass be trippin' about them phones. You can get a street charge... Oh well, like I said, I'm just checking up on you and hope that there is no love lost. If you need anything that I can help you with, don't hesitate to get Officer Landon or any CO to contact me for you, ok?" Lt. Gibson instructed him.

"I appreciate that, lieutenant," Jay responded. Now he wondered if she heard his conversation about Landon. He definitely didn't want to blow Landon's spot or get the Lieutenant suspicious about him and Landon. That's all he needs. He knows that she can get fired or moved off of the section for even a rumor.

"See you around, sexy," she said, spinning in her Nike boots and prancing down the tier in the direction that she came from, singing *"I Shoulda Cheated"* by Keisha Cole. Landon stood up soon as Gibson strolled down the tier in her direction. She waited to see just how long Lt. Gibson was going to be talking to her friend. She wished that she had enough courage to tell her girl about Jay, but she didn't want Gibson to tell the other girls. She's embarrassed to be falling deeply in love with Jay because the relationship goes against all that she held onto for years; her dignity. Now, she's starting to lose it. Like, really, really, lose it. Gibson cheerfully returned to Landon after her conversation with Jay. Landon also became noticeably a little jealous.

"What were y'all talkin' 'bout for so long, girl?" She asked, being nosey.

"I complimented him on his swag and then I asked to see his package," Gibson lied to tease and get a reaction from her girl.

"You did what?!" Landon became shocked.

"Shiiiiiit! He got the goods, girl," Gibson said. "You sure you never peeped when he took a shower?"

"That's it! Get the hell off of my tier, you nasty huzzy!" Landon began tugging on Gibson's arm and pulling her into the hall and away from G section. She got boiling mad. She can't wait to talk to Jay about this shit. Gibson hit a nerve. Any other time, they would be laughing and giggling about something like that.

"Damn, L! You ain't gotta be so serious. Calm down... Are you going to the bar tonight? I think we need to talk, girl. You've been acting shiesty as hell." Gibson began to admonish Landon.

"I'll be there. I don't know what you're talkin' about but, I'll see you there later," Landon said to Gibson. She began to leave, walking up the hall and heading into the direction of the medical unit.

Landon turned to hurry and check Jay's ass. He's not going to play with her like that! Landon charged onto the tier and to Jay's cell. He stood outside of the cell talking to Uncle Twin. She walked straight up to him and slapped him across the face. It wasn't a really hard slap, but it echoed on the tier. Jay grabbed his face, surprised. Landon marched back towards her desk as quick as she marched to slap Jay's face. Uncle Twin laughed at his young comrade.

"Boooooy, you are playing with fire," he said to Jay while still laughing. Jay stood there holding his face and shaking his head back and forth in disbelief.

Gibson sat at the desk by the entrance to the medical unit. She worried about her girlfriend. She's never witnessed Landon so uptight. Now she *knows* that the reason for her change of behavior has to be a direct result of the affair that

135

she's having with Jay. Gibson began to think about the things that Jay said on the phone about her girl being wrapped around his finger. She knew that Lacy Landon was vulnerable for a man that could penetrate the invisible defense shield that makes her appear tough as nails. She *is* tough, but all it will take is for that right man to make her give in. Jay has all of the characteristics of a real strong man, with the exception of his criminal lifestyle, which makes him so wrong for Landon. He's straight hood without any care for the future. His life is for "here and now" and he does what he has to do to conquer all foes. His BGF family comes before even Tiffany and the children; although he won't admit it. His actions shows this. Maybe he won't take advantage of her, but it is highly likely that he will by the way that he talked about her to his comrade on the phone. Then the thought came to Gibson about Jay's hoodrat girlfriend that caused Blackwell to lose her job. She has to get Landon's attention about the love affair to ensure that she won't jeopardize their money. She really loves Landon. That's her girl. The relationship between Landon and Jay just can't be trusted.

Candace walked into the medical unit on her break. There were guys sitting on the benches waiting to be seen by the nurse for medication or for whatever medical reasons. It was busy and Candace could see the lieutenant engaging in a heated exchange with one of the inmates. She waved at the lieutenant to let her know that she's around and wants to see her. Candace also noticed G-Loc among the inmates that sat on the benches.

"Hey, Miss Simms!" G-Loc yelled, excited to see her. G-Loc and Pimp are almost inseparable in the jail. This is one of the rare occasions that they couldn't pair up. G-Loc put in a request to the medical unit's sick call. It's important that they move together, most of the time, because of their positions in the organization. They always have each other's back and they both are fearless members of the set. Simms did notice another Crip sitting close to G-Loc and yet another one standing close

136

to the glass entrance.

"What's crackin', Loc? Where's my big homie?" Candace asked him.

"He's back on the tier. I'ma' tell him that I saw you. You want me to give him a message for you?" Before she could answer another familiar voice filled the medical unit.

"What up, babyma... I mean, Miss Simms!" In pops Red Mike. He walked in accompanied by three other Bloods. These groups put up with one another in the jail and on the streets, but it don't take much to have them at odds and beefing. Actually, most of the groups don't like Bloods. They tolerate them. There are a lot of Bloods and they will start shit and are violent without being provoked. Some use numbers to start a lot of stuff. One of the acronyms for B.L.O.O.D is Building Leadership Over Oppressions and Destruction. What they demonstrate the most is destruction and oppression to anyone that isn't Blood.

G-Loc remained quiet and the friendly smile that he had for Candace abruptly disappeared. He turned his attention to his own comrade that sat next to him. G-Loc whispered a word or two and positioned straight into observation mode. Red Mike, noticing the attention that his presence came with, toned his voice down and moved closer to Candace so that no one could hear their conversation. Lt. Gibson watched all of this while continuing to conduct her business with a couple of inmates that were in her face vying for attention. However, she did admonish everyone to quiet down so that they could hear the names being called for screening.

"Daaaamn, baby momma, you act like I ain't even in the jail, yo. What up wit' 'dat?" Red Mike asked.

"Come on now, Mike. Why should I be concerned about you being in the jail? You don't do shit for me or your daughter. Just 'cause you locked up don't change a damn thing," Candace scolded, making sure that G-Loc witnessed the conversation. She's not dumb and *knows* that the encounter is going to be reported to Pimp. After the statement that she made to Red Mike, the nurse called G-Loc. He stood to answer the call of the medical personnel. He and Mike exchanged frowning glances at one another, then they both looked away without saying a word. The guy sitting with G-Loc followed him into the sea of offices and examination rooms. He stopped short of the cubicle where G-Loc's screening took place to post up. Mike and his boys were chuckling among one another at the sight of their movements before turning his attention back to Candace. Then he resumed the conversation in the slick manipulative manner that she'd grown accustom to and often anticipated.

"Damn, Miss Simms, I apologize. You don't have to get all upset," he said. He leaned in towards her and asked, "Can I talk to you alone somewhere?" Candace looked around to see where they could get a private moment. She then looked at Gibson and nodded her head towards Mike. Gibson shrugged her shoulders at first, but then gave a quick nod towards the hallway outside of the medical unit.

"Come on," she said, leading the way. Mike told his boys to chill so that they wouldn't follow him, then he and Candice walked out of their sight. "Now, what's on your mind?" She asked, folding her arms.

"Yo, you need to go by my mother's house and get that bag she got for me," he ordered Candice as though giving instructions to one of his boys instead of asking for a favor.

"Oh, really? What's in the bag?" She inquired.

"There's a couple o' ounces of loud and some tobacco in the bag. I told my mother that you should be there tonight or in the morning," Red Mike continued in sly way.

"You got it all figured out, don't you? What's in it for me?" She asked. She wanted to see what he would say. She didn't have any intentions of doing anything like that for him. In fact, she decided not to help him at all.

"Damn, baby momma, whatchoo' mean by what's in it for you? You can't take care of that for me? You go uptown every day. It ain't like we not cool or nothing, damn!" He said, arrogantly.

"Boooyyy! You must be out of your mind. Who's going to take care of my babies if I bring you that shit and get caught? You damn sure ain't! I'll be damned if I risk my job for your deadbeat ass," Candace responded.

"You do shit for that nigga, Pimp. He always got weed and brown. What's up with that, yo?" He asked as if holding something over her head. "Plus, I know you too well. You're too smart to get caught."

"I don't know what you're talkin' 'bout. I don't bring a thing in this jail for Pimp," she answered.

"You lying. Do you mean to tell me that you can give him some pussy in the gym, but you ain't bringin' in shit for him? Get the fuck outta' here!"

"First of all, that's my man and if *I am* givin' the business to him, it ain't none of yours, so let it go, Mike. I ain't bringing Pimp nothing and I damn sure not bringin' any weed or tobacco in here for you," Candace said, "And tell them flunkies of yours to mind their business!" She expressed, clearly upset.

"Ok, ok! Chillax, chillax!" Mike pleaded. One of his boys looked into the hall to check on him.

"Look at that! Just like on the streets. You ain't learning nothing in here. What do you have, four children now? You have three women with babies? This is your first time locked up, too. I know you got money. Why don't you take this time and evaluate your life, grow up, and don't be afraid to go to somebody to help you with that money so that you can get out of them streets?" Candace begged Mike in anguish.

"Look, I don't want to hear that Oprah Winfrey save the world shit. Then again, my bad, my bad," Red Mike relented. "I tell you what, Why don't you let me give you these two one hundred dollar bills that I got in my pocket and call me up to the gym so that I can get my nuts out the sand? You can buy our daughter something real nice with this."

139

"You just don't get it, do you? Life ain't all about sex, money, and drugs, but you too damn dumb to realize it. You can't make a career out of breakin' the law, or you gonna spend the rest of your life back and forth in places like this and you'll always be a grown ass boy. Worse yet, the life you live just might get you killed. You don't care about your children, your mother, or me. I love me and I'll be damned if I allow myself to be used for your pleasures. Why don't you be a man? Use that money you got to manipulate into a legitimate business. People do it every day. You might even do well for yourself. Oh, I forgot; you's a fool and happy with being a dummy that's in charge of imbeciles and idiots. I could hate you but, I don't...

"Let me tell you something else. If you were half of the man that Pimp is, I would suck your dick in here every day, if that's what you want. I would come to your cell and let you hit it from the back, too." Then she grabbed his crotch before continuing. "But, if you think that I'ma let this inside of me ever again, you might as well bend over and give that ass to one of these horny old heads in the jail to get your rocks off." She let him go and backed away. Suddenly, G-Loc and one of his boys walked out of the medical unit. Red Mike's face grew twisted with anger. He turned beet red. He moved to grab Candace but, she backed away before he could reach her. She folded her arms again, then hissed, with much venom,

"I dare you!"

"Fuck you, bitch! Fuck you and that broke ass nothing ass nigga you got... Who you looking at?!" Mike woofed at G-Loc. They began walking towards one another.

"Who the fuck is you talkin' to?!" G-Loc responded. Candace jumped in between the both of them and turned to face G-Loc. She grabbed him and turned him around in the opposite direction. He eased up to retreat.

"G-Loc, please go ahead and don't pay him any mind! Please, for me!" She begged. He and his comrade reluctantly continued on in their way back to the section. They both were strapped with razor sharp folding blades and were more than willing to use them. G-Loc retreated out of respect for Pimp and Candace. Somehow they all knew that this incident would be the beginning of some serious shit.

Mike stood there watching Candace restrain G-Loc and began grinning sinisterly. "You Crabs don't really want it with us... Bddllaat!!! He yelled, giving a call to alert any Bloods in the area. By the time his boys came out of the medical unit, G-Loc was too far off. "Fuck them... come on," Red Mike said, leading the way back into the medical unit. He completely ignored Candace. Once inside, he quietly, but visibly agitated, sat down onto one of the benches that inmates use until they are called. Gibson looked at him and got up out of her seat. She motioned for the officer assigned to the post to come back to the desk. She had to catch up with Simms.

"What's going on, girl? I can tell something' ain't right by the way that the goons came into medical," Gibson said, huffing and puffing when she caught up to her young friend.

"It ain't nothing, Ma. I handled it, for now. I hope things don't get out of hand," Candace responded.

"I don't know, Simms. Your baby daddy looks shiesty as hell. I've been around thousands of 'em. The way he looks now, he's up to something in that head of his," Gibson informed her, apprehensive. "Plus, he got a lot of followers, too. That's a deadly combination."

"You are so right about that," she agreed. Then she switched the subject.   I'm on my way to lunch. Can you come with me so that I can show you what the real estate agent, Mr. Tucker has for me?"

"Sure, girl. Come on," Gibson said, interlocking her arm with her young friend's as they strolled into the direction of the Officer's Dining Room. "Tucker is a sweetie and I love him to death. He'll fix you up."

Lt. Gibson and CO Simms walked through the line with trays choosing their meals for the evening. They sat at the table to eat while continuing on with the subject of Simms' house shopping. Candace Simms is about to be 20 years old and in almost a year since she's has been on the job she never believed that so many good things could happen for her. She purchased a car and is close to buying a home. What more can she ask for? She developed a genuine love for Lt. Gibson because of everything. She appreciated her friendship with Landon, Hope and Bee as well.

While continuing the conversation, a distress call came bursting through the radios that both women wore with their uniforms. The officers were instructed that the location of the fight is in the medical unit. Gibson and Simms looked at one another. The eating abruptly stopped. They both ran to the medical unit.

By the time the two women arrived on the scene, along with other officers abandoning their posts to stop the violence, there were two female medical personnel working on a Crip member that didn't leave the medical unit with G-loc and his comrade. Blood was splattered everywhere when Gibson and Simms got to the medical unit and the two ladies that were working on the guy barked orders. They worked at stopping blood spewing from the young man's neck and torso. There were three other officers struggling to subdue a short muscular guy that resisted, yelling, "Bddllaat, Bddllaat!"

Mike and a couple of the other blood members sat on the benches looking at the spectacle before them. After hand cuffing the suspected assailant, he was forcefully escorted out of the medical unit and on his way to lock-up. Hope, Landon, and Bee stood with Simms. They were also a part of the cavalry of COs that now crowded the medical unit. Gibson began to take control and give order to the chaos. The victim, now stretched on a gurney and being wheeled away with a monitor to measure his vitals, desperately waited for the EMT to arrive at the detention center.

Bee and Landon retreated to their post, along with the other officers present at the melee. Simms and Hope remained at the scene of the aftermath, quietly talking among themselves and stealing glances at Red Mike and his boys. Mike and his boys remained seated. Looking as though he didn't have a care in the world, with his legs stretched and arms folded, he chuckled with his crew. Both of them knew that he motivated the mayhem. They know his work.

"What's up, Glo?" Mike spoke to Hope. She moved closer to him out of everyone's earshot before responding. Simms walked close to Lt. Gibson.

"Don't call me that. Call me by my last name," she reminded him. Then she asked covertly. "What happened in here?"

"Come on, yo? What do you call yourself doing? I hope you ain't tryna' play me. You *iz* the police, ain't choo?" Mike responded.

"Awwww, nigga, please! I don't give a shit about the dumb ass games that yall supposed to be grown ass men be playing. All yall do is kill and hurt each other, anyway. We grew up together and we're homies, but since you takin' it like that, just forget it!" She snapped at Red Mike.

"My bad, yo. You know how real shit is, Glo. Anyway, I guess the crab got outta' hand and he needed to be tightened up. You feel me?" Mike said, looking at his two blood brothers that sat with him laughing and giving one of them the signature handshake in affirmation.

"You need to stop it. I'm going by your mother's house in the morning so that I can tell her you're over here showing off." Hope said, getting confirmation on what she and Simms already suspected. Mike instigated all of the trouble.

"You need to get that bag from her for me when you go by there. My baby momma on some bullshit. You know I'ma look out if you make it happen," he said, getting serious.

"I'll give her a number for you so that you can call me and I'll look into it for you. I'm not making any promises. You just have to chill out and keep the violent shit to a minimum so that things can run smooth, you got me?" Hope advised her homeboy.

"I got you, Glo… I mean, Ms. Hope," he said, smiling with his ruby encrusted gold teeth shining. She walked away from Mike and began talking to some of her co-workers. By this time, Simms went back to her post as well but, Lt. Gibson stood boiling mad. She hate these type of power plays among the so-called gangs. She know that Mike did this to get Simms and her son's father attention. That is his personal bullshit. It now has the potential to start a gang war in the jail that could be bad for everybody; and Gibson, for one, isn't prepared to do all of the overtime hours or seeing all of the bloody crime scenes. She also thought about Simms.

"Lock him up and lock his ass up, too!" Gibson yelled, pointing to Red Mike and indiscriminately choosing one of his boys.

"I ain't do shit! What da' fuck you locking me up for! Officer Hope, why is she locking me up!" Mike pleaded to his homegirl.

"I'm the lieutenant, not her, and you look sneaky; also, because I can! Get them outta' here, NOW!" She yelled to four huge goon squad male officers that are her designated henchmen of the moment. Mike wanted to buck until he heard Hope's voice and saw the look in her eyes. Her eyes advised him to chill out and not make the situation worse. He complied. However, while being escorted from the medical unit, he mean mugged the lieutenant with a deadly and fierce look. Gibson refused to look away or flinch, returning an equally ferocious gaze. He frightened her just a little. They all do in these very intense moments, but she refused to let anyone see her back down or cower. She's still "the boss".

After sending all of the inmates back to their cells and housing areas, Gibson finally relaxed a little and sat down exhausted. Hope stayed with her after calling the P-section officer to lock her section down. Hope and Gibson talked about Mike and his connection to Simms. Hope surmised that she will do all that she can to talk to Mike about not causing more trouble. This isn't the streets. A prison beef between gangs can produce more victims than a street beef. Even faster. A can of worms, or better yet, cells of niggas with knives can be opened. The two women talked longer until Hope realized that she had to get back to her section.

On her way to her post, she thought about a conversation that she and Max had about how easy it is for a war to start in the jail with so much tension among the brothers. Max called every blackman his brother. Max told Hope that black men are so insecure about themselves that competition makes them feel worthwhile. It's natural to compete, but black men compete wrongly to the detriment of themselves. They are always challenging to one another. Now, with the gangs, individual challenges turn into group battles. She found herself moving fast in her haste to talk to Max about the potential beef that is almost certain to arise and to ask his advice about keeping the situation under control since it involves her friend. She knows that he is sure to give her some good insight.

Thinking Max always keeping her informed and captivated, she's beginning to develop a fondness that is surprising her. He's unlike any other man that she has ever met. He's humble, yet strong. He always seems to know more than the person he's talking to without coming across as arrogant. He didn't associate with a lot of people, but he never hesitates to hold court so that he can share his knowledge. Thoughts of Puddin' didn't consume her mind so much anymore. They are being replaced with thoughts of Maximillian Muhammad. She needs to know more about him and thought to ask him about his crime. Is he a murderer? She can easily find out but she want to hear what he has to say. He is intimidating, but not in a scary way. It's more like a guardian or fatherly way. She can tell that they are around the same age.

Hope got back to the section and went straight to the dorm where Max sleeps.

"It's sanitation time, Max!" She hollered into the dorm, unlocking the grill and walking away real professional like. She hid her anticipation well. Max came out of the dorm and immediately retrieved a broom and started his job of sweeping and mopping the tier. Inmates began yelling to Hope for frivolous reasons, as usual, just to get some attention. She entertained their petty request, but let everyone know that once she sit down to do her paperwork, do not call her for anything! However, she let Max know that she needs to talk to him about something important. They usually talk every night anyway, but, he can tell that this is a specific and pressing issue. He decided that he should move quickly and not give into every inmate that wants him to pass, deliver, or retrieve things from other inmates.

Max mopped the length of the hall. Approaching Hope's desk, he paused, leaned with his left hand on the desk and held the top of the mop with the other, he crossed his legs.

"What's on our mind, Miss Hope?"

"I have a friend who is a CO in the jail. She's young and have two baby daddies that are in here locked up." She began explaining.

"Oh yeah?" Max replied and began to ponder before he spoke. "That's a delicate situation. It can cause problems for her if they don't already have an understanding. It sounds very volatile... Do they get along?"

"No, and one of them is a Blood and the other one is a Crip," Hope said, warming up to the meat of the meal that she wants Max to swallow and digest.

"Holy smoke!" Max yelled with his eyes bulging. Hope laughed. "Are you for real?"

"I sure am," she said, and then explained what she knew about Mike getting a Crip hit because Simms refused to bring him stuff in the jail. She also explained how she don't want to see Red Mike get hurt because they grew up together, although she is a couple of years older than he. She explained how hard headed and arrogant that Mike is, on top of having

146

some money and influence.

"Do you know that ten years ago Baltimore didn't have a so-called gang problem? That didn't mean that there weren't any Bloods or Crips around. They were very few in number," Max began. "The influence of the media and the music is what helped to foment a lot of young people in the city to join. We here in Baltimore are always jumping on somebody else's bandwagon. We Johnny Come Latelys and we don't support our own. What gets to me is that we won't fight for proper knowledge that will free us from being poor. Some of us will join the armed services because we are poor and fight foreign enemies that helps to make America rich. We'll also kill each other for next to nothing right here on Greenmount Avenue. In years past, we were killed because of our skin color and because a lot of white people view us as less than a human being. Today we will viciously kill, rape, and rob one another. Nowadays, we're killing each other because of colors and what different group that you happen to be with. It's just sad!

"Sister Hope, it's going to take the BGF and the Sunni Muslims in the jail to stop this one. Right now, it's too early to tell how far it will go. We'll just have to see how the blues retaliate," Max said to Hope. He loved looking into Hope's eyes when talking to her. A lot of the black women her age don't care to hear proper knowledge. They are justified because a lot of black men go to prison and get really smart just to come home and act so dumb.

"I think you are right. Maybe it's a little too soon to tell how violent this situation can get. I believe we are in store for more," she said.

"Sister, a man named Na'im Akbar once wrote that black people built the pyramids; now we destroy our neighborhoods in frustrated explosion of rage, irresponsibility, and neglect. We reached high civilization through the dignified leadership of African Queens; now many of us have become abusers and destroyers of black

147

women and black femininity. We introduced medicine and healing to the planet. We've now become drug abusers and merchants of this illicit trade and destroyers of our own lives. We have descended from scientist who studied the heavens, to being reduced to clowns that degrade ourselves and brutalize one another at the delight and for the entertainment of others.

"We need to search for and develop into that higher human awareness that almighty God bestowed upon us and that the giants of our ancestry were so in tuned with," Max explained, feeling compelled to share his thoughts. This is her moment and she knows that she had to ask her question, now.

"Max, you are so brilliant and you have a pleasant but strong demeanor. I need to ask you a serious question. You don't have to answer, if you don't want to. I just like you because, you are so different from any man that I've ever seen come through the jail and on the streets. So, what did you do to get yourself in here?" She finally asked. Max looked at her intently. Then he dropped his head and turned away, not expecting such a question. He thought for a moment and then decided to answer.

"Ten years ago, I was a demon. I didn't care about anything but money. Making it and taking it. Nothing could stop me from being the meanest nigga around... Anyway, one day I and an associate of mine planned to rob a dealer in South Baltimore. We were finishing up robbing the guy with a score netting us $30 thousand and some drugs. I just had to prove a point to my partner. He wasn't a friend or anything. He's just someone that I knew. He set the whole caper up and chose me to help him pull it off. I had to prove to my partner in the crime just how wicked I could be. I put my .45 point blank to the mark's head and pulled the trigger. That is the first time that I've ever looked into someone's eyes and felt pieces of their life's flesh, blood, and bone splatter back into my own face. In that split second, that person went from being a living being to a dead body and a memory. I felt an extraordinary evil inside of myself. It's an inhumane like feeling. Then the fear came. A fear so strong that it had me believing that I could do it again. That frightened me! I looked at my partner in crime and I contemplated his demise. It's very hard to explain, but I live with seeing that incident played out often in my mind when I'm sleep and awake, it doesn't matter. I made a decision to change and get rid of the evil inside of me from that moment up until this day. That was the end of my murderous campaign into the life of the streets. Today, I'm in here because the partner that I went on *that* sting with and who got half of the loot committed a crime recently and he is a three time loser facing twenty-five years without the possibility of parole. Maybe I should have smashed him, too. Well, anyway, he was stopped with a lot of drugs in his car. So, now he wants to give me up concerning the one incident that changed my life and made me a person worth the air that Allah has given me to breathe," he explained to Hope, with watery eyes that were now filled with the pain of his memories. "I was only eighteen, but, if I have to pay for my crime, may Allah bless me to get through it. All that I can ask for is His mercy," concluded Max.

Hope had to get her handkerchief out of her handbag to stop the flow of tears that poured from her own eyes. "You aren't that person anymore. I just know that you aren't," she said sympathetically.

"Well, it's still hard for me to believe that I'm not and I've studied to learn myself and others to see what makes us want to destroy one another with so much malice. We are all a design that comes from concepts housed in the mind of Allah. How dare we, who are so much less then he, destroy any part of his creation; let alone to destroy a man who God has given dominion over everything that is his. God gives us his earth and his glory and we heap death and destruction upon it! Who are we and how dare we show such non-appreciation to Him in this manner? I work on myself daily so that I can teach my family the better principles of His world," he explained, once again.

"You have a family?" Hope asked.

"You are on it with the personal questions today… No, I don't. But, I do want a Queen that I can adore and who's not a slave to this material world. There's nothing wrong with luxuries because we are God's best and as long as we work for it and meditate on it, we deserve and should have the best of things. That's part of God's gift of dominion. There are just too many of us that worship a lot of things instead of worshipping the mind, heart, and spirit of one another who are the closest thing; or should I say, being to God on the earth. I'm looking for a woman that I can worship and that worships me so that we can give our collective worship to our Creator…

"Now, I have a question for you, Miss Hope?"

"What is it?" She responded.

"Why are you a lesbian?" Max asked her. Hope never expected him to ask her such a question. She would usually take offense to someone questioning her sexuality. Coming from Max, she felt a slightly embarrassed but not offended. She wasn't ashamed and she respected him a lot. Anyone else would have gotten the blues. Any other man, that is. He has every right to ask her, due to the questions that she asked him. Before answering, she thought just how good it would be for a man like him to teach Lamar. She took a deep breath and then she started.

"Well, women turned me on when I was young. I am in love with the strength of them after becoming so weak and beat down often by the hands and actions of men. We are so absolutely strong and weak. Delicate, so to speak. This has always attracted me to the same sex. As I got older, I witnessed women that were close to me suffering behind the deeds of men. I've never been raped or anything close to that but, I have family and friends who were raped and abused by men so often. I've witnessed women suffer after giving all of their heart and soul to a man only to have him killed in the streets--leaving her to hurt and struggle with a family until the strength to move on is found. Some women go on a rollercoaster ride of emotions and struggles with their men going in and out, back and forth to prison. I've seen women die a thousand times being abused and beat up by men, only to take the man back again and again with promises not to hurt them again. Then there are the ones so scared of their men that it makes them slaves to whatever his whims are. I've seen the pimps, liars, and the users. The killers and the dealers that have lead our communities to hell with their childish, selfish, and whimsical desires and attempts to charade as men, but are merely grown boys. I've comforted many women through their pains inflicted mostly and overwhelmingly by their men. I've been comforting them since I can remember and I've developed a certain disdain for men. So, I never wanted to be with a man. This is the very first time that I've ever shared that with any man, period," Hope ranted in disgust and becoming a little agitated that she let her guard down to such a degree.

"Come on Max, it's time for you to lock in."

Max could see that Hope grew uncomfortable with her answer. However, he just had to ask one more question. So, after he put the mop and bucket away, he walked up to Hope and asked, "Sister, how many men have you ever been in a relationship with?"

"Well, let me think… I've never had a relationship with a man but, I've been in love, maybe, three times in my life with women. I have someone who I'm in love with now, but we're not together because, we're having problems… Now, come on so that I can lock you in," she calmly ordered Max. She stood from behind her desk and began to pull the keys from her belt to lock Max in.

"Ok, ok… I just have one last question, if you don't mind?" He could tell that she became unnerved, but he tried her anyway.

"Damn, Max! You're really making me pay for asking you that question. I should have kept my damn mouth shut…

"All right, all right, but this is the last one! I talked too much already," she said exasperated with Max and his questions.

"How many men have you been with?" He asked her, looking into her eyes.

"Well, let me think… none." She answered softly.

"What do you mean none? Do you mean to tell me that you've never been with a man?" He asked her, even more surprised. Max could not believe that this gorgeous black woman has never had the strong gentle touch of a caring black man.

"That's what I said." She revealed again, as a matter of fact.

"You're still a virgin, with your fine precious self?" Max asked. It was more of a compliment disguised as a question. Hope stared at him and rolled her eyes instinctively. She began walking to the dormitory where Max slept and opened the grill. He followed closely. He went into the dorm, then turned to look at Hope as she locked it. "Good night, Officer Hope," He said, holding onto the bars of the grill.

"Good night, Max. I'll see you tomorrow," Hope said, shyly. She walked away smiling without turning around like a schoolgirl.

Chapter 8

Elliot was filled with anticipation waiting to be let out of the bowels of the Clarence Mitchell Courthouse located in downtown Baltimore. The judge released him with a sentence of probation and a suspended sentence. The anxiety inside of him craved for that ultimate feeling of relief that is a pleasure more gratifying than sex. Being set free from jail! He was escorted from the holding cells that held all of the inmates awaiting their turn to be judged and exonerated or convicted by one man or twelve citizens. Coming up from out of the garage and onto Guilford Avenue, he began to walk slowly at first. He picked up speed with his head held high as he trotted towards his destination. It's a brisk autumn day. Elliot moved smiling and cheerful, oblivious to the weather that one would normally need a jacket for. He's warmed by the rush of emotions that excite him from the numerous thoughts that flood his mind. The first thing that he has to do is go around the way on Lanvale and Rutland so that he can catch up with Bighead Charlie. He didn't have any money in his pockets because it is in his account at the jail. He'll have to get that on some other day. So, he did what most of the newly released prisoners do. He walked.

Approaching the block, Elliot spotted the usual suspects. Everyone that he walked past commented on how good he looked. He's always been built pretty solid, but now he is a little more bulked from lifting weights and exercising. Plus, he hasn't been using drugs every day like he did when he was previously home. In fact, Elliot held firm about not getting high at all within the past two weeks before his eventual release. He has a lot to prove to himself about not using drugs so that he can finally make some real money and get paid. His girl assures him that she has a job in place for him so that he won't have to hustle.

His girl! That thought surprised him, too. Elliot had grown very fond of Lt. Doreatha Gibson. She remind him of

153

his old girl Gina, who really cared about him a lot. She let him know that he can stay with her and all she want from him is to be a real man so that she can share her world with him. Now that he is home, he really wants her to see that he can do his part and more. His mother and his brother will soon see that he is his own man. He decided to call Gibson after he gets up with Charlie. He saw one of the home girls in the middle of the block on Crystal and Rutland.

"What up, Pam?" Elliot yelled, walking up on her. Her eyes went wide with her mouth open and her hand went across her chest as though she held something inside of herself.

"Elliot, is that you?! Mmm, mm, you look good! You're just shining all over the place. Come over here and give me a hug!" Baldhead Pam yelled, surprised to see Elliot looking so good. She's use to seeing him ashy and worn in the face by a lack of rest from chasing drugs and not eating properly. He also wore a fresh pair of sneakers and jeans, with a shirt that fit. Unlike the usual baggy clothes that he wore because of weight loss from using drugs. He walked over to Pam thinking that she never showed him this much love before. He gave her a hug and noticed that she held him tight and pressed her body completely against his. After the quick embrace, Elliot asked if or not she saw Charlie around. Pam allows Bighead Charlie to use her house to cap his dope and vial his coke for his shops. She and Elliot are both part of Charlie's team.

While they discussed the possible whereabouts of Charlie, the undercover Organized Crime Division policemen that locked Elliot up drove the car onto the sidewalk, jumping out and rolling right up on Elliot. "So, you made it home, huh, bitch?" The cop that everybody in the neighborhood calls Crazyhorse asked him.

"Fuck you! I ain't doin' a damn thing wrong. I'm clean as a whistle. I just got out of the bing about an hour ago," said Elliot. Crazyhorse and his partner Runnin' Man are familiar with Bighead Charlie and his whole set, including Baldhead

Pam and Elliot.

"You will be, soon as you catch up with your boy Charlie... Ain't that right, Pam?" Crazyhorse snickered in her direction.

"Come on, Crazyhorse! Ain't nobody doin' shit. Yall always messin' with somebody!" Pam responded. Crazyhorse walked up to face with Elliot. Elliot swelled, unafraid by the memory of the fight that he had with Crazyhorse when they locked him up. Elliot was digging in his ass until Runnin' Man and the other back up OCD officers collaborated on giving him an old fashion police ass whooping. Elliot can tell that Crazyhorse still harbored ill feelings about Elliot handling him in the fight.

"Don't worry, bitch. As soon as you think you're gonna move some work for your man, I'ma' bring your junkie ass down so fast that the devil gonna' have to give you a hand to help pull you back up," sneered Crazyhorse. "With your bitch ass." Crazyhorse and his partner went back to the car and drove away towards Federal Street.

"Elliot, them whores been on Charlie's ass hard ever since Lil' Tavey got killed. They blame Charlie because Tavey worked for him. That's why he ain't out on the black now. We been chillin' ever since... Come on. Let's go to my crib and I'll hit Charlie up on his phone," Pam said, grabbing Elliot's hand to lead the way.

Pam called Bighead Charlie on his cell phone once they got into the house. Her five year old and her three year old were in the house alone taking a nap, so Pam went to the store. She also had four more children who were in school. She is a very nice looking short haired woman, who is also fat to death. After having six children before the age of 27, with four baby daddies, she spend her days hustling with Bighead Charlie and chasing boyfriends. She don't care if the latest boyfriend has money or not as long as he helps her with the children. She usually has about two or three different boyfriends a year. They all have to accept that Bighead

Charlie is the real man of the house. He and Pam only had sex two times and that was a long time ago.

While waiting for Charlie, Pam offered to buy Elliot a bag of dope. She call herself treating him and looking out for him on his first day home. Once Elliot declined the offer, Pam became even more impressed. He explained to her that he's not getting high anymore. It's time for him to get paid. *This* Elliot turns her on. She lit a blunt and offered it to him. He didn't even hit that; although he hadn't planned on refraining from the weed. Right now he wants to remain focused and see Charlie before even thinking about doing anything with drugs. Pam asked Elliot if he wants to stay in the back room of her house until he gets on his feet. What she's really doing is trying to get him in her clutches and sex him up so that he won't leave. She never looked at him like this before. He's so fresh and confident.

Charlie arrived glad to see his main runner. Elliot was a big part of Charlie's business. Most of the customers that don't live in the neighborhood knew Elliot first, and all of the white customers comes to Charlie's shop because of Elliot. Things run smooth when Elliot is on the scene. It will be a good thing for Elliot to take his position back because of all of the heat that they are getting. Bighead Charlie became encouraged by Elliot being free and home to open the shops up again. After falling back and chillin' from selling anything in the past ten days or so after Tavey got shot, Charlie gave Elliot $200 for his pocket and offered him some dope. He just got to get Elliot charged up and back on the block. He did do okay without Elliot, but he's no fool. His young ass know who run the shops for real, and along with good drugs, Elliot made the clientele what it has become. Elliot is the best on the block. Nevertheless, Elliot refused the offer. Charlie don't like it that Elliot is not getting high, but he didn't show it. He figured that he will be sniffing smack in a few more days, or probably even later on that night. At any rate, Bighead Charlie got to get him back on the block.

Elliot joined Charlie and Pam in smoking a blunt. The three of them laughed about Elliot almost beating Crazyhorse's ass the day that he was arrested. Elliott continued to stress to Charlie how bad that he wants his own package and how he promise that he is not getting high off of the dope anymore. Charlie let Elliot know that he needs him to put the shops back in order and how good it is that Elliot is uptown just in time to break out the new smack that will be coming in a few days. He emphasized that the smack they are getting is a Bomb! Elliot let Charlie know that he will help him get things started but, he still wants his own package to work so that he can move around at his own pace and in his own time. This is a wise decision for Elliot because he knows that if he jumps straight out on the block like Charlie wants him to, he will be hounded by Crazyhorse and Runnin' Man until they lock him up again. He's not scared of them, he just know that they are wild cowboys and their passion to bag him, along with not knowing the neighborhood like they think they do, is exactly what Elliot uses to get away with shit. This time around he don't want or need that type of attention from OCD. It's time to rise above the corners. He's done the corner for too long. It's all about the next step for him.

Time passed. Elliot and Charlie said their goodbyes to Pam. They both got into a new Yukon Denali that Charlie drove. It's a truck that he bought for his girl. Elliot expressed how bad he wants a new ride and get money. He repeated to Charlie how he now has his head on straight. Charlie listened as he transported Elliot to his mother's house. Before the pair departed, Charlie gave Elliot more money.

"Here, yo," Charlie began. "Call me as soon as you get a phone with this hundred. The number is still the same."

"I got you, potna... Thanks, lil' homey. We gonna' do this here," Elliot said. They shook hands in front of his mother's house before he stepped out of the truck.

Elliot had to see his mother. She worried about him a lot. So much so that she almost paid his bail, but Elliot's brother advised against it. She knew that her son needed some tough love and she prayed on the decision. She decided to leave him in the good hands of the Lord. Seeing her child look this good was a sign that she'd made the right decision.

"Look at my baby! You look mo' and mo' like yo' father the older you get, with your handsome self," She said, hugging her child. "That girl's been callin' here for you, too. She had me worryin' if or not you went in that old neighborhood, first. She checked up on you at the courthouse and they said that you were released some time ago. She called about three times. Tell me you ain't fix'n to fool with them same ol' low lifes. We moved from that neighborhood, your father and I, so that you boys can have better; praise God."

"Mamma, I'm fine. Everything is all right. I'm glad to be home, too," he said, hugging his mother and changing the subject. "You said that Doreatha called for me?"

"She sho' did, and she wants you to return her call as soon as yo' butt part this door. You best call that child. She's been pretty good to me these past few months while you were away.   She really sees a lot in you. I hope you don't ruin that girls feelins," Elliot's mother said.

"Ma, I like her a lot. She's been good to me, too. I still have to get to know her, but as far as I can see, she seems to be special... Let me go and call her," he said, getting one more hug from his mother before going to the telephone. His mother beamed looking at her son and wishing that his father was alive to see him looking this good. He sure enough didn't look this good at the funeral. All tore down and sucked up.

"Hey, bay!" Gibson answered her phone. "Well, it's about time that you called me. Whatchoo do, went to see one of your other bitches? I knew that you was full o' shit. My girlfriend at the courthouse said that they let you go almost three hours ago. All yall niggas is just alike. You don't know what's good for you."

"Yoooo! Hold up, Boo! It's not like that," Elliot said, in his defense. Gibson was pissed off. She'd taken a day off from work to spend time with him. "I had to go see some people that put a few dollars in my pocket."

"Yeah? I thought that we talked about that. You said that you are gonna give yourself a chance and not rush back to the streets," Gibson reminded him. "I got what you need!"

"Now, look! I'm a grown ass man and I had some things to do! Now, is you comin' to get me or not?!" Elliot barked. That's the shit that turns Gibson on. She loves for her man to take charge.

"I'm on my way, Elliot," she whimpered.

"Now, that's what I'm talking about," he said before hanging up the phone. He continued to talk with his mother and his Aunt Shirley before Gibson arrived. Once she arrived, she came into the house with her bottom lip hanging and looking like a spoiled little girl. They both apologized to one another before the embrace that turned into a passionate kiss.

The two of them went shopping for clothes and Elliot bought dinner at the Rain Forrest Café in the Towson Town Center. They ended the night sipping on champagne, listening to Ladawn Black's Love Zone on the radio and sharing stories of their lives with one another until the ambiance of the night, along with the happiness of Elliot being free, led to a night of wild passionate affectionate and bonding sex.

Gibson took off from work for the next three days. They spent that time hanging out and getting to know one another on this side of life. Elliot even made her breakfast every morning. He did stay the night at his mother's house one time. That was the second day that he was free. His Boo stayed with him, too. Gibson helped him get a job driving a van for a cleaning service. That's all he had to do, along with unloading supplies. Bighead Charlie had to wait for Elliot a little longer because the neighborhood stayed hot, but Elliot didn't care one way or the other He likes what his life is becoming with Doreatha Gibson in such a short period of time. He continued to keep thoughts of getting paid in the back of his mind and now he only sniffed dope once a week.

Elliot was fortunate to be at home or to leave Steel-side when he did. Before he left the jail it was in the air about the potential war between the Crips and Bloods. He more than likely would have never been involved in the war, but just being a resident of the jail in the time of a jailhouse war had an added miserable effect on the misery that is so much a part of pretrial detention if you are involved in it or not. It's depressing to witness the maiming and murder of people and the feeling that at any moment someone can be attacked. A lot of times the men that were attacking one another didn't have a thing to do with what initiated the war. It becomes about what side or what color you represent, or who your homeboys are. A lot of the combatants don't even know one another. Friends or foes. A sad and pathetic reality!

The war in the jail is now on the rise. Upon hearing what occurred in the medical unit, Pimp and G-loc ran all of the Bloods off of their section. There were about twenty five Bloods and only fourteen Crips, but Pimp and G-loc went extremely hard on the enemy. Their spirit for battle transferred over to the soldiers in their set on the tier. No one died in the battle yet, but out of the seven critically wounded, only one was on the blue side. Retaliation came swift. The leader of the Blood's set in the jail called every one of the brothers who were leaders on their section and made a calculated plan for them to go at every Crip at the exact same time all over the jail. Their leader's name is Moon. He is one of the most ruthless, conniving, manipulating, and wicked geniuses to come off of Edmondson Avenue. He's feared, well respected, loved, and revered by all of the sets in the city. He's fighting a homicide that he knows will be thrown out of court. However, he's been in the jail for four years fighting his case. City officials are using the system to keep him off of the streets as best as they can. Never mind the violation of Hicks; which is his right to a speedy trial.

After the synchronized assault on the Crips, the jail

was in pandemonium. The battles grew bloodier and now three lives were lost after the synchronized attack. Everywhere the blues and reds ran into one another they went at it. They went at it in the gym, in the yard, at work in the kitchen, and also the Library. They were stabbing one another at Sunday church service, too. They wouldn't dare bring the battle to Friday Jumma service. That would have been disrespectful to the Sunni Muslims. Nobody disrespected Jumma! They beefed in the medical unit and even when they were being escorted to court. All of this started because a grown man couldn't have his way with a woman. The fools went at in front of their families during visits!

The chief of security was going absolutely nuts. He had no choice but to call a code red emergency and place the entire Baltimore City Detention Center on lock down. Mass Control went into effect. There were escorts for all mandatory movements such as medical and when an inmate came off of the section, they had to be handcuffed. All activities were cancelled. Including family visits. The violence had become senseless. It was going on just because. In a few short weeks four lives were lost. Those are homicides that never got counted among the Baltimore city's homicide toll.

To maintain order and bring the violence to a minimum all of the Crips were put on a section of their own where Pimp and G-loc are located. The Bloods were put on S-section. This way the administration can monitor the situation and minimize the violence. In the annex the reds had the second and third floor, while the blues had the first floor. The reds always out populate the blues. The Crips are growing in the city but, BGF run shit in the Maryland prisons and Baltimore city. Although there are less Crips in the jail, the casualties of war were just about even; with only a small edge on the side of the Bloods.

Despite all of the mayhem, Uncle Twin is still able to maneuver around the jail under the guise of trying to get a grip on the violence and trouble that went on. The security chief like and respect Twin. Twin basically use him as a means to an end. The money! Sometimes Twin will plant knives and direct the chief on where they will be. They are never the best weapons. Information like that ingratiates him to the chief. Uncle Twin also will occasionally get him drugs and plant a few phones. This is so that the chief can present those things to the warden and his superiors. It's all a matter diplomacy. One hand washing the other because everybody has to answer to somebody. The officers believe that Twin has more influence over their boss than they do. Gibson can't stand Twin's relationship with the chief. She respects Twin but, she really don't care for him too much. There is just no way, she thought, that an inmate should have that much power, no matter how much she needs him. This is why she keep her words short with him.

Things began to get out of hand so bad that the chief made a decision that hit a lot of people where it hurts. The only thing that he could think to do is to stop the inmate population from ordering commissary. That's right, COMMASSARY! This will slow down the biggest operation in the jail. The war is officially out of hand and has to be stopped. Twin tried his best to convince the chief to keep the store open to no avail. Twin got mad about his money flow being bothered. He is about to go to court soon and he's trying to save every penny that he can. He don't know what his fate will be, so the money that he makes is to insure that he can continue to help his wife pay bills if he do time, or as a down payment on a new Benz in the event he is released. He was making a killing in the jailhouse war because he used the tightening of security to go up $50 more on everything. By him being one of the only inmates to move around the jail during the war, he transported just about all of the contraband. Now there is no way that this shit can continue without him putting his foot down. These hoppers are too damn violent! They have to be stopped.

Candace and Bee couldn't see Pimp and G-loc in the

gym anymore. It became really hard. Candace would send Pimp a pass when she worked in the medical department so that he could talk to her. It's hard for them to be alone in there. She would get him to walk in the back and pretend that she need him to help her with something just to steal a kiss and tease one another. Sometimes, she will fill in for someone else that has the post just so she could see her man. She felt extremely guilty about the violence that kicked off in the jail. The weight of all the bloodshed was on her shoulders. Everyone did their best to convince her otherwise. The only things that she found solace in are getting the home for her family and seeing Pimp when she can. Every time she looks at her daughter, she is reminded of the bullshit that Mike started. He's ridiculous with all of the things that he began to do in the jail. He has several gullible followers to use because of his money and his status within his set.

One day after the roll call, Candace saw her big break to get closer to Pimp a little more privately. His name was on the list to be escorted to the medical unit on her shift and she is assigned as the escorting officer. She got happy thinking about being close to him.   Walking on the section to round up the inmates for the medical unit, Candace went directly to her man's cell. "Heeeeyyy, sweetness!" Pimp jumped off of the top bunk with a big old Kool-Aid smile on his face.

"How're you doing, Daddy. I couldn't wait to get up here to see you today. I miss you sooooo much. I'll be glad when all of this is over and you can come home to where you belong," she pleaded to him. They chatted briefly before Candace handcuffed him with his hands behind his back through the bars of the cell door. She hate doing that to her man. It just don't feel good at all. After securing Pimp and getting his cell door opened, she held him by the arm and led him in the direction that they will be walking to the medical unit. While walking throughout the jail, they both expressed much concern regarding the war of the Bloods and Crips that she believes that she is the cause of.

"Stop being so hard on yourself for the actions of that no good ass Red Mike. He used you for a reason, but that doesn't mean that he wasn't going to start some shit anyway. People like him always do. Their misery never lets you down...

"I got an idea. Do you think that you can get me on lock-up to talk to him?" He asked her. Some people love to feel important, so he thought that maybe he can personally appeal to Red Mike for the sake of peace for his family and all of the problems that came as a result of this jailhouse battle.

"Well, let me see who is working the lock-up section and I can possibly get you over there for about five minutes." Candace replied. She called the section. The officer working lock-up was cool. Candace asked him for the favor of letting Mike on his tier.

When the two of them arrived onto the section, Pimp advised Candace to let the tier officer escort him to Red Mike's cell instead of her. He figured that if Mike see Candace and him together, then Mike will feel like he has something to prove, or jealous at not only seeing Pimp and Candace together, but the fact that Pimp is doing things that he himself can't do; such as get out of his cell and go anywhere in the jail when it is locked down. The officer running the lock-up section obliged Candace's request for him to escort Pimp to Red Mike. He knew a little about what's going on because of the rumors. However, he didn't know which co-worker had the Blood and Crip baby daddies that were beefing. To his surprise it's the young CO Simms that he thought to himself is a cool person. He didn't mind helping her out at all.

Mike had his mirror in his hand that he stuck between the bars so that he can see who is walking on the tier. His face squinted before recognizing exactly who it is that's walking on the tier and then stopped in front of his cell. He couldn't believe the nerves of this nigga, but he remained calm and not show his fear.

"Well, well, well. What do we have here? What do you

164

want, Loc? This better be important," said Mike, pulling his arm inside and tossing the mirror on the bunk.

"Mike, I know that you don't give a fuck about me and probably won't mind blowing my brains out, but I want to be a man and ask you to call your boys off and I'll call mine off. You gotta know that this war is affecting a lot of people and Candace feels like she is the cause of the trouble. She has been upset and it is starting to interfere with the way that she has been with the children. She is a good mother and your daughter needs her to be in a better mind frame. We both are not out there on the streets helping her raise our children, but we are in here making it difficult for where she works. She also has no choice but to take the stress of us beefing home, too. This beef has her worried about which one of us is going to get killed first, yo," Pimp said, humbly.

"Man o' man! You sound like yall crabs had enough. If you can't stand the heat, get the fuck out the kitchen, *Pimp*. Ha, ha, ha, ha, ha!" Red Mike put extra emphasis on Pimp's name for sarcasm. "Yall crabs needed to be cracked open. So, I guess you got enough, huh? You want to tap out for my babymomma, huh?" Mike wanted to come off of lock-up too, but he had to keep his game face on and act like he don't care. Pimp stood in front of Mike's cell trembling with rage, but held his peace and hoped that the fool couldn't detect his rage because he wants to put an end to the mayhem. Red Mike continued to run his mouth.

"I guess that we can come to some type of cease fire or truce. I don't want my daughter to go through no trouble that came from me putting the big hand on some niggas in jail. But, yo, you should have thought about that before yall hit my pups on yall tier. The call is not mine alone, but I guess that I can talk to Moon. He did say that this war is fucking up the business. I just hate when you crabs get out of line and don't understand that warring with us is a no win situation. You did good to come to me and talk this thing out, even though I don't like anything about you. I don't see how my babymomma got hooked up with you in the first place. I thought I taught her better than, but I'm not gonna make this my personal vendetta. You just give me a couple of days and I'll have somebody call you. You do have a phone, don't you? Oh, I almost forgot. Candace brings you shit, so you good." The officer could feel Pimp tremble while holding his arm. He understood why. Red Mike is such an idiot and a natural shit starter. The officer's fifteen years of service in the Baltimore City Detention Center made him recognize Red Mike for exactly who he is.

"Thank you, Mike. I am glad that you can see the benefits in ending this bullshit. Plus, I know that you are getting tired of this cell. We all are," is the only words that Pimp could spoke before leaving this impossible foe.

"Shiiiiiit! We locked-up anyway! This ain't nothin' for a soldier," Red Mike responded. He lied to appear tough like he can handle it, but in truth, staying locked in the cell is driving him mad no matter how much weed he smokes.

"So, it's settled then?" Mike asked to reaffirm the decision.

"I didn't say that. I said that I will call you in a couple of days, damn, yo. Don't put words in my mouth. I think that we can probably end this, but it's not my call, so I'll let you know."

"All right. That's good enough for me." Pimp finished and looked at the officer to let him know that he's finished talking to Mike.

Walking off of the tier in cuffs with the officer leading the way, the officer and Pimp heard Red Mike yell out, "Tell my babymomma to give Michelle my love; ha, ha, ha, ha, ha!" By the time they got to Candace, Pimp had a single tear roll down his angry face. Candace didn't utter a word. She just kissed the track of his tear because she could see that her man was terribly disturbed by her daughter's father.

On the day that the prison population went back to normal, Candace worked utility. That meant that she would be wherever she is needed in the jail. The officer of J section took his break an hour or so before the shift was over. Candace broke her neck to relieve her co-worker that worked the section for the day because that's where Pimp slept. Bee was still assigned to recreation, but soon as Candace took over J-Section, she invited Bee. She didn't have anything to do for the day but hang out with Candace and holler at G-Loc. G-Loc turned Bee on. She became extremely fond of him. She liked kickin' it with her young girlfriend and the two men. The main topic of the discussion was everyone being glad that the fighting is finally over for now.

Bee brought G-Loc and Pimp something to eat from the officer's dining room and Candace let the tier workers, Crips, top Muslims, and guys who are a little more strong and savvy than most run all over the tier and stay on the institutional phones for as long as she ran the section. She let her co-worker know that he didn't have to come back after his break and that she will wait until the 11-7 shift officer comes in to relieve her. Pimp and G-Loc were both glad to get their perks back. They informed Bee and Candace that a couple of female co-workers had become rubies; female Bloods.

"Are you serious?" Bee asked, surprised.

"It's about five of them that I know of," Pimp said, confirming what G-Loc revealed.

"Boo, you might as well jump on our team. You should, too, Bee. Yall already unofficial Blue Diamonds. You might as well make it official." Pimp suggested to his girl.

"Boooooy, are you sick?!" Candace frowned.

"Look, I love you and all, but you can forget that! Hmph! It's bad enough that I brought a blue Caddy. Bitches already think that I'm one because of you. I don't need that shit all up on my job. Why I wanna be a Blue Diamond? I go through enough shit being a *black* woman. I don't need any added pressure as a gangbanger. I don't need that label for me or my children to possibly be put in harm's way. You got the game fucked up," Candace raved. "Besides, I pray that you got your priorities straight when you come home. I ain't gonna

167

keep going through this dumb shit worrying about you all of the time. Crips, Bloods, BGF, UTG, FTC; fuck all that shit. Yall asses should work at being real M-E-N.!" She scolded.

Pimp and G-Loc were both chastised by what Candace said. Pimp could see how the job, the children, the hustle, and the responsibility of being the main issue in a jailhouse war began to change Candace's attitude. She became more mature. He had a lot to think about concerning their future; and although his veins bled blue, he will have to put his life in perspective and become a leader for his family. Candace needs some help and a break. He saw it in her eyes.

Lock-in time came, so Candace rounded everyone up and locked them into the cells. G-Loc and Pimp are cell partners, so they were the last two to lock in. G-Loc was trying to pay Bee for sex, but he didn't have any money. As much as she likes him, she never broke her number one rule--no money, no Funny! However, he did get his feels on. That beats a blank when you're behind the wall.

While Candace and Bee were in front of Pimp and G-Loc's cell, the 11-7 shift officer walked onto the tier to take over. Candace spotted him first.

"Bee, look," she said, backing out of the way for Bee to see the 11-7 shift's relieving officer. It was none other than Officer Paul Powers.

"Girl, fuck him," Bee said, rolling her eyes after they spotted one another.

"Come on. Let's hurry up and leave. This is his section now, girl," said Candace, urging her along. "You know he might run his mouth about us fraternizing with Pimp and G-Loc."

"So?!" She spoke loudly, prancing a step behind Candace and walking towards the front of the tier where Paul stood with his hands on his hips. Once he recognized that she became bothered by his mere presence, rage filled his heart. He fought back the desire to put his hands around Bee's neck and then squeeze the life out of her. This one friend can't do

168

anything but beat and claw at him once he denied her oxygen until her eyeballs bulged out of their sockets. Maybe he can't handle four of them bitches, but two won't be a problem at all.

"Are you gonna just stand there, or are you gonna take these keys... Damn!" Candace stood impatiently holding the keys out to Paul. He snapped out of his trance and lightly snatched the keys. Candace didn't take the bait. She ignored petty Paulie.

"Well, I am just shocked to see you and a co-worker conversing with the inmates at lock time when you're supposed to be waiting for me at *this* desk to relieve you," he stated in a professional manner. "I know that you don't need any help to handle this post. Or do you? If you do, maybe this job ain't for you."

Candace noted Paul's sarcasm and continued signing the books while ignoring him. "Come on, girl," she said to Bee, rolling her eyes at Paul. Paul delved his head into his paperwork, doing his best to disguise the contempt that he felt. Listening to the two women laugh and giggle into the echoing hall made him burn inside. He knows that he is the source of them sounding like two cackling wenches. Now there isn't a doubt in his mind that he will make Belinda Berry beg for mercy one day soon. He smiled thinking of seeing her this morning as she was taking her children to the babysitter and to school. He had her routine down pat. He couldn't stand to see her all up on the men that she met. She must have been with them while they were seeing one another. That discovery sealed her fate more than anything. Even the ass whipping that she and her friends put to him was not as worse.

Paul got up from his desk to take count. Reaching Pimp and G-Loc, he stopped and stood there to take a quick inventory of everything that he could see as possible contraband. He was being an asshole CO.

"Aaaaaaaay, give me those two extra sheets!" he said, like a true police.

"Awwww, come on Powers! Why do you gotta' be

sweatin' those sheets like that?!" G- Loc said, agitated. "You don't even live here! Go home with that shit! Some fucking sheets?!" He continued to complain. Pimp wanted his man to calm down and let Powers take the sheets and leave.

"Is that an open razor? I think you need to flush that in the toilet," Paul said, spotting something else that they aren't supposed to have.

"Come on with the bullshit, Powers! Ain't nobody fuckin' wit' 'choo! I need 'dat razor for cutting shit out 'da magazines for my photo album. Why would I keep a weapon in the open like that?" Pimp asked, straining his voice.

"Look, yall got a choice; either you give me those sheets and flush the razor down the toilet, or I'll just call a shakedown crew and see what else yall got in there that yall ain't 'spose to have," Paul threatened. G-Loc handed Paul the sheets, reluctantly, while Pimp flushed the razorblade. They didn't want to take a chance on him sending a shakedown crew in the cell. Their phones were hidden in the cell next to them and they had an almost undetectable stash spot in their own cell that held the weed and tobacco. They couldn't let it be it found unless the officers really earned their money by finding it.

"Thank you, gentlemen," Paul said, throwing the sheets towards the front of the tier and out of the reach of the inmates in the cells. He then continued on with his count.

Paul let quite a bit of time pass before deciding to get Pimp and G-Loc's cell searched. While Pimp slept, G-Loc was curled up under the covers with a female on the phone. The shakedown officers crept onto the tier. No one noticed. Suddenly, G-Loc and Pimp's cell door opened.

"All right, I need the two of you to get up out your bunks and step onto the tier!" The shakedown officer ordered them. Pimp jumped up fussing. G-Loc got caught off guard. He didn't know what to do, so he slid the phone in between his ass cheeks, and then appeared from under the covers. He looked at Pimp to forewarn his comrade that he was dirty.

They both stepped out of the cell. One of the officers began to search the cell while the other one instructed Pimp to undress on the tier down to his boxers. Then he instructed him to drop, squat, and cough. Pimp did as instructed in a swift motion, then pulled his boxers up and stood. Next, G-Loc's turn. He wanted to run, so he did! Having nowhere to go, he threw the phone in someone else's cell. The officer, caught by surprise at G-loc's burst of action heard G-Loc yell into a cell for whoever to flush it! He couldn't afford to let the administration get some of the numbers that were programmed into his phone.

"Hurry up and flush it!" G-Loc hollered again. He and the C.O. began scuffling. The distress code was called and the officers punished G-Loc for fighting back. He still had his clothes on and they never got the phone. He can stand going on lock up. What he could not afford was for them to get the phone with important criminal contacts and a couple of numbers that belonged to female officers. He hated that asshole Powers for what he'd done. He made a promise that if he ever see Powers on the street he's going to deal with him. Pimp, now mad that his man is gone off of the tier had to think fast. He would have jumped in the fight, but he knew that he had to stay in population for his homies. It's not a big deal for what G-Loc went on the hammer for, so he held his cool. They also had weed, tobacco, and knives around and no one else can run shit like them.

Paul left the tier that morning feeling very good. He was able to take Bee's jailbird gangbanging boyfriend down. He even had the chance to punch and kick him while he and the other officers had him cuffed. He should have never tried to run and then attack one of the officers. Don't the dummies understand that Paul is with the toughest gang in the jail? They are "THE POLICE!"

Paul entered his car on Eager Street. He drove up to Greenmount Avenue and stopped at the light. A potato chip truck stopped at the light on Eager Street facing him and going in the opposite direction. Paul didn't notice the driver of the truck at first, but then the driver's face and build became familiar. The light changed and the truck drove into the intersection to make a left turn. Paul drove past him and made a u-turn to follow the truck driving southbound onto Greenmount Avenue and then turning right onto Madison Street. Paul wrote down the license tag number while the truck waited for the big red gate that led to the back of the city jail to open. The potato chip truck driver was Bee's delivery man that Paul saw her with on Edison Highway. Paul must definitely check this out.

Chapter 9

A very anxious Lacy Landon remained in her seat after the roll call still thinking about Jay. Lately she has let her mind take control and wander off with him in her thoughts a lot.

The day before Jay's court date his attorney came to let him know that his proceedings will end with his case being placed on the courts stet docket due to the lack of concrete evidence. The case stet is to last for one year. This means the case could be re-opened within a year if more evidence is discovered or if Jay commits a compatible crime that will suggest the likelihood that he committed the first crime. So, Jay is to be let free. Landon hurried herself to the inmate traffic control center on the way to her post so that she could look at the court dispositions of the men scheduled for hearings. This is Jay's court date and the anticipation was killing her. After being involved with him and risking so much, it will be such a relief to have this man home for her exclusively and without restrictions. She didn't see his name on the return sheet. That can mean that he is still downtown waiting on his hearing, or that he is finished and waiting for the inmates to be transported back to the jail. She started to call one of her girlfriends in transportation to see what is going on, but she decided against it. She feared that it will probably raise suspicion. It's only 3 o'clock anyway, which is still early for the late court returns. The last returns won't come back until five or six p.m. She's wound up, but once she realized that she would see him before he is released, she made a sigh of relief and didn't waste any time heading to her section for the count.

As usual, while taking count, the inmates on the tier began making request and complaints. A lot of inmate services and requests were backed up due to the jail being on lock-down. Now that the lock-down is over everybody on the tier bombarded Landon with questions and asking for passes. They needed to run around and make moves. She ignored every last one of them. The only inmate to get her attention in this moment is Uncle Twin.

"What's up, Twin? Do you think he's going to be all right?" She asked, lowering her clipboard and stopping directly in front of his cell. Twin rose from a sleeping nod and took a long look at her before he spoke. In front of him stood such a classy lady. He can see that she is setting herself up for failure. He admired Landon, but he also know that this is a lesson that she has to learn. Jay won't ever choose her over Tiffany. Landon has a lot more going on and is a much more mature woman of substance. Tiffany is straight hood, but she worships the ground that Jay walks on. She loves him way too much to allow him to live on this earth with another woman. She put in too much work for him and their children. Jay knows that Tiff will kill him dead, or at least try. Leaving her is not an option.

"He's gonna be good. His lawyer ain't no joke, and if that's what he said to Jay yesterday, then that's what he meant. I know he was smiling this morning and couldn't sleep just waiting to go to court. He was in a good mood, unlike the dudes who aren't sure what's going to happen in their cases. Besides, he ain't come back yet, so you'll be the first to know before his family, I guess," he said, assuring Landon.

"I hope you're right. We are supposed to see Beyonce at the First Mariner Arena tomorrow night. I can't wait! I want to show him a really good time. I bought a new Gucci ensemble to go with my Blahnik Monolos and I have another outfit that I bought for his after party from Victoria's Secret," she revealed to Twin, smiling with a starry-eyed look on her face.

"What color is the Gucci shit?" Twin asked.

"Oh, it's a cream color and I can't wait to see what he'll buy to match with me when we go shopping. I guess that you know that I won't be here tomorrow. I hope he'll like the CLK. He can drive it, if he wants to," she said. "Let me finish up my count... Do you want me to hit your door when I finish?" She asked Twin.

"I sure do. The way things have been going, my business should be wrapped up in a minute," hinting to Landon that he is just about finish with all of the weed and tobacco. The dope was gone a long time ago. Half of it was gone, anyway. The other half was personal for Uncle Twin. He never ran dry. This run everybody's money looked good.

Landon finished her count and let the President of the I.A.C and the leader of the BGF out of his cell to attend to his institutional ways of the day, after the count was cleared. When the count cleared, Jay popped up on the tier pumped up and smiling so bright, like the happiest man in the world. Landon and Twin also began to smile knowingly. Jay had that look they'd both seen many times over the years. Twin experienced that same elation several times in his life, but this was the very first time that the look of being released from one of the inmates meant anything to her. She wanted to cry and jump into his arms. It took all the power of her being to restrain her and stay seated at the officer's desk.

"I'm uptown, YEEEEAAAAHHH!!!!" Jay yelled on the tier. "You hear that, boo? A nigga made out just like I told you! My lawyer deserved every bit of that seventy five hundred! Unc, it's on and poppin', ya' heard!" Jay went straight through the grill and headed towards his cell. "Hit my door, CO!" He ordered Landon. The order went with a lack of attention towards her. She hit his cell door and then sat back at the desk. She and Twin could hear Jay and all of his comrades yelling back and forth to one another. Most of the men yelling were asking Jay to leave them something. They asked for clothes, tennis shoes, weed, tobacco, his phone, money, pictures and his information so that they could get in touch with him while he was uptown to ask for more. Jay obliged them all.

"You know, sweetie, Jay is a good dude. He's still young, but has good strong qualities about himself. You gotta ask yourself, is your patience ready to be tested with his whims?" Twin said this, then walked abruptly back onto the tier to give his goodbye salutations to his young protégé. Landon could understand where Twin was coming from. She had fleeting doubts a time or two about giving herself to Jay. He was just so strong and handsome. On top of that, he kept niggas in check. Getting involved with him earlier on made her feel as though she was on a plane with a parachute strapped to her, waiting to jump. However, she was resisting and afraid but something was behind her pushing and pushing until she finally had to let go. She was freefalling, and it felt dangerously good. When would she pull the chord on the parachute? Or did she know how to?

Uncle Twin waited for Jay by his cell. He knew that his young comrade was excited and saying his goodbyes to his BGF brothers. He'd been in the jail for almost a year. Twin understood the feeling that Jay was having; hoping that he himself would be celebrating just the same in the coming month. Jay noticed Twin standing in front of his cell, so he cut all other conversations and walked towards his mentor to pay homage for taking him up under his wing. Twin definitely helped him sharpen up with being a leader of "the pack wolves."

"Hamjambo," Jay said to Twin, pulling him close into a manly embrace, greeting him in the Swahili vernacular that they used.

"CeJambo," Twin responded likewise.

"Unc, man, I can't thank you enough for tightening my boot straps. I got mad love for you, and if you need anything, don't hesitate to get in touch with me. I promise that Tiff and I won't get married until we know what's going to happen with you next month," Jay said. "I want you to be a part of it."

"Man, I would love to see you and your Bonita tie the knot. What you gonna do about her?" Twin asked Jay, pointing to Landon, who was sitting at the desk.

"Unc, she cool people, but you know ain't no future with that! My sons' mother would smash the both of us.

Especially at seeing how fly the bitch is. We could stay cool, if she plays her position. If not, I just view her as a pastime. You know, help me past the time away," he said.

"Well, I just hope that you never told her you loved her, or given her the impression that ya'll was gonna be together, because if you did and you fuck over her, God bless you. I warned you that she was a little off. You listened to me about a lot of things, but I believe that this one was the most important, and you didn't pay me no mind. The dick rules, and the dick wins most of the time, but the man often loses in the long run...Is you going with her to see Beyonce?" Twin asked.

"We 'spose to go...Why?" Jay was curious to know what Twin wanted to say about that.

"She prepared the whole day for you...Peace, comrade," Twin answered and finished the conversation. That's when the jail telephone to control rang. They all knew that it was probably the court release call for Jayson Hill. Landon called him to confirm the call. He'd already given everything away and made his farewells. Now it was time to face Landon.

Jay walked up to the desk while she was writing his pass that would allow him to travel through the jail. "So, you know what time I get off...What time are you gonna' call me tonight?" Landon asked him. She passed him the pass along with five twenty dollar bills so that he would have some cash to get where he needed to go and do a few things, but Jay had $800 already from hustling.

"I guess I'll call you around 'leven thirty or so," he said.

"You want me to come get you from wherever you are?" She asked.

"I don't know. I'll let you know when I call you," he said, with a hint of agitation. He noticed that he sounded a little harsh and capped it up by kissing her on the cheek. Then he said, "Don't you know that I love you," just as Uncle Twin was coming up to the desk to ask him about the Soledad book. Twin heard it but, he pretended not to and asked Jay about the book.

"Oh, I almost forgot about that. Can you get that book to the guy Maximillion for me?"

"I sure will... Come on. I'll walk you downstairs," Twin said. They walked off the tier and down the hall. Jay looked back and saw Landon looking at him with her back resting at the doorway, and her arms folded. She didn't say anything or wave as she watched him until he was out of sight.

Twin and Jay walked to traffic. They both laughed and joked with the officers. The officers made fun of Twin losing his walking buddy and right hand man. After the laughter and jokes, Twin warned his young friend that he is really playing with fire. Jay said that his mentor is underestimating his pimp game, and that he will stay in touch with him to let him know what the business is going to be once they are both free. Then Jay was officially released.

Twin walked away after the officer came to escort Jay to J.I. building where he will be processed out of the door. He was on his way to take Max Muhammad his book. All of the jailhouse politics started to weigh on his shoulders. Manipulating the drugs, weed, cigarettes and phones for money, or whatever pacified the natives and gave them something else to focus on besides violence is *his* doing. Being a mediator or peacemaker between prison battles and wars is also another hard job. These are the torn spirits of giants who are powerfully at war with one another. They are fueled by hate, fear, ignorance, and anger that *he* has to lead and guide. "Wheeeewww! Hard job, hard job," he said to himself, strolling along through the jail.

Instructing Jamma, or his BGF family is a tedious process, too. Making money continued to motivate him but, overall, it's past his time to move on. The very limited person to person per square foot is getting to him, along with the smells, sounds and lighting of the jail. He didn't have to worry about the food. It's the worst! He never ate it. Officers bought food for him every day. He usually has three or four dishes per shift. They share home cooked, fast food, sub-shop and restaurant meals with him. He's homesick. It's time for him to go so, none of it matters anymore. He figured to go ahead and deal with his charge and not postpone his next court date. He will either be free or in prison doing time.

First, Uncle Twin went to Q-section before making his rounds to collect money to return Max's book. Twin reflected on a time when he was a lot more disciplined and lived his life by the words of comrade George Jackson. The revolution ran through his veins and the things that were being revealed to him concerning black people and their suffering, paralleled with the struggles of all oppressed and indigenous people on the earth were monumental. It was knowledge that empowered him and those that learned as he did to fight for the cause of BGF: JAMMA. It was all about fighting for change. Then the smack flooded the community and there began the death of the movements; slowly, but absolutely. Drugs, money, and materialism soon followed. That goddamn Vietnam War!

As the years progressed the knowledge was used to manipulate the young aggressive brothers in prison that were the enforcement for extortion. Today things are out of hand to the point that greed, ignorance, and violence Rules!

Twin walked to the dormitory where Max slept and saw Officer Hope standing at the grill talking to Max. He walked up on them making comments about the inmates that were hypnotized watching The Maury Pauvich Show.

"Peace, Brother Max. Here is your book. My young comrade wanted me to make sure you got it back. You know that a man's word is his bond. He wanted to keep his word to you. He wanted to keep his word to you. He says to tell you thanks and that he's grateful to have had the chance to learn from reading it," Twin said. He continued, "He went home today."

"Thank you, brother. You think he got something out

179

of it?" Max asked referring to the book.

"I'm sure that he did. He studied it all of the time. He wanted to be up on comrade George," Twin responded.

"Yeah, we need to develop some of those brothers' minds to bring to birth some modern day George Jacksons. This is the best time because nobody expects much coming from us now more than ever. Today the masters can go to sleep without fear that anything will ever touch him and his world." Max said.

"I suppose you're right. The struggle is *ever* on," Twin said before turning his attention to Hope. "How are you doin', Officer Hope? I know you glad the lock down is over."

"Well, actually, I'm glad that the fighting is over. The lock-down wasn't too bad for me because I didn't have to be worried with everybody's bullshit. Now, shit is back to normal and the niggas is getting on my nerves, *again*." she said, putting emphasis on again.

"Well, Officer Hope, this is Steel-side. It's not just a job, it's a fucking adventure," he said, laughing. "Well, I guess I'll be going," Twin said, before strolling away.

Max and Hope said their goodbyes to Twin as he walked off. They both continued to watch the men and women on the show make a spectacle out of their lewd, degrading and promiscuous sexual practices. One woman with four men on the show that took paternity tests to determine which one of them is actually the father sat in her chair listening to the cheers and jeers as the men were introduced.

"She's a mess! She had the baby only to set the child up for failure. Some women are just so dumb. They will let men sell fantasies to them just for an orgasm. Some of them just want to fuck, too. No protection or nothing. This is so damn trifling," Hope commented to Max, while watching the show.

"Uh-Huh," Max responded, continuing to give most of his attention to the television.

"Here comes Maury with the results," she said,

expecting to see one of the men become a father on television to a child that he doesn't love by a woman that he loves even less whom they both produced out of a moment of insecurity, insincerity, passion, immaturity and strictly stupidity. Sex, the American way.

"When it comes to 6 month old Dominique, Brian, you are not the father!" Maury announced. The guy named Brian jumped up out of his seat like he won a car on a game show and began to dance. He then stretched his arm with a finger in the young woman's face and made an open declaration.

"You's a ho! I told you (bleep), I told you I wasn't the father of that (bleep, bleep) baby! You a (bleep)!" Brian yelled and then directed his tirade to the camera and the studio audience that joined in on the indictment of the young female's indiscretions as though she was a side show. And she was! Maury had to calm Brian down and get him to take his seat so that he could get on with the business of finding out who fathered the child.

"Mark, when it comes to baby Dominique, you are not the father!" The same scene just about repeated itself with Mark and then another guy named Roy.

"He's at the last one now, Max. She ain't move a muscle. I bet if she could shrink, she would be about an' inch tall in that chair. This last guy must be the father," said Hope, silently praying for the young woman.

"Yo, 'dat bitch ain't shit!" yelled an inmate watching television. They loved Maury. They huddled up to the television like clockwork every morning, noon, and as many times the syndicated show aired.

"She freaked out, fuckin' all 'dem dudes at 'da same time!" Another one hollered.

"Bitches be some scandalous hos!" Commented another one. "I bet you he ain't the father, neither."

When the last envelope was opened and read, the results were also negative. This meant that the little infant child was fatherless and her mother remains alone in raising

181

her. The young woman could think of nothing to say or do, so she ran away backstage until there was nowhere else to run, then collapsed. She balled up like a fetus on the floor. Her face, covered by her hands, she cried in shame. Maury followed along running behind her with the cameras following him to comfort the woman, but not to let her escape the public humiliation, with a promise to test any more men, without cost, that she had sex with and are willing to come to the show. It was such a dramatic and disgraceful scene.

"She's a dumb bitch!" One of the inmates yelled. He was joined by others who were expressing the very same sentiments.

"That's a damn shame," said Hope.

"Can you let me out to clean? I've seen enough of that," Max said, shaking his head. Hope opened the grill and let Max out into the hall. They both walked towards her desk. She sat at the desk and looked at her friend. She could clearly see that he was bothered by the television show. She didn't believe that it was that serious.

"Come on Max, that's just how shit is. Nobody cares about what's right or wrong anymore. They just do what they do," she said.

"You're right, and that's just sad. You'd think that all that's happening negatively, along with more access to information in the world, people should not want to still wallow in ignorance," said Max. "People love not knowing how to be better because knowledge demands responsibility to do something and people, especially poor black people, have become immune to the tragedies. They are even expectant of them. On top of being lazy, we are willing participants of the tragedies we deal with and are around us because it takes much thought, work, and responsibility to use the knowledge that will rid us of the daily tragic shit that we endure," he said venting. "We are happy not knowing and that in itself is a tragedy."

"Huh? What does that have to do with that dumb ass

girl laying with those men and not knowing which one is the father?" Hope asked.

"For one, it's tragic that Maury will disrespect and debase the women, and even more tragic that the women and men that come onto the show to parade their ignorance never realizes the depths or the consequences of displaying their ignorance for entertainment concerning a child. A child is the most precious being to us all because we don't know what invention, discovery, answers, healing, or saving will come from such a child," Max continued on. "There are different races of women on Maury, but there are mostly black women that come on his show with the most ignorant of men. On top of that, our women are now showcasing themselves in videos, on television and at strip clubs as whores with their clothes off and praised for having the fattest ass. Years ago most of our women looked at such behavior with a frown and in disgust. It was filthy and nasty and most of them shielded a lot of it from the children. They were protected from the perversions of wonton sex because, with sex comes the most awesome of responsibilities. Today our women act as though they invented the filth and do their best to be looked at as the nastiest of the nasty. The children are now mimicking that same behavior with the women cheering them on in song and dance. The behavior distracts them from not only the important aspects of life that will make them good human beings, but by being captivated by a sexual lifestyle, they fail to see the world at large."

"Max, you always say that men are the leaders and from what I see, most women do the things that they do because that's what men want from them. When they give them what they want, most men shit all over them," Hope complained. "Then we are left to lead children with the hurt of abuse and abandonment."

"In a lot of cases, you are right. The majority of women want a *gooood* man, but they aren't good women. A lot of our women don't even want to qualify themselves for a good man. They chase what they know ain't right and it's all a distraction. The television and the cell phone and the medium of entertainment play a role in our mating lives as well. We used to be forced to take roles in Hollywood that portrayed us as crooks, thugs, pimps, junkies, whores, killers and drug dealers. This is what was and still is offered to us as actors. Now, we beg to be seen as this; not just in videos, movies and music, but in real life. We can put down this behavior as a way to change our circumstances." Max expressed himself with a lot of emotion. Hope felt the connection to the things that he said because he made it so plain. She began to feel admiration. She wanted to see more of his mind on such a serious subject, so she began the questions.

"Well, Max, what can we do about these things and who do we blame the most- niggas aint shit, most of the time -the man, or the woman?"

"Woman, we are so far gone that blaming anyone or anything don't mean a damn thing. It's only a distraction and a big waste of time to play the blame game. Keep in mind that the roles of black men and women throughout the history of this country have been criss-crossed. It's been going on since the slave trade and the effects of that deadly trade is reflected by the madness of today in black people and America at large. We must re-awaken the original attitude of the men and women who were the builders of the best and highest civilizations known. We must demonstrate a builder's attitude within the fabric of our daily lives and in everything else that we do. Anything short of this will continue to perpetrate the confusion and degeneracy so prevalent in our communities. It's in the perverted sexual orientations of freakism and group sex, along with promiscuity that also must be changed because, it endangers and helps to destroy the black family structure. Collectively seeking to find solutions to our problem, black men and women must STOP seeing each other as the enemy; which we so often do. We must band together to win victory over the enemy of ignorance, along with any other enemy that stands in the way of a true unity that will and can change the condition of how we simply relate to one another. We must *establish victory* over enemies who view every good thing we do for ourselves as a threat to others' existence because they will seek to define, control, and co-op every aspect of our lives, and in particular, black male and female relationships," Max explained his position.

Hope fell in love with Max's mind. His answer to her question was waaaaay over the top, but also worthy to believe in. She feels ready to do her part like a dutiful solider. Without thinking, before she spoke, she blurted, "What are the requirements that a woman has to have to be your woman, Max?" The question sounded more personal than it should have been. Once it was asked, she pushed aside any apprehension that she might have had for asking the question and wanted badly to hear his answer. Max grinned and laughed at his thoughts before speaking. He began to respond.

"First and foremost, she has to allow me to protect her because, I will give my life to protect my woman. By giving my life, I don't mean in death, but I do mean that every day that I breathe will be dedicated to the protection of her. Not just from physical harm, but more importantly, protection from a world full of negative forces that work constantly to destroy our peace. She cannot stay in a frame of mind that she doesn't need a man for shit because, that will sew a seed to dictate that she can be in any way independent of me. It's also not just required of her, but is *she* also qualified in being the opposite but equally good woman that she wants in that good man. The root meaning in relationship is to relate. To relate means to have a connection that we identify with equally. As the man, Ms. Hope, I represent the head. Not as a ruler, but as the maintainer of peace. Peace is the absence of confusion and the presence of harmony in relationships. This harmony is love, peace, and happiness. That will be our exact formula to success because, without love, you can't have peace, and without peace, there can be no happiness. I understand that love is more action than feeling because feelings alone are never enough to stay committed to a person. Success in relationships is achieved through the process of selflessness, which is to place your partner's wants, desires, and needs before your own. True love is reciprocal; meaning it exists on both sides. So in producing my woman's happiness, I will have also produced my own. Her nature will lean towards fulfilling my wants, needs, and desires," explained Max. Hope became very attentive to him with her elbow on the desk and her head leaning to the side. Max saw that she took in every word and decided to make the conversation more personal.

"Now listen at this... Let's suppose that you and I became down for one another. I would strive in understanding those parts of you that are misunderstood. Oh, it would take work to deconstruct the wall that you've built around yourself due to past hurts and experiences that are akin to being a black woman but, anything worth having is worth working for. The achievement of possessing the invaluable beauty that is you will be the greatest investment or sacrifice that I can ever make. I will do absolutely whatever is necessary for you to love me so that you can love me in the way that I need you to. I would always put you before my selfishness to prove myself worthy of you through dedication of comforting, protecting, and honoring you with a constant display of affection that shows that your worth is more than I can afford. All of this I would be willing to do and be, not merely just for your sex, but for the reward of being yours and you being mine. That reward alone is enough. That's the kind of devotion that's needed to raise the best of children because, that reward is the actual experience of heaven on earth." He finished.

"Come on, Max, you have to lock-in," said Hope, nervously moving things around on the desk and fidgeting. She stood quickly and walked swiftly to the front of his dorm and unlocked it. She stood a little off and held the grill open for him to go in.

"What's wrong, Miss Hope?" Max asked, surprised at the sudden change in Hopes demeanor while walking to the dorm.

"Oh, nothing. I just have to use the bathroom," she said. Max walked into the dorm. Hope tried to shut the grill before Max could see the tears that began to well up in her eyes. It was too late. She tried to turn her face away but, Max spotted her crying. He remained silent as she ran away from in front of the dorm after locking it.

Hope called for an officer to relieve her from the post. She had to get her nerves together. She realized that not only did she love this man's mind but, she was falling in love with everything about the man. The way he looked and the way he sounded. She couldn't wait to come to work and see him, and even when she wasn't at work, she would daydream and smile about something he may have said or one of his many facial expressions. What he'd just explained to her touched her so deeply that she wanted badly for him to be the one. But, he might possibly go to prison for the rest of his life. Even if he did, she wanted to always be his friend and promise herself to this man completely. If he didn't come home, she would remain a lesbian. She wanted desperately to feel every part of him in every way.

After half an hour of getting herself together and making a few moves, Hope returned to her section. She didn't say anything to Max at all. She did see him studying and decided to leave him alone. When it came time for sanitation she let him out and avoided any attempt at a conversation. Max could feel the tension and didn't force a conversation, either. After finishing his work, he stood in front of his dorm. Hope called for him to come to her. He walked up to the desk.

"Open your hand, she whispered and looked around to make sure that no one is being nosey. The coast was clear, she said, "I'ma put something in your hand and you hurry up and put it away, ok?" Max agreed, and then Hope pushed a small cell phone in his hand and said, "I'm going to call you tonight. Now go ahead and lock-in." Max put the phone in his dip, and walked away from Hope smiling from ear to ear.

Later that night, after getting off of the job, Hope declined an offer from Gibson to join her and Simms for a quick drink at the Icon. Landon rushed off to a hot date. Gibson, Bee, Simms and Hope discussed how Landon began acting ever since she started messing around with Jay. She never talked about it. However and as it so often happens, rumors began circulating throughout the jail. No one approached her concerning the situation but, they all worried. They knew that Jay had been released earlier in the evening and figured that their girl was on his heels.

After getting into her car, Landon called Jay's cell phone and became furious when one of the inmates at the jail answered it. The inmate continuously called back trying to get a conversation out of her. *'Now I gotta' change this number,'* she thought. The last thing she needs is an inmate in the jail to be calling her all the time. Isn't that what she did with Jay? She didn't view Jay like the rest of them. Images of him sexing her took over her mind and she caught a quick hot flash.

It was almost 12 am when Landon got to her home on Lothian Road. She entered the door and that's when her phone rang. It's a different number from the one that's been continuously calling her all night and damn near burning her battery out.

"Yeah," she said, with an attitude.

"What up, Boo?" Jay's voice came back.

"Where are you? Do you want me to come get you?" She asked him, excited.

"Well, I'm cool, I'm cool. I'm with some important people and I gotta' get a few things straight on the money tip, feel me?" He answered. He tried to push her off.

"Who're you with, your sons' mother?! Nigga don't lie to me!" She screamed into the phone. "You gonna' fuck around and see a side of me that ain't for no bullshit! Don't play me Jay!"

"Who the fuck is you talking to like that?! Didn't I just tell you that I'm taking care of some shit?!" Jay responded defensively.

"You're fucking with the right one now, Jay! You said that we was gonna hook up tonight. Now, I understand that you might got shit to do, but you rather play Monopoly than to play Lacy Landon, nigga! Fuck it! Just be a man about your shit and tell me that you were on some bullshit the whole time! I'm a big girl! I can handle it! But, please-I'm only going to say this to you once-do not fuckin' play with my feelings and emotions! Now, do whatchoo' do!" Lacy Landon let her frustrations with Jay turn into anger.

"All right, All right!" He hollered into the phone. He began to think about what Uncle Twin told him. "I'mo' get up witchoo' later, boo. Calm down and give me your address. I'll call you when I'm in front of the door, ok?"

"You don't have to wait on anybody. If you need me to, I'll come pick you up," Landon offered more calm.

"That's okay. I'm good. Plus, I know that you're probably tired from working all day and I know that I'm going to be awhile," he said, doing his best to sound sincere. He knew that Tiffany wasn't having him be any place other than with her, as long as she's been waiting and for all that she's been through while he's been gone. Jay didn't care how mad this crazy bitch Landon is going to be tonight. He just wants to calm her down and decided to himself that he'll get up with her in the morning. Once she see him free, she'll want to fuck his brains out and all else will be forgiven. Landon gave him the address and Jay promised that he'll be there before the night is over. She admitted to him that she is tired and then she apologized for her attitude. Jay also apologized and told her to keep the phone close so that she can hear it once he's outside of her door. They both said I love you and hung up. Landon ended the conversation with a smile and Jay with a sigh. What is he going to do?

Landon got herself a drink, first. Second, she lit a candle and listened to some music, while taking a nice hot steaming bath. Finally, after all of these years, she found a man that she can be with. He even reminds her of her son's father. That's another issue. Jay is only six years older than her son. She is glad that he lives with his grandmother most of the time. She don't want to feel like she's disrespecting him by having a man as young as Jay. Maybe her son will like him, too. Maybe she's planning things prematurely. She has to be careful because, although she wants him, she don't want to hurt anyone if he plays with her heart.

Meanwhile on Lakewood, Hope dressed for bed, and like a giddy adolescent in high school, she couldn't wait to get to her cell phone. She wants to talk to Max while relaxing in the comforts of her own home and comfortably in her bed. The phone rang just as she went to grab it to call Max. She looked at the screen and saw the name "Puddin-pop". She became annoyed at being interrupted in her plan to talk to Max. She don't want to keep him waiting up half of the night. She also hadn't heard from Puddin' much, but they still talk from time to time. The concern for each other's wellbeing and on account of Lamar is important to them both. Hope didn't worry about Puddin's safety as much anymore and longing for her to be with her.

"What?" She answered, sounding bothered.

"Well, excuuuuse me, queen. And just how are you doing tonight?" She asked with a slur. Hope can tell that she's been drinking, as usual.

"I'm good. What up witchoo'?" Hope responded.

"I'm ok… I was just thinking about you real heavy so, I decided to call you to tell you that I miss you and I want to spend some time with you," Puddin' purred.

"I miss you, too… Where are you?" Hope asked. Not because she have any intentions of going to get her but, hoping also that she isn't still hanging in the projects. She misses her, too, but just not as much as she did a few weeks ago.

""I'm with Yolanda and Rashon down Douglass," she answered.

"Oh, I figured that much," Hope said. A part of her wanted to end the conversation. Puddin' loves the projects.

"Well, watchoo' ask for then?" Puddin' responded, getting smart. But that's her.

"Just forget it. Stop taking life for granted and do something more than hang out and stay in them projects doing the same thing every day. It's not that you are there but more about what you are doing in you every day practices while you are there, damn," Hope said, not caring how Puddin' takes it this time.

"Please, don't start it. I just want you to come and get me," Puddin' said.

"Come get you for what?" Hope questioned.

"I told you that I miss you and I want to be with you. Didn't you say you miss me too?" Puddin' asked her lover.

"Yeah, but where are you when I really need you? Besides, I'm in bed and I don't feel like getting up," Hope replied. Now her agitation became felt.

"Well, I'll just get a hack to bring me up there. Can you pay a hack to bring me to the house?" Puddin' asked. On any other occasion Hope would have made sure that she and Puddin' got together. Especially when it comes to making up. But right now, she's not turned on by Puddin'.

"Why don't you just call me tomorrow before I go to work? Maybe we can hook up and have lunch or something," she said.

"Glo, who the fuck you got up in there with you?! If another bitch is up there just say so, but if you lie to me, I'mo' come up there and bust your damn windows out!" Puddin' threatened.

"Look, I don't have time for this shit! Ain't nobody in here with me, but if I want to fuck somebody it ain't none of your business! I don't say shit about you being with them trifling bitches in the projects. Now, I told you that I am tired and I'm not coming down the steps to open no door and if you want to see me, call me in the morning!" Hope declared.

"Well, excuse me then... Glo?" She began again.

"What!"

"I need a few dollars for some shoes and to get my hair done. Can you pleeeaaassse help me?" Puddin' asked her. Puddin' did miss Hope, but she also missed the things that came with her being Hope's girl the most. Hope loves her still but, she's not in love with her anymore and this conversation makes her understand why.

"Puddin', I'm really tired. Just call me tomorrow and I'll see what I can do, ok." She offered. She just wanted to get off of the phone.

"All right, boo... Glo, I love you," Puddin' said to her. She really meant it, too.

"I love you, too," Hope responded. Then she hung up.

Hope laid on her bed with her phone in her hand down at her side. She began to reflect on Puddin' and their relationship. The desire to be with Puddin' is diminishing.

"Oh!" she screamed. Forgetting about calling Max. She dialed his number with much enthusiasm.

The phone finally vibrated at the jail as Max waited on his bunk for the call. It was after 1 a.m. and long past his bed time. He answered the phone and there began one of many, many, late night conversations.

Morning came and Landon found herself awakened by the sounds of *"Dangerously in Love"* by Beyonce coming from her phone. It's the same number that Jay called her from quite a few hours ago. "What do you want, liar?" She asked, groggy. She peered at the clock on the dresser and it was going on 9 a.m.

"Ain't da' address 5410?" He asked her.

"What the fuck do you think? Stop playing dumb?"

She wasn't in a mood for game. With hurt feelings, all she wants to do is scratch out his eyeballs out.

"Well, if it is and you have a pretty ass CLK directly in front of your house then, I'm standing on your front," Jay said as a matter of fact.

"I should just leave yo' ass outside for lying. Don't come bringing me no seconds after freaking off with your children's mother. Damn chicken. I ain't no dumb bitch, Jay, and if I come to that door, I might just bring my gun with me," she said, getting out of bed and putting on her silk Victoria's Secret mini robe with the matching panties and bra. She held the phone to her ear.

"Come on, woman! Just open the door!" He said, like a man in charge.

"Give me a minute," she said, hanging up the phone and going into the closet. She reached in and pulled out a double action Smith and Wesson .40 caliber automatic. She released the clip and saw that the magazine was fully loaded. Then she put the gun back into the closet before going down the stairs and opening the door. There he stood smiling in her face as though nothing is wrong. She unlocked the storm door and then she turned to jump on her sofa, snuggling up to one of the velvet pillows to escape the slight draft that came into the house from the opened door. Jay entered the house and then shut the door behind him. He stopped to gaze at such an immaculate home. Looking at Landon in this beautiful setting made him think about pictures in a magazine. She looks so fine with her pretty legs folded inward and hugging her pillow. All of her tables are glass and the room is carpeted with chocolate brown to match the huge velvet sofa, loveseat and armchair. All of the furniture stood accented with a tiger chaise lounge chair, chandelier, and an étagère filled with pictures. There's also a 50 inch television on the wall, an entertainment unit on the other wall that held a stereo, a numerous amount of old school CD's, and various glass knick-knacks. The windows are draped to match the room.

This is the first time that Jay had a chance to see her out of uniform. *'She is beautiful!'*

"Is that your car in the front of the house?" He asked.

"Yes it is... What happened to you last night?" She asked Jay. He walked to Landon and sat down next to her then put his cold hands on her legs. He watched her uncovered parts get chill bumps and began to take his jacket off so that he can nuzzle up with her. She smells so good to him and all he can think of is how regal that this woman is. She is definitely a dime-piece in a lot of ways. Then he gave her a cock-and-bull story about business and getting drunk with his best friend who gave him a thousand dollars to go shopping with. He promised and he swore to her that he wasn't with anyone. Landon didn't believe him and made her mind up to excuse him this one time. She's going to sex him so good that he won't want anyone else.

"Do you have any condoms?" She asked?

"Yeah," he answered. She got up and grabbed his hand and led him to her bedroom. He couldn't believe how Landon lived. She unrobed revealing opened crotch panties, laying on her back on the queen size bed, she moaned, moving coyly and seductively under his body. He entered her. Holding him tight and wrapping her legs around his back so that he could be all the way inside of her, she rolled him over and mounted him and rocked back and forth, fast and then slow, like riding a horse in the rodeo. Then she placed her hands on his chest and sat up on him in a squat position. She dug her fingernails into his chest and moved up and down very slow, looking at the dick go in as far as it could go. Then she looked at it until her pussy held just the very tip of him. The both of them came. After catching their breaths, she didn't hesitate to give him head until his toes curled and then put it on him once again.

After sex, they showered together. Landon left the shower first and dried off. Walking around the house wearing nothing but a towel, she fixed him breakfast in the afternoon. Jay loved the neatly furnished house. Everything appeared exquisite. She took good care of herself. He never expected Landon to have so much going on without a man.

They finished eating and drove to Anne Arundel County so that they could shop for Jay. He picked clothes to match what she planned to wear at the upcoming concert date. They pair walked into a jewelry store where she proceeded to spend over $3000 on a watch for him to wear. He also picked out a leather blazer to match his shoes. The two of them had a lot of fun talking and hanging out. She let Jay drive the entire time that they were together. They even talked about doing something for his sons together. He sold her all the usual dreams. She had to keep stopping him several times from calling her Miss Landon and get him in the habit of calling her by her name. Besides that, their day went pleasant.

Jay let Landon know that he had some business to take care of and promised her that they will eat dinner at the steak house, in the Pier 5 Hotel, at the Inner Harbor before going to the show. Jay called one of his friends and Landon drove Jay to meet the guy on Baltimore Street and Broadway in Fells Point. They both agreed that 5:30 would be the time that Jay will call her so that she can pick him up and they can spend time together before the show starts at 8:00. They exchanged long kisses after he loaded the bags into his friend's car and they held one another as though they never wanted to part.

That same day, Elliot enjoyed the beautiful weather while driving the work van from the job that he got by the connections Doreatha made for him. Doreatha Gibson is the best person that he could have met at this point in his life. Her looks aeren't the best only because she started showing signs of aging, but she isn't too bad for him. She also has a little bit too much gut. Elliot loved thick women and she definitely fit the bill for that. She can afford to lose a couple of pounds around the mid-section. Overall, everything went perfect. In the past three months or so, life became sweet for Elliot. The job started him off with $7.50 an hour, but after 30 days he receives a two dollar raise. His responsibilities are to transport the employees to Baltimore County by 7 a.m., check up on them at 12 during the lunch hour and then pick them all up at 3 p.m. or later. A lot of times they didn't finish at three and worked overtime. Elliot then uses the van for whatever he wants to as long as he is on time to transport the workers. Occasionally he's needed to run an errand or so for the company. Elliot began doing well for himself and only chose the weekend to sniff dope. He drinks a little heavier on those nights so that Gibson doesn't get suspicious. He's giving her the dope dick when that happens so she never questions it.

Elliot continued to deal with bighead Charlie. Charlie let Elliot run the shops completely, now that he isn't out in the streets chasing drugs. He could tell that Elliot still sniffed dope once in a while, but it didn't interfere with Elliot running the shop. He let Elliot re-organize the entire shop and paid him $2000 a week to do it. Gibson bought him a Buick Park Avenue just as soon after he started working. He meets Charlie at 5:30 in the morning and then take the dope to the stash house on Crystal Street. He opens the shop and make sure that it is up and running by six. Then he drives to work. After dropping off his first set of co-workers, he goes back around the way to oversee his other co-workers. He's now in uniform and when all of the dope is sold, Elliot collects the money and goes to meet Charlie to re-up with more smack for the house. Bighead Charlie is hardly ever seen in the neighborhood.

Elliot is falling in love with Doreatha Gibson. They spend a lot of time together when they can. It's mostly at night when she's off. She cut back on going to the Icon, but she still gives her girls at least two nights a week. Elliot's mother loves his new girl and seeing him work and do well gives her a better spirit about him. Elliot and his woman took her and Aunt Shirley to the Olive Garden for dinner. He even will give Aunt Shirley a twenty dollar bill from time to time; though she always try to give it back and tell him that she don't need it.

Elliot saved his money now and things happened for him. He's getting money more than he envisioned and he has almost $25,000 saved up on the low. He and his brother are getting along a lot better, too.

This is the day that Elliot is going to cop a new ride. He'd been shopping around and a dealer told him that he'll take his '96 Buick as a $2000 trade in and $2000 cash for any car within on the lot. Elliot stood out on the block thinking about which car he's going to get when Baldhead Pam come to tell him that they need more dope. Elliot smiled. This is also payday! Things are turning out real good for West Nile, which is the name of their product on the block. He put the call into Charlie and instructed him to meet him at spot A. It's almost 3o'clock, so Elliot chose the gas station on York Road and Northern Parkway on his way to pick up the work crew. That's point A for him and Bighead. He went to Pam's house, counted the money and saw that Pam only had about 30 caps of dope left. This will be sold before he gets back. That will be the last run of the day for him.

Driving up York Road, Elliot saw a Lincoln Navigator. It looked like the 2008 Navigator on the car lot. He could see himself pushing the shit out of the Navi!! He thought about the SC430 Lexus that he knows is perfect for him. It's much smaller than the Navi, but he can open up the luxurious sports car on 695. A few months ago he sat over Steel-side with plans of doing his thing. Now things began to happen. He know that Charlie needs him. More than anything, he thanks God that he blessed him with a woman like Gibson. She don't know that he is getting paid because he takes his money to his mother's house to stash. Soon he will take a nice piece of his money and buy her a big ass diamond ring. Maybe in another month or so. She really deserves it.

Pulling into the service station, Elliot spotted Bighead Charlie sitting in his truck in a parking space reserved for people who only want to use the convenient store inside of the gas station. Elliot drove to a pump. He looks like he's getting gas. Elliot observed the surroundings before moving quickly towards Bighead Charlie's Denali. He got to the truck, opened the door and climbed into the passenger seat.

"What up, Elmo?" Charlie greeted him.

"Here, yo. I kept my two and this is your two. I'mo' make sure everybody else gets paid out of the pack that you getting ready to give me," Elliot said, handing Charlie the money.

"Are you getting that whip today, yo?" Charlie asked him. Then he hit the hood of the truck where he puts the stash.

"Yeah, I'mo' get something' slick, too," Elliot said to him.

"Come on, yo." Charlie said, getting out of the truck. Suddenly, unmarked cars appeared from everywhere! By the time that it dawned on Charlie and Elliot what the hell is going on, it was just too late. Charlie remained stuck standing on the ground between the door and the inside of the vehicle and Elliot never had a chance to open his door because the Navigator that he passed earlier had him pinned into Charlie's truck with a white guy and a black one pointing guns at him with police badges around small chains on their necks like medallions. They counted about five unmarked cars in all before the regular police came to the scene with two guys yelling for them to put their hands where they can be seen. All guns pointed at the pair. Then the sirens!   At the forefront of the gang of OCD officers stood Crazyhorse and Runningman.

After being cuffed and laying with face on the ground, Crazyhorse began to gloat. "I told both of you whores that I am going to get you. You guys think that you were so slick. We've been watching Elliot for two weeks. Oh yeah guys, Pam's house belongs to us, too." Crazyhorse said laughing. Then one of the OCD officers handed Crazyhorse a brown paper bag. He reached in it and pulled a freezer sized zip-lock bag out of it filled with 500 capsules of heroin. "We got both of you bitches dirty, ah, ha, ha, ha!!!"

Landon stood before her full body length mirror styling and profiling. Her Blahnik Monolo shoes are a perfect match to go along with the Gucci suit. She checked herself over several times while waiting for Jay to call her. She did her best to ignore the fact that its 6:30 and when she finally decided to give him a call to see what's taking him so long, the answering machine picked up the call without a dial tone as though his phone was turned off. She didn't get upset!

'Maybe Jay's phone needs to be recharged. Surely he wouldn't pass up a chance to see Beyonce with Ne-yo opening up the show,' she thought to herself, putting on her diamond earrings. "Come on Jay!" She said out loud, walking down her stairs and becoming antsy. "Please don't fuck my night up." Now she got angry.

Lacy Landon lay on the same spot of her sofa with her legs tucked inward in the very same position that she sat in earlier that morning. The only difference this time is that she is beautifully dressed. Her shoes were kicked off and she didn't snuggle into the pillow, either. She propped her head up so as not to mess her hair up. That took her beautician hours to make perfect. Listening to a Destiny's Child CD, she waited on Jay to call. The song *"Survivor"* came on, which is exactly what she needed to hear. That's why she loved the young girl Bey. She remembered that this is also Simms's day off from work. She looked at her Cartier and its 7:10, so she decided to call her and invite her to go to the show. At first Simms protested not having anything to wear, but Landon convinced her to find something nice to put on. She told her that she didn't care if she put on a jean set and sneakers. She needed a friend to tag along with her because she got stood up and didn't want to waste the ticket. Now convinced, Candace screamed into the phone excited to be seeing Bey perform live in concert.

"Hurry, and get down here!" She yelled, agreeing to go. Landon put on her shoes.

Landon drove her car into the projects and parked

behind Simms's car. She stepped out of her Benz looking like The Queen of The World with a bag in her hand that held a half pint of Remy Martin. She spoke to two young ladies sitting on Simms steps. The girls smoked weed, so Landon called Simms to let her know that she's outside waiting instead of coming upstairs. She then offered the girls some of her drink, which they did accept. One of the girls ran into the house to get two plastic cups. They both introduced themselves as Shania and Kierra. Landon opened up her Gucci handbag and pulled out a half of a blunt and then lit it. They commented on Landon's car and how good she looked tonight, also, that she definitely don't look like she smokes weed. For whatever that means. Plus, it's Kush haze! She took some puffs and then passed it on.

"I'm ready, girl," Candace said, dressed in a one piece Chanel jumpsuit, Jimmy Choo's with big Chanel shades. She looked gorgeous, but not as good as Landon. "Girl, I had to put this together real fast. When in doubt, one piece it out."

"Shit, I thought you were going to put on sneakers and jeans. You're fine, girl. Isn't she?" Landon asked Shania and Kierra, teasing her girlfriend.

"Mm, hmm," one of them said. Landon felt the hate. Then she didn't help but to notice that they sucked her weed all the way down before Kierra passed her the roach.

"That's ok. You go ahead and kill it," she said, regretting that she didn't go into Simms house to smoke.

"Oh, we goin' in the Benz? Let's do this shit," Candace said, ready to go and singing, *"To the left, to the left."*

They talked about Shania and Kierra most of the way to the show. They both had another blunt so they stopped to get another half of pint because Shania and Kierra sucked all the drink up, too.

"Girl, I should be closing the deal on my house in a month or so and I'll be glad to get the fuck away from them two freeloading and hatin' ass wenches. I can't stand they project asses." The subject of who stood Landon up surfaced. Candace did wonder if or not it might be the BGF guy in the jail named Jay. Everybody knows that he made it uptown.

The women were jammed to the music in their front row seats. Ne-Yo is smaller than they imagined him to be from seeing him in the videos and on television. He did all of his radio classics and went into a Michael Jackson tribute. You can tell that he is more than an artist, but an entertainer that will become an Icon for the time. Then the moment that everyone waited for came. Beyonce made a grand entrance with her all girl band and did more than enough to live up to being the headliner of the show. After Ne-Yo's performance, she had to show that she is worthy of top billing. Make no mistake about it, she is. She opened the show with *"Crazy in Love"* and took it from there. All of the women in the arena, it seems, were at a girl power revival with their "I can be strong without a man," songs and "loving a bad boy," songs. The arena went crazy with *"Irreplaceable."* Landon really enjoyed herself and also glad that she chose to get a friend and still come to the show. Although she craved Jay and is furious at herself for getting caught up with an inmate knowing that they can't be trusted, her choice to come to the show turned out to be good therapy.

Beyonce sang *"If I was a boy"* and the song left the women in the arena in tears. Candace took a glance at her girlfriend and she knew that the words of the song meant something more to her. She ended the show with *"Single Ladies"* and everybody's tears washed away with Beyonce impressions and declarations. In all, the show proved to be a spectacular event and the two women shared praises of the performance while leaving.

Candace and Landon walked into the picture line when Candace spotted Jay walking with a short and pretty young woman a little older than she but younger than Landon. "Look Landon! Ain't that the guy Jay who went home yesterday over there with that girl?" Candace asked, directing her attention with a nudge and a nod. Landon's blood started to boil, but she kept the explosion inside. However, she moved abruptly out of the picture line and walked up to the pair with Candace trailing.

"Hello Jay, I see that you made it home," Landon said with a pleasant voice, holding her hand out. Jay definitely got caught off guard. He grew paranoid every moment that he and Tiffany were at the show. His greatest fear became a reality. Candace also spoke to Jay. She would see him in the gymnasium with Uncle Twin all of the time. She took notice that Jay is dressed nice and his watch and bracelet are exquisite and classy with the way he dressed. Then she looked at her girl and thought to herself about just how much that her girl and Jay looks like the perfect couple with what they both wore. *'Oh my God! He did stand her up!'* Candance began to think.

"Oh, how are you Ms. Landon and Ms. Simms? Baby, they work over Steel-side," Jay said in a nervous rush. He prayed that Landon don't blow the spot.

"Damn, Jay, it looks like you shoulda' took her to the show. Y'all matching. Y'all should take a picture together," Tiffany suggested. Go ahead, I don't mind. She wore a Pink set. The pair looked odd. "I told you that you on some GQ shit tonight, Jay. The two of you look like yall should have been here together Jay. You still coming home with me. Go ahead. Take a picture."

"Oh, I can't take any pictures with him. If someone see it, I can lose my job. You do look good, Jay. I could have picked those clothes out myself," Landon said, still being nice. "Your jewelry shows that you have good taste."

"Well, it's good seeing y'all ladies. Take care," Jay said, pulling Tiffany on. Candace looked at Landon and witnessed it all on her face.

"She's not bad looking, but she ain't got shit on you girl. His *own* woman wanted him to take a picture with you, bitch," Candace said. She's telling the truth, too.

"That's Miss Bitch, girl. Don't forget the *Miss*," Landon said. She was glad that she held her rage inside. She wanted to Jet Li or Matrix the fuck out of both of them in her Gucci shit. They are lucky she had on modeling shit for a modeling bitch.

Landon came clean to Simms about having a relationship with Jay. She was hurting by what he'd done, but the both of them enjoyed the concert and the night went well. That made the situation bearable. Candace loved how Landon kept her cool. Landon still can't believe that she held her peace. "Girl, I coulda' ran to my car, laid on his car and shoot the fuck out of them both," she said. She meant it, too.

While Driving Candace home, Landon's cell phone rang. It's Gibson on the other end crying. She wants her girl to meet her at the Icon. She just got off work and is on her way there. The bar is the destination for the queens.

Landon and Candace walked into the bar and people began to stare with gawking eyes. The two women wore fashions finest walking to their seats at the bar. Bee also sat at the bar listening to Gibson.

"What's the problem, girlfriend?" Landon asked before Mr. Junior came to take their orders for drinks. Everybody greeted one another.

"Girl, I'm at work thinking that everything is sweet when my homegirl calls me cursing and fussing about the police taking a work van that belongs to her cleaning service! Apparently, Elliot has been arrested for drugs and he was at work with the van when it happened so they confiscated the van and the city has it on drug hold. I swear to God that's what I get for messing with street niggas! That's all they know and that's all they wanna know! My goodness, you would think that after being locked up so much for the same shit it will register that the game ain't for him! Maybe others, but not for him! Plus, my Boo's doing so well," she explained while sobbing. "He is different, too. He's really trying to be a man for me and I thought that he appreciated what is growing between us, but I just can't take it. I'm through with them jailhouse ass niggas," Gibson continued to cry. It's hard for them to see her like this. She is the strongest of them all. Everyone believed that Elliot had the possibility because her program changed along with her being happier. Now she is crushed!

"Give me a double, please," Landon said.

"We goin' through it together girl. Check this shit out..." Lacy Landon finally came clean about the relationship between her and Jay. She let them know everything! First, the part about having sex in his cell, all the way up to taking him shopping to buy the jewelry after standing her up the first time. Simms took over the rest of the story and talked about how good they looked if they were together at the show. The moment elicited an uncomfortable silence. She apologized and they all went back to talking about the no good bastards. That's when Landon's phone rang.

"What the fuck do you want, boy?! Don't call my phone anymore!" She said ending the call and not giving him a chance to talk. He called back.

"Talk, Jay!" She started. Everyone looked at Landon while she listened to him. Then she put her phone down and hit her drink. She put it back to her ear and Jay continued to talk. "Whatchoo' say? Ah, huh... Let me think about it... Oh, ok... I'mo call you when I'm on my way." She ended the call and rose from her seat.

"Girl, leave his ass alone. Take it from me, he ain't shit!" Gibson said.

"I know, girl. Trust me. I got this," Landon said, a little tipsy. She walked out of the bar and then to her car hitting the trunk to open. She grabbed a gym bag and shut the trunk. She opened the passenger door and got a 16 shot Glock .9 millimeter out of the glove compartment. She went back into the bar and walked directly to the women's restroom, where she changed into her dark navy blue hooded sweats that she work out in. They are supplied by the job. It had a gold insignia of the badge for the detention center. The yellow insignia was so small that you couldn't see it at night. "I need you to take me somewhere, Doreatha," Landon said. Then she dialed Jay's number. "You said the basketball court, am I right?" She looked at her friend and continued listening to Jay on the other end of her phone. "Are you coming or not?" She asked the lieutenant ending the call again. Gibson drowned her drink and then she followed her girl out of the bar.   Bee and Simms followed suit as the four of them ducked into the dark green B.M.W.

The women drove to the O'Donnell Heights housing projects to meet with Jay. He asked Landon meet him on Toone Street near the swimming pool and the basketball court. "There's the pool; turn here," Lacy Landon gave Gibson directions from the back seat of the car. They spied a small crowd of guys on the court from the firelight of the cigarettes and lit blunts. Landon put her window down and then called Jay to the car. He trotted towards the Beamer eagerly. He knew that it had to be Landon; although the car looked a little creepy because the windows are tinted and he can't see the inside of it, but he recognized her voice. She opened the car door but didn't step out. She waited until he moved closer, then she sprung from the car!

"Don't move or get loud. If you do, I'ma kill your bitch ass," she whispered menacingly. Her girls sat mesmerized and silent inside of the car. Jay began to plead! She didn't hear a word of his begging.

"Get on your knees, bitch," she said to him. He fell to his knees and tried to put his hands in the air. "Put your hands down before I bust your motherfuckin' ass." The guys on the basketball court couldn't see her holding the gun on Jay. It's just too dark, the car is a distance from where they are on the court and most of the street lights are shot out. All they can see is Landon's dark figure and their man on his knees. They took it for granted that he's just begging for the pussy and trying to get back in good with the fly CO bitch that he'd been bragging about to them. They laughed at Jay and continued to smoke the weed.

"Damn, Boo! I'm sorry! It ain't that serious!" He yelled, trying to get the attention of his boys. He can't tell if this bitch is serious or not.

"Shut the fuck up before I hit your head! Yell just one more time like that again and you're dead! Now turn around on your knees, WHORRRE!!!" She hissed like a B-more bandit, dragging the r. Jay began to think about the warnings from Uncle Twin. This is a mad bitch and he just didn't see it. His life is in her hands at the moment and he's shook. He followed exactly as she instructed. His boys stopped laughing when Jay turned with his back to the figure on his knees with his head bowed. It looks like he's about to be executed. Before it registered what's really happening. BOOM! BOOM! Came with two quick fire flashes! One of Jay's homeboys pulled his gun out to shoot back but, he hesitated because he didn't want to make a mistake and hit Jay. Jay jumped up from kneeling and ran into the line of his sight. Once Jay moved, his man let off some shots at the figure running to get into the car. She stopped short of the door, turned, planted her feet, took aim and then licked off about ten more shots at Jay's homeboys before jumping into the B.M.W. Gibson drove fast away once she heard the back door of the car shut. Then she took a quick glance to make sure that her girl sat safely in the car.

They returned to the Icon safe and sound. Landon went to the restroom to put her concert clothes on. She collected almost $400 from her girls and then handed the money and the gym bag that held the sweat suit and the gun to Mr. Junior to dispose of. She ordered another double shot thinking about the two bullets that she put into each one of Jay's ass cheeks while her girls laughed and joked, calling Landon about a thousand crazy bitches. Finally, she pulled that parachute cord and eased into her landing.

Chapter 10

This is the day of reckoning for Twin. The final countdown! His lawyer let him know on his last attorney visit that the state wants ten years out of him. Twin can't imagine doing ten years at 47 years old. Not with a ten year old daughter. He already believes that he wasted a lot of time not being a father to his oldest son and daughter. His son is doing 15 years for attempted murder but his daughter works for Johns Hopkins. She's 23 and raising her young son alone and Twin knows that their lives would be better had he not been so selfish with his choices. His little girl means a lot to him and he's been around most of her life. To do a ten year bid will kill the growth and development of the relationship that they share. Sure, he'd been away before, but never for too long. This time he realize that he just got to give his entire life of the streets up for his child. He knows deep down in his heart that he's going to do some time so he prayed to the God in his life that it won't be ten years. The façade of Uncle Twin aside, Irving Randle must face the reality that prison is going to be his future for a few more years.

Uncle Twin let Ochie know on the night before that he's going to be the official commander of the family. Ochie went to court and his case got postponed for another 4 months. He has the most seniority in the jail and by having such, it makes him the highest in rank. Twin let him know how to see Officer Landon if he don't come back with another postponement. Twin knows that will be unlikely. Ochie will also take over as the acting President of the I.A.C. until a vote is cast. He's automatically going to win the election. They got to make it look good. Ochie will also be moving in Twin's old cell. Twin believes that Ochie is a good man for the job. The only drawback that he has concerning his homeboy is his propensity for violence. Ochie like putting in work even though he don't have to. Ochie can be diplomatic but only after flaunting power. This won't ingratiate Ochie to the Chief of Security at all. So, instead of introducing the two men, Twin just let the chief know who to contact when shit gets too crazy and he can't get a grip in the jail. Twin is sure that Landon will like Ochie because he is a natural leader and can follow instructions as well as enforce. He also money minded. Twin laughed when he thought to himself of how Ochie asked him to see if C.O. Berry can give him the pussy for a thousand. Well, now Ochie will probably be able to put his own bid in with a few COs. Even some that he didn't know will take money for sex. Depending on how good of a commander can be, he will have a variety of choices and chances to get sex in the jail. Twin emphasized confidentiality. That and the money will get him anything but out of the door. If he wants that bad enough, one might never know.

Waiting in the bullpen to go to court, Twin spotted the young guy, Pimp. A lot of the young comrades were vying for Twin's attention, making jokes, offering him weed and cigarettes. All while crammed into the bullpen at receiving area waiting to get shackled and chained to be transported. Twin directed most of his attention to Pimp. He really liked the young man's style and could tell that he was responsible. He thought that he and G-Loc were both two up and coming gangsters that would one day run shit. They were capable to do it on the streets as well as in the joint. It didn't matter if they were together or apart. The both of them had Twin's utmost respect.

"What up, Pimp? I see you're goin' to court today, too, huh?" Twin greeted him with a solid hand shake and his usual gold toothed smile.

"Yeah, I gotta face this shit today. My lawyer says I might have to take a year. I got almost five months in so, I'll only be down a couple more months at the most. I'll probably have a lot of probation, too," he explained.

"That ain't too bad. I'm facing 40 because of my record. Ain't never killed or hurt anyone. Drug charges. This will be my sixth major incarceration, but they're talking about giving me ten. I hope I can talk 'em down some more. If I can't, so be it, but ten better than blowin' trial and getting 40," Twin informed Pimp. If I was younger, I'd take it to trial!

"Damn, Unc! I feel you. My girl told me to take the deal so that I can get home and help her with the children. She makes a lotta sense, Unc. I don't want to live like this. I don't mean no harm, Unc, but ain't choo' tired of this shit at your age?" Pimp asked.

"HEELLL YEEAAH!" Twin answered.

"How the hell do you do it, Unc?" Pimp wanted to know.

"The exact same way you gonna do it if you don't help that little sweet honey you got with them babies. I see why she had you and that other kid goin' crazy in the jail. She is a diamond! Plus, my people tell me she got it going on," Twin said pointing to his head to indicate that Candace is smart. "My interactions with her shows me that she is good peoples, but she young, Pimp, and if you not around to keep her focused on a solid life, you will lose her to many, many, other influences or distractions. She could get a positive nigga and build a life with the family you could have, or she could get involved with other influences that could use her and introduce her to all things wrong. She could be fuckin' niggas in this jail, or kissing bitches and being a flunky for whoever leads her. Where will you be, in prison?" Twin could tell that Pimp listened closely.

"Nawww, Unc, my Boo don't get down like that," Pimp said.

"How old is she?" Twin asked.

"Twenty," Pimp answered.

"She's not like that yet, but the power to be like anything I mentioned has potential. Who knows, she may not fuck one of these inmates, but a lot of these CO dudes be on these women wheels, too. If *you* can get the pussy in the jail, just think of how good another nigga's game can be. She might have just a little attraction to him if you *ain't* around to be her everything when she needs you to be. You're in prison doing a ten year bid. Get the point?" He explained.

"Yeah, Unc, I see," Pimp said, realizing the truth of what Uncle Twin revealed to him.

"Pimp, I have a lot of regrets and even though I saved up a nice piece of change to help my wife in case I get some time, my biggest regret is that as much as I've been around for my daughter, I'm about to deprive her of what she needs most in her life that will ensure she'll feel secure beyond measure. I'm about to deprive her of her father. If only I could think beyond Wild Wild West Baltimore City and not live to represent streets that ain't even mine, I could have been a father to my older children. I left them insecure and less confident. Now I'm about to do the same thing to my little one. Pimp, you are a serious young dude and if you continue on the road to being a gangbanger, then you'll reach the stars in no time. I mean, Shorty, you a G already. But, believe me when I tell you, all of the time that you will waste being Big Pimp, or Big Homey, in the streets and in prison, you'll miss out on being a Big Man. The life that you will live won't amount to shit. It's not so much that you have to be a goody two shoes or a Positive Pete ass nigga, but if you live for your children and that fine woman that you have, your life will be a lot better than living for the streets that you don't own, niggers who only use you for strength and doing shit that don't even matter in the real world. Last, but not least; the drugs and guns don't amount to shit. In the beginning of it and in my day, it meant a lot to get money and come up. That life slowly died off. Today, and for y'all, it is a sure and absolute quick death on all ends. Especially the spiritual one. Some of us got past the game. Almost none of y'all are making it out of the game. You'll go down in the joint or down in the dirt. What the fuck is that shit about, Shorty? And don't blame that shit on me and my generation. It's not *all* our fault, either…

"Pimp, don't live your life just to collect regrets, feel me," Twin said to Pimp. They shook hands again and then

Twin reached into his sock to pull out a joint for Pimp to light. The both of them smoked it without sharing. Twin didn't even pass it to his comrades. He saw a lot in Pimp and now Pimp looked at Uncle Twin in a completely different light. He never imaged that the OG would kick it to him like that. It really made him think. He thought about nothing but Candace, Lil Pimp and Michelle the entire morning. He and Twin started their morning off like that and they stayed together from the bullpen to the van. They were both assigned to the same courthouse, too.

G-Loc knew that his man was going to court today and that there is a strong possibility that he won't be coming back into the jail. Pimp passed on a cell phone, two ounces of weed and five cans of tobacco. G-Loc got himself another phone, but he couldn't wait to own the one that Pimp had. That phone had a video camera, internet capability, and people could send him pictures from their camera to his. Pimp made sure that his phone's photos were filled with X-rated pictures of a lot of females that they both knew. He's scheduled to be let off of lock-up today. He's been behind the door for forty days. He was glad that Pimp didn't get involved in the altercation. He still made sure that Candice loaded G-Loc's cut of their weed money onto G's Green-dot accounts as well as send Loc weed to smoke while he did his lock-up bid. Pimp is supposed to take a year in court today, so he wasn't going to get a chance to holler at his man before he left the jail to move on to the Diagnostics Center, where you are processed from detention into a prison sentence and serving time. G and Pimp built a strong bond together. They planned to get with one another on the streets. They thought a lot alike.

G-Loc figured that he could make about $800 off of one of the ounces and then smoke half of the other one. The money that he makes off of the last half will buy him a new clothing package. He wants to be fresh by next week and he is going to make sure that he send his baby sister enough money to hook him up a nice package. He wants Bee to see him still handling his business no matter where he was at in the jail. Bee kept it real with him and he likes her style. That's why he don't have a problem giving her whatever she wants for some pussy. Not many dudes can do it like that in the jail. Loc counted himself among the best of survivors.

"Gregory Ronald Butler Junior, are you packed up and ready to get off of lock up?" The female CO that had been working the tier for the week startled him from his thoughts. He didn't really care for her too much because, he knows that she is ruby. She wore red dreadlocks.

"I' be ready in a few minutes. Am I coming off of lock-up this morning or in the afternoon?" He asked.

"Not right now but, you'll be coming off before lunchtime," she informed him.

"Good," he said, jumping up to get his things together. Lunch time on lock-up is at 10 am. It's about 9 right now. He'd grown tired of being up in that cell anyway. He wanted to be out at the first moment's notice.

After the CO informed G-Loc about coming off of the hammer, she walked to the end of the tier to the very last cell where Red Mike slept. G figured that she was going to do that because she always did it when she came onto the tier. He could hear her laughing and giggling back there and it really irked him. He didn't hate but, he knows that Mike stays up for no good. They eyed one another on the tier when the other one would be out for his hour walk. Only one inmate would be on the tier at a time but, they used that time to stretch their legs and walk around. G-Loc wanted to do something to his ass. He peeped the whore in his eyes but, they gave their word to Uncle Twin and the Iman that they will keep the peace. It won't be to anyone's benefit to beef with the BGF and the Muslims together if the truce line got crossed. The truce had been called right before G-Loc came over to the lock-up; so why is Red Mike still on lock-up? That's very unusual. Maybe he'd done some shit to keep his ass locked down. Some scared guys will do that to look tough and not face the prison population. Anyway, G-Loc's time is up and he can't wait to see Bee Berry.

"Did you get that money from my mother?" Red Mike asked the red dread CO. She gave him about 50 e-pills and an ounce of Sour Diesel weed. She was scared to bring the Diesel in at first because the aroma was just too strong. However, she wrapped it up good and her White Diamonds Perfume made the scent non-detectable.

"Yeah, your mother looked out for me real good. She even fixed dinner and wouldn't let me leave until I had a plate. I'm glad that I stayed," the young female CO explained herself to Red Mike.

"Are you sure the team gonna' be in the gym when that crab comes through?" Mike asked her.

"Of course, I'm sure. He has to go through the gym to get to his section anyway. They'll already be on point. The sections will be inside of the gym at 9:45 am until 11:00. He should be coming off at around 10:00," she said to Mike. She'd been asked these questions what seemed to be a thousand times. Mike wanted to make sure that everything is on and poppin'!

"Go ahead and get low. I'm gonna holler at Moon to make sure that this crab gets caught. ...You coming down here after count to hit me off? You ain't gave me no head in about a week now," Mike said to her.

"Boy, you worryin' too much about the wrong things. I got choo today before I get off. I promised Mom dukes that I would take care of her baby," the CO said in a sultry voice.

"I should see you later then," Mike said, pulling out his phone to call Blood Moon.

"Speak, young blood," Moon said, answering his phone.

"Man, the crab swimming your way today. Are you gonna catch him for me? I already got the stack in place for the pups," Mike said to Moon.

"The timing is perfect because I hear that Uncle Twin

ain't even around and it's a good chance that he ain't comin' back in the jail. Ochie takin' over. He's dangerous but he can't think like Twin. He's a killer and not a leader, so, I got him. Before long, I'll have him on our side. It's time for us to take this motherfucker completely over for when our family members have to take a fall. They will be good when they hit Steel-side. That's what it's all about. I should be leaving here soon but, I want to leave the family on top," Moon expressed to Mike.

"That's how it's supposed to bang, anyway, ya heard?" Mike agreed.

"Don't worry about the crab. I should be in the gym myself to make sure that a couple of the pups hunt him down," Moon informed him. "Oh, and the other situation concerning the cheesefish sub with extra ketchup got ordered last night."

"You talkin' 'bout my situation?" Mike wanted Moon to verify that the witness in Mikes's case got killed the night before at a subshop in West Baltimore. This bit of information made Mike even happier. "My enemies are now at my footstool... ha, ha, ha, ha!" He laughed.

Mike was so excited to see his plans come to fruition that he started throwing up all sorts of signs in his cell and dancing around. He directed his glee to no one in particular. That nigga G-Loc will soon catch the wrath for getting in his business between him and his baby mother at the medical unit. The truce put everybody to sleep and G-Loc being on the tier with him made Mike a little too uncomfortable. This plan is just perfect. All good plans take some time.

G-Loc packed his belongings and sat on the bunk. He waited on the cell door to open so that he can go back into population and onto J-section where Pimp left his stash. Tying his lock-blade knife to a shoulder strap of the wife-beater that he wore under a t-shirt, he buttoned up the shirt that he wore because in population, anything goes. He stays ready for whatever.

The C.O. popped G-Loc's door just before the food

cart came to the section. Red Mike waited to hear G's cell door open and for the tier officer to call out his name, which is the signal to call Moon to ensure that everyone is in place. G-Loc grabbed his bag and slung it over his shoulder. The CO gave him his pass to travel to J-Section. There is a shortcut from the side of the jail where G-Loc is, onto the other side that went through the gym. When the officer opened the grill for G-Loc to make the shortcut, he could see guys alongside of the wall talking on the inmate telephones. He inattentively heard the irregular bounce of the basketball, along with the screeching of the rubber soled sneakers coming from the players on the basketball court. It felt good to be off of the hammer. He looked to see some familiar faces of allies. He didn't see anyone. One face stood out to him above everyone. The face changed his attitude immediately. The nigga Blood Moon! Their face fighting began instantly. G-Loc felt someone pat him on his back three hard times. He looked to see who hit him on his back but, then he quickly recognized it for what it is. An attack! He instinctively moved, dropping his bag and reaching for his knife. That's when the battle began. G-Loc battled for his life!!!

Doreatha Gibson felt let down by Elliot. How could he be so stupid as to allow himself to get caught up in the streets in such a short period of time, yet again? He's been becoming a fixture in her life compared to other guys that she decided to have a relationship with. He appeared to be really getting his shit together. He spent time with her on her days off and he was very thoughtful with her, his mother, and his Aunt. Maybe she should have let him know that he didn't need to be doing anything to get extra money. She should have let him know that she had enough money for the both of them. He must have known that anyway. He embarrassed her so bad to her friends that gave him the job. She laid in her bed thinking about how much she misses him. She changed the locks so that he can't get into the house and she didn't accept his calls. She even put his clothes in bags so that he won't have to come to her house. She left them on his mother's porch and just drove away. She called his mother to let her know that his things were there. Doreatha also let Elliot's mother know that if she need anything that she should call her. She just had to cut all ties with him after what he's done but, She and Elliot's mother developed a special bond. Better to cut him off now than to get caught up in his street shit later. Why didn't he want to grow up and leave the streets alone?

It's been over three weeks since she's heard anything from Elliot. She began to rub his the side of the bed where he once slept.

Elliot and Bighead Charlie made bail on the day after their arrests. Pam was lucky to have sold all of the dope before the raid began. The police arrested her and two of the workers in her house for a bag of weed and a .38 Smith and Wesson. The worse part of it all is that Crazyhorse ransacked her place and trashed a lot of her things *after* not finding anything. Her children were terrified. This is the Baltimore City police. She felt more protected and served by Bighead Charlie.

Elliot was crushed that Doreatha changed her locks and wouldn't take his calls. He knew that she was a tough black woman, but damn! She wouldn't give him a second to repent. Elliot has also been depressed. His sense of self-worth that's been building up into becoming a man that he's always envisioned himself to be with a woman. He's always wanted a car and a nice place to lay his head. Now all of his wishes has been shattered. Maybe he is meant to be a fuck-up and never amount to much. The depression that he feels, along with the stress of catching a new case and also violating his probation is killing him inside. Lately, all he does is stay dazed by the demons of worry and uncertainty. It has been weeks since he tried to contact Doreatha.

He decided to try just one more time to recapture what they were building; and even if he can't do that, he wants to at least give a sincere apology for being such a disappointment.

He stopped at the Eastpoint Mall on his way to her home and he picked up a diamond friendship ring. An engagement ring just isn't proper now.

Elliot drove into the townhouse complex and spotted Doreatha's B.M.W. He sat in his car for a moment, before getting out. He had to face the fact that she could possibly have company. His heart beat moved fast and then he became instantly filled with jealousy. Springing out of the car and marching to her door, he knocked on the door a little forceful. Seconds passed before she popped her head out of the upstairs window to see Elliot looking back up at her. They were both delighted at the sight of one another but, pride stood in Doreatha's way and Elliot didn't want to make light of the situation. Both of them checked their emotions and remained expressionless.

"What do you want?" She asked, mean spirited.

"What, do you have company or something?" Elliot asked, but he was really thinking out loud. He didn't mean to ask her that but, it was too late to take it back.

"Who the fuck..." She started to respond but changed her thoughts and cut it short while pulling her head back in to shut the window.

"Droeatha, wait!" He yelled, stopping her. "Please let me talk to you just this one last time? Can you give me that much?" She left the window for a brief moment and then returned to the window to toss him her keys. She didn't feel like walking to the door. She put on her housecoat and jumped back into the bed, pulling the covers up over her and tucking the sides in tight. This will thwart any attempt of him trying to touch her. Elliot came up the stairs into the room and then he sat at the bottom of the bed. He began to give it his best shot.

"When you met me I had no intentions of changing. Truth be told, I thought you was just some kinky broad who just wanted to get your rocks off. You gave me some head in the medical unit! Wow! I was whipped after that and would

217

have done anything you wanted me to do. I would have stabbed somebody if I thought that you were messing with them, too. You changed my whole outlook on you when you started doing things for me and we began to talk on the phone. I really liked the fact that I was getting to know you. Then you hollered at my mother and she liked you, too. That's when it happened... I thought about changing for the better but, I still had plans for the streets, too. That's how I roll. Boo, you chose me and the life that I lived with you was almost like a dream come true. It was amazing! I had a job, a woman and I was getting things going on and doing well in the streets. I was getting my respect back and people were seeing me come up after I had been a fuck up for so long. You gave me the confidence that I could be better than a petty corner ass hustler who only hustled to get high, buy clothes, and use the streets as a playground. That's who I really was. Being with you made me feel like a man but, I also felt like the streets owed me because, I'ma hustlin' motherfucka'! I'm good at what I do and I have something to prove to myself. Now, I meant you no harm. I only wanted to make you happy. At first, I didn't know what would become of us but, once I realized what was going on between us, I fell in love with our life and I loved showing you how much I appreciate you. I was also loving what I now realize is a big ass, dumb ass lie. The playground of the streets is an illusion that keep mothers in prayer, has no retirement plan for 99% of the players, and the players pay with their life and freedom, or the life and freedom of others. The streets are destructive to all black people in the United States of America. The only thing that can replace the love of the streets for black people is a better love for and from themselves, which is the black family. Now, and once again, these streets are threatening my freedom and the faith, trust, and support of my family. Family strengthens freedom, faith, trust, and support in one another. With you in my life, along with my family, I know that the answers will be revealed to me on how to best let go of the streets. You just *can't* take that part of what you've given to me away. You can be hurt, mad, angry, upset and you can punish me, Lt. Gibson, but you can't turn your back on me. Just remember, you chose me," Elliot wiped the tears from his eyes, reached in his pocket, and then gave Doreatha the ring.

"This is *beautiful,* Elliot," she said, looking down at her hand with her fingers spread apart, admiring the one that she slipped the ring on.

"What about your probation, Elliot. Won't you get a lot of time with the arrest and the probation combined?" She asked him with concern.

"That's just it, Boo! My lawyer told me that he can beat the charge for $10,000. It's almost all of the money that I have. He said that although they've been watching me, there is no evidence that I had anything on me but money at the time of arrest. Bighead Charlie's truck is not in my name, nor is it in his name, either. His lawyer says that Charlie also has a fighting chance. My lawyer says that if push comes to shove, he'll get me whatever the probation judge gives me and run it together with the time that I can get for the arrest. He will make sure that I get the same thing, which means that I will get 3 years at the most," he explained.

"That's not too bad, Elliot. All I can say is that most of y'all men do not know what you are made of. The streets rob you of things that you can do beside drug dealing, robbing and conniving. You can make a better life for yourself than the life that the streets can offer you, most of the time. I see wasted minds every day and a lot of us: meaning your woman, don't expect too much from yall anymore. Keep this in mind; God's creation moves, grows, changes and fulfills. A seed is planted, fed, watered and it starts to grow. There is a process that takes place before the bud blooms into a magnificent flower. Black men in the hood, most of them, never want to take the time to grow. They want to sprout up overnight by selling drugs. Don't get me wrong, I understand the temptation that fuels the trap. It's that almighty dollar but, for us, sprouting into a flower overnight only happens for a few out of thousands. However, for some of the few and for most of you, the streets come with death, wasted life, undiscovered potential and a lot of degradation. A lot of people of importance that make real life decisions of substance look at y'all as pure fools and assholes. The streets keeps them eating off of the misery of your incarceration, death, and the broken families. You all become experiments, studies, and guinea pigs for the system. They all eat off of you. Soon as you get too comfortable, they bring your asses down, then me and my girlfriends get paid and make a career out of being a grown dumbass blackman's babysitter... You are right, I did choose you because I need a man. Most of you that are in jails and prisons are the best of fearlessness, strength, and honor but, the damn streets, drugs, guns, cars, money and pussy are making y'all niggers not worth the air that God gives you to breathe. Why? Everything that God gives you is being wasted in the streets, prisons and graveyards. I *need* a man, Elliot. The black woman in the streets need our men, Elliot, to change our streets into a better place instead of continuing to perpetuate this living hell and delighting at being the devil's runners, boo! **YALL NEED TO LEAD US OUT OF THIS SHIT!**" She angrily yelled to emphasize her point.

"Now come here," she said, holding her arms out, inviting him to a hug. They held one another in the closest affections. The embrace lasted minutes. Then they kissed. That's when Doreatha's libido began to throb but she caught herself. She played it off cool and eased Elliot away from her. She rubbed his face lightly with her hands and looked into his eyes and said, "I'm not going to abandon you but, I need to work this hurt out of my soul. Now, you have to leave so that I can get up and ready for work, ok," she said. Elliot smiled.

"I got you, Doreatha," he responded. He wanted to demonstrate real love so, he resisted the urge to feel her body as his own. He kissed her on the cheek and departed feeling full of a fresh spirit that replaced the emptiness and gloom of depression. It disappeared.

Pimp was surprised to see Candace, his mother, and the children for a show of support in the courtroom. Not only did he care about the issue of her being a correctional officer coming to surface and putting her job in jeopardy but, he also knows that this is also the day that she will be going to settlement for the house. Everything's going according to plan.

Pimp received 3 years of probation for 4 of his charges and a year in the Division of Corrections. The judge gave him time served, which meant that he should be home in another 2 months or so. The question of his child's mother's profession never came up in court, and after Candace gave a quick character testimony, she hurried off to keep her appointment with the real estate agent.

Uncle Twin's case had also been adjudicated rather early in the day. His lawyer spent most of his proceedings holding secret sidebar discussions with the judge and the state's prosecutor. The judge occasionally looked over the two counselors' shoulders to give Twin some stern looks while listening to the pros and cons to help in the decision of how much time that he intends to mete out for this repeated offender of the law. Twin's attorney put up a hell of a battle for his client. After the clandestine conversations of the court, his lawyer stood beet red with his neck-tie loosened. His efforts got his client a ten year sentence with all but 4 years to serve at the DOC, with the remaining 6 years suspended with 3 years of probation. Twin has almost two years inside and will probably serve 8 months to a year more. He became so happy that he quietly and slowly cried openly. No one in the courtroom detected how he wished that he'd chosen another path in life or how much he prayed to himself, asking God to please give him just one more chance. He is the happiest man alive accepting a guilty plea agreement. This meant that his daughter will have him around a hell of a lot sooner than he believed. He thought about how he's getting too old for this courtroom drama. After over 30 years of law-breaking his agenda must be concentrated on making a sincere effort to retire from the life of crime.

Uncle Twin and Pimp were both relieved of an astronomically heavy burdens. It's the burden of an unknown fate from the courts. A lot of pressure has been released with knowing that they will be free soon. Unlike what's going on in the minds of the six other prisoners who rode in the same van from the court building and back to Steel-side. One of the young guys received 50 years for an attempted murder; another one got life and 20 years for a body, too. There was an eight year sentence, a six year sentence, and the remaining two were to be released that day from Steel-side. The moods on the van ranged from somber, to satisfied, to happiness.

When the crew returned to Steel-side with the big time went straight to T-section onto lock-up. Besides the inmates to be released, the rest of the court returns got their property and went onto C-section. They will stay there until the next morning when the Maryland State Division of Corrections comes to start the process that will send them to one of Maryland's many prisons. Uncle Twin and Pimp paired up as cell buddies. They were both now short-timers and not considered a maximum threat to one another and they both will be going to a minimum security prison.

Once they got settled in the cell, Twin asked the tier officer if he could be let out to move around. She informed him that Mass Security Control is in effect. She then went on to let him know that an inmate was stabbed up seriously this morning and had to be sent to Shock Trauma. He remained on life support. It wasn't until a sanitation worker came onto the tier to clean up before anybody found out that the victim was G-Loc. Pimp was furious but there isn't anything that he can do. They found out that the hit came from Bloods and then Uncle Twin felt betrayed. He's smart though. He knows that it is a power play because everybody in the jail knew that he would be in court and, more than likely, not coming back. Twin wrote a short letter to Ochie and gave it to the sanitation worker. He told him which officer to give the note to that will ensure its delivery before the night is out.

"Damn it, Unc! G is my man, yo! I hope and pray that he makes it. What's fucked up is that I know that bitch ass nigga Red Mike has something to do with it. I just know he do, Uncle Twin. That shit got his cruddy ass name all over it," Pimp barked angrily.

"If that's the truth, then I know Moon got his hand in it. He's a demon seed, too," Twin said to Pimp.

When the shift changed, Candace, Bee and Lacy Landon came onto C tier. Candace wanted to see Pimp. Bee and Landon wanted to say their goodbyes to Uncle Twin.

"Hey, Boo," Candace greeted Pimp, walking up to the cell and speaking in a weary manner. "I guess that you heard about G-Loc by now."

"Yeah, I sure did. It's only one person that I can think of that he might have had beef with. Even still, there ain't nothing that I can do because I'm leaving the jail but, when I catch that whore uptown, I'm gonna..." Candace cut him short.

"You gonna what?! You ain't gonna do jack shit but come home to your family and raise your son because, It ain't nothin' that you can do for G-Loc but pray that he pulls through. Now, I signed all of the papers for the house so that we'll have us somewhere nice and hidden to live when you come home. It's a community and not a damn hood. You got choices to make about our lives, Pimp. I refuse to be your babymomma that works over the jail, who makes moves for you every time that you get locked up. I want a family and I want you to partner up with me into making it happen. Now, you don't have to want the same thing but, just let me know now so that I won't look forward to you being my man. I will just concentrate on taking care of my children and you'll be watching me do me," she explained her position to him.

Pimp looked over to Uncle Twin thinking about the conversations that they were having all day. Twin gave him law. On the low, dudes would talk behind Uncle Twin's back. They couldn't understand how this oldhead who sniffed smack all the time and really wasn't a mass murderer could be in charge of the most notorious and feared crew in the jails and prisons of Maryland. Not only that, the oldhead really ran shit and he wasn't a big dude. Pimp could see that this brother had a serious mind. Maybe even more than can be contained by one person so, he has to express *his* oneness with others. He is really good at what he does. Now Pimp understood clearly all of the talk that Twin shared with him about his regrets. Pimp can tell that if Uncle Twin would have used his mind for something other than "the game" or "the streets" he would probably be in a better situation and more relevant to the cause of freedom for his people.

Twin looked back at Pimp and shrugged his shoulders. "I told you that she is a winner, yo. So, get uptown and win some of those challenges with her. Fuck winning beefs and wars with your homies. We only killing our own army at the end of the day," Twin said.

"Y'all right but, G is my man! He's my brother! I just want him to pull through."

Pimp, Twin, and Candace briefly discussed if or not Mike was the cause of it all. Twin needed to get to the bottom of it before he left the jail so that he could give Ochie proper instructions. No matter what happened, somebody will have to understand that men must keep their word in all situations. That's what keeps order. After teasing back and forth with Bee Berry about how much he's going to miss her and how he's coming to that Icon Inn bar that they talked about so much to find her. Twin asked Bee and Candace if they both can let him have a word with Officer Landon. The two women excused themselves and headed to their post. Candace began saying goodbye to her man and Pimp let her know that he will be in touch to let her know where he's going in the system.

"I know which one that is. I haven't smelled that one since I first got here," Twin said to his friend about her perfume. This is the closest to a private conversation that can be had with Pimp in the cell with him.

"Which one is it?" She asked playfully.

"Elizabeth Taylor's, Black Pearls," he said, with that gold toothed smiled.

"You stay on point, don't you?" She gave him his props.

"Oh well, I do my best... Miss Lady, I need you to get my homeboy Otis Ricks down here to me. You think that you can make that happen? I already let him know to see you if I didn't come back but, due to the circumstances of the situation, I need to see him," Twin knew that Landon could probably pull it off, even though the M.S.C. is in effect. For one thing, Ochie is supposed to move into the cell previously occupied by Twin on Landon's section. He is also the new president of the counsel; which means that any excuse can be made to get him out of his cell. Landon agreed to get Ochie to him as quick as she can and want for something else. It's as good as done. He had something else that he had to talk to her about a couple of weeks ago but, the timing seemed to be perfect now.

"You know what, Miss? I tried to tell the kid that you not right. You know that I fucks with you and I saw it coming but, I just want you to know that if you were anyone else, I would have given the word. I know that it came from you with Shorty. He wasn't hurt bad, but I still want to know who you put on him?" Twin asked her concerning Jay. He didn't say any name so that Pimp can't know who or what he's talking about.

"Man, do you think I'm scared?! Trust me, Twin, I gave him what he asked for and I warned him ahead of time! I did what I did and that's that! He's lucky to be alive! Now, I need to ask *you* a question. What's up with the guy Chicken? He just moved on the tier the other day and I like him," she said, smiling.

"Oh shit! You turned out now, huh? Yo is cool. He my man, but he ain't connected to us or anybody else. He got his own boys. He's from Lanvale and Barclay Streets. Compared to my boy, he is a general. My boy is serious but, he just a sergeant... Just be careful, Miss Lady," Twin advised.

"Please! I'm just fine. It's not that serious and I'm glad things happened so that I can see. I'll tell you something; it was fun enough to try it again and that guy Chicken is the truth."

"I hear that shit! You crazy, Miss Lady, and I'm gonna miss you," he responded.

"I know you're gonna visit us again, aren't you?" she asked, sounding sarcastic.

"Noooo! This is it for me. I'm too old for this shit and I need to change," Twin said like he is in confession.

"I've never heard you sound so serious... You stay up and I'll get your boy down here, ASAP," she said, then walked away.

Landon got Ochie down onto C-section after talking to Lt. Gibson. They let Ochie use his newly appointed position to walk around the jail after he switched cells to move onto J-section.   The lieutenant wanted to see him and check him out, anyway. Although she knew who he was, she wanted to get a feel for what type of man he could be. Being an older guy made him cool with Gibson off the top. After she checked him out, Landon let him know that Uncle Twin wanted to see him.

Twin was filled in on what happened to G-Loc. Pimp listened to every word as he sat up on the top bunk while Ochie stood in   front of the cell talking to his comrade, who leaned on the bars inside of the cell. Ochie confirmed that it was a set up because Blood Moon was in the gym when it happened. Moon sent a message back to Ochie, after Ochie sent somebody to see what happened, that G-Loc had violated and he would see Ochie when the doors hit to let him know what it was about. One of their sources denied what Moon suggested and confirmed that Red Mike put the hit on G-Loc and that it was meant to go down because Uncle Twin would be gone. Moon was rumored to be taking over the jail now that Twin was leaving.

"Do you think I'mo stand for that comrade?" Ochie asked Twin.

"You better not! What I want you to do is find out who specifically hit G-Loc, and make sure that they feel it. Also, I don't care what you gotta do to get the kid Red Mike, you just make sure that he gets gotten, ok? Let Muk'min know that the truce line is crossed coming from the red team, which means that they'll have no refuge in case of an all-out war... Ochie, here," Twin said, reaching down in his pants and pulling out a balloon with four grams of heroin. He bit the balloon and put a little on the back of a book before tying the balloon again. "You take this, comrade. I'm through."

"You sure, man? You know you gonna be sick soon as you get over the Doc house," Ochie said with concern.

"I guess that's the price that I have to pay to do it right this time. That's the point," he said with the gold toothed smile. "Hamjambo."

"Cejambo... I love you homeboy," Ochie said to his friend.

"I love you, too," he replied before they shook hands through the bars. Ochie walked off.

Twin sniffed his last bit of dope and he and Pimp smoked the weed that they both had before going to DOC. They were up all night high. Pimp made a vow to quit smoking weed, too. His logic is that if his woman can do it to get a job, than he can, too.

The pair laughed and joked all night. Candace brought Pimp his dinner and also more food before leaving. Uncle Twin had quite a few of the officers bring him farewell wishes and outside dishes. Steel-side wasn't too bad for these two. A lot of men had horror stories to tell or stories better left kept to themselves. Some stories were traumatic. Then there were those like G-Loc's. He will never get to live with or tell his story. It's over.

All in all, Twin and Pimp got about two hours of sleep before the CO awoke all of the detainees transferring out of the city's jail to go and serve their sentences within the Division of Corrections. They were placed in the C-section day room. There were six BGF comrades, four Bloods and along with Pimp were 2 Crips among the 16 men to be transferred. An eerie silence filled the room at first, until everyone huddled up into their own and began to converse. Tensions were in the room but, when they all saw Uncle Twin, it made everyone hold all ill feelings inside.

The men were quietly talking to themselves until the unimaginable happened. The day room's door opened to protests coming from two detainees, handcuffed with their property in both hands dangling between their legs.

"I don't know what the fuck kind of games y'all playing, but somebody needs to tell me what the fuck is going on!" Blood Moon yelled. The day room door was shut behind Blood Moon and Red Mike. The pair stood there close to the locked door trying to figure out just where they are going. Neither one of them had a court date. All they were told is that it is an administrative move.

Turning around to face the men in the dayroom, and in a split second, Mike and Pimp's eyes locked. Pimp stood there. It registered that one of the men coming into the day room is none other than Red Mike, *and* that his hands remained cuffed in front of him, he gave Red Mike a ferocious kick to the middle of his chest that sent him crashing into the wall. Moon ran to position himself between the arch rivals and the other Blood members followed suit ready to attack Pimp. Uncle Twin jumped in between Pimp and the Bloods with his comrades and Pimp's homies positioned for an all-out war in the little small day room. A few knives appeared from everyone, but the Bloods recognized that they were clearly outnumbered.

228

"Lookie here," Twin began with that gold toothed smile. He looked side to side to take a survey of what is about to take place. "Moon, you and I know that you and your little pink bitches is gonna step 'da fuck back no matter what happens. If they don't, I'm instructing my comrades to cut your motherfuckin' throat and rip your snake ass head off," is all that Twin said. Moon stared at Twin hard and then he looked at the cuffs on his hand. He knows that he is at a complete disadvantage and that no matter how it plays out, the main objective is to kill him. He looked down at Mike, then back to Twin.

"At least let him stand up again," Moon said. That is all he could think to say. Twin agreed. It really didn't matter because, once Red Mike got to his feet, everyone stepped to the side and Pimp smashed his fist into Mike's nose. Blood spewed out from in-between his cuffed hands as he grabbed his face while falling into the same spot that he'd been helped from just seconds ago. Blind fury overcame Pimp and that's when he started stomping on Mike. He kicked and stomped his face into the wall until he slumped over, and then continued to stomp some more. Mike was out cold and his face became an unrecognizable bleeding mass. Several knots and lumps formed on his head before Uncle Twin pulled hard onto Pimp's arm just enough to put distance between the last stomp and Red Mike's face. His face now matched his name-Red Mike.

"Ease up, Pimp! That's enough, yo!" Twin yelled.

"I wanna stomp that bitch's brains out!" Pimp gritted. Twin pulled him back just in time because, the CO opened the door a few short moments after Pimp stopped punishing Mike. When the officer saw Mike's battered body lying still, he hurried over to him to check his vitals. He also called on his radio to have a stretcher sent down to the section because, there is an inmate that needed emergency medical attention. The officer just happened to be the very same CO that escorted Pimp to Red Mike's cell when the truce was initiated. He looked at Pimp, then he looked at Red Mike, again. He turned to face Pimp with a smile on his face. The duty sergeant came to the section with a few officers in tow like they were going to lock someone up for the assault. He looked at Twin and then to Moon, along with the inmates in the day room standing around quiet with the *"I didn't see nothing"* look, before he spoke. He saw the cuffs on Moon.

"Is that the Federal guy?" He asked the tier officer.

"Yes sir. The beat up one is, too," he reported.

"Get him outta here and into a cell. I guess we're already going to hear it from the Federal Marshalls when they find out that one of their guys have been attacked under our watch," said the sergeant.

"Whatchoo mean that I'm one of the federal guys?!" Moon asked, wide eyed.

"Like he said, the feds are coming for you and your partner. You boys are in the big leagues," the C.O. said. "Let's go."

Moon was escorted to an empty cell by the tier officer. When the officer got back to the day room, it was time for the rest of the inmates to be cuffed, shackled, and moved on to the next phase of their experience. Twin asked the officer about Moon and Mike. All the tier officer could tell him is that it is true that the feds are taking them to the Maryland Correctional Adjustment Center, better known as *"Supermax"*, where the violent of the most violent inmates in the state were housed. They also have a section strictly for the holding of federal detainees. That's where Moon and Mike are headed.

"I wonder what the feds want with them niggas." Twin queried.

"Me, too! That's serious," Pimp said.

"Right! I wouldn't wish them boys on my enemies. Ain't no telling what that shit could be about?" Twin and Pimp talked about that all the way to the DOC.

The state couldn't make a good case with Moon, so they contacted a U.S. Attorney, recognizing the potential for the mayhem that can follow with a person like Moon being released. They started their own investigation, which lead to Moon's cell phone number. With the recorded conversations, they were able to bring federal racketeering indictments that involved, drug dealing, extortion, conspiracy to murder, as well as murder for hire and attempted murder charges. The hit on G-Loc was the final chapter that also closed the book on the indictments. Red Mike's charges mirrored Moon's and also included two State Correctional employees. Moon and Mike were both facing life with the feds. Moon also faced the death penalty. The Federal Government classified him as the head of the investigation.

Chapter 11

Bee was mad that she'd lost two sources of income at one time. Her pockets felt the effects of Twin being gone for a couple of weeks now and G-Loc's lifeless body continued to be supported. Why wouldn't she miss at least an extra 8 or 9 hundred dollars every week between G-Loc and Twin? She also wanted to get in touch with G-Loc's family to offer condolences. She liked him a lot.

The jail was still locked down and the inmates were out of everything. Bee was hurting for money. That oldhead guy Ochie stayed on her heels. She wondered if Uncle Twin said anything to him about her. Ochie had muscles and looked good for his age. He wasn't playful as Twin. He seemed to be a borderline stalker. Bee can tell because her pants stays tight and she always see him in the gym with *every* section. She needed a catch anyway. Bee decided to proposition Ochie but, she needed to give it a few more days to figure out her approach. He appeared to keep his business to himself and once she noticed his obsession for privacy she discovered that he lead the BGF. So, now he's about to do business with her people. He became more attractive to her. On top of that, Ochie told her that he's about to go to prison for at least 15 years. The thought of hitting him off for a fee turned Bee's bad girl on just knowing that she can be his last piece.

After doing her running around early in the morning, she headed over to Hope's house to pick up the new package. The Queens chilled for a couple of weeks after the two young dumb ass gang banging CO blood bitches got caught up into the federal investigation. She couldn't believe that her girl Simms's baby father turned out to be so damned shiesty. She figured that he got what he deserved for what he'd done to G-Loc. She knows that just about anyone that the feds snatch from Steel-side are going to get time. From the sound of their situation, they were facing some major time and will more than likely be in prison in another state.

Bee parked her car and knocked on Hope's door. Hope opened the door with her cell phone pressed to her ear and turned back into the house leaving Bee standing there without saying a word.

"Hello to you, too," Bee said out loud to herself, coming into the house and locking the door.

Meanwhile, Paul Powers parked his car at the top of Madison and Lakewood streets to watch Bee go into the house that she always enter into on the days she meets that potato chip guy at the 7-Eleven on Sinclair Lane. He doesn't know what the connection is concerning the house on Lakewood and he really don't care. He waited patiently until Bee came out of the house and then he followed her to the shopping center and the tobacco store. This will be the day that her world comes crashing down. He is sure that Major Parker knows something about what Bee does because he has pictures of them meeting and going to the Renaissance Hotel in downtown Baltimore. The Major adamantly denied to Paul that he knows anything of what CO Berry is up to and he got Paul to keep everything quiet about his improprieties with Bee so that the matter can be disposed with as little attention possible. Paul made the Major agree to make sure that Bee and anyone involved in whatever she's hustling will pay dearly. He called the Major to put him on point that in about an hour and a half, Bee will be at the designated location with the goods. The plan is to take her down first and then follow the delivery man. He emitted a sinister laugh after ending the call to the major.

"Who're you talkin to?" Bee asked Hope, while looking over the weed that she placed onto the table and pinching a bud from the pile to roll up with. Hope never answered the question. She just held her finger up so that Bee could stop distracting her from hearing what Max relayed on the other end.

"I'll get the suit for you... That's o.k... You don't have to get anyone to bring me any money, Max... Uh, huh...

233

Well I'm coming anyway, because I want to be there... I won't get into trouble because no one has to know who I am, Max. I'll be just another spectator in civilian clothes... OK... Look, I'll talk to you later. I have company... Yes, I work today... OK, I'll see you then," Hope promised, ending the call.

"Max?! Who was that, the guy in the jail that you be talkin' about all the time? " Bee asked her.

"Well, yeah," she answered. "He's my friend."

"Well, honey hush," Bee said, flopping to sit in the chair. "Don't say anything until I finish rolling this blunt, heifer." Bee and Hope began to weigh and separate the packages while Hope attempted an explanation concerning her and Max's relationship. Her eyes displayed an extra spark of light when talking about him. She went on and on non-stop talking. She expressed a lot about how much intelligence Max has and how well he is informed. Bee listened to her intently, and could tell that Hope really fell for Max beyond what she is saying so, she decided to put a little bait on the hook to see if she bites.

"I understand how you can fall for him. He *is* fine," Bee said.

"I look beyond his physical appearance but, yes, he *is* a nice looking man." Hope said.

"Ah, ha! You gonna give him some, ain't choo?! Bee asked like she discovered America.

"Girl, you got to be outta' your mind," Hope answered. "How did you get that out of what I said? That's because you just nasty!"

"And you right because, first of all, you ain't beefing about me asking you that and you didn't say *"I ain't had dick since dick had me,"* which means that you thinkin' 'bout that shit," Bee said, like a detective. "You gonna buy him a suit? Huh!"

"Yes, he asked me if it isn't too much trouble to get it for him. He doesn't want his aunt to get it for him because he says that she is a little too homely," Hope explained.

"You're going to court with him too?" This bit of news surprised Bee.

"Yes. He's my friend and he's facing a life sentence. I just want to be there for him either way it goes," Hope said.

"Well, I ain't never hear you express anything other than contempt for niggas. This attitude that I'm seeing from you is quite different and I hope that he makes out in court because I want to be the first one to know it when he put it in you and break that ass off something proper," Bee said and then choked after hitting the blunt.

They wrapped up their personal weed and finished that part of the business. Bee put everything in her oversized purse and said goodbye to her girl but not before teasing some more about giving Max some head.

Hope locked her door and rolled herself another blunt. She only took a couple of pulls off of it before putting it out. A blunt will last her for two or three days since Puddin's been gone. In fact, she still has weed from the last package. When Puddin' was around, she would have had to buy weed before the package came.

Her mind drifted back to Max and his court date. She decided to wear a skirt to blend in with the family and supporters, but more importantly, to impress Max. He joked about the way that she dressed. She shared with him some pictures of her and he teased, calling her Butchie. It was all in fun and not meant as an insult or an attack. Hope became self-conscious about her style of dress for the first time in her life. She decided to call Landon and get her to go shopping with her for Max's court date. Since she is going to dress up, she felt she had to do it with class and style.

Pudgy placed the last few boxes of goods onto his hand cart when he saw Bee's car come into the parking lot. He pulled the lift gate down in the back of the truck and leaned the cart waiting for Bee to park. Pudgy heard that Bee used to be a stripper and every time he saw her, thoughts of her dancing naked on a pole and dropping her red ass like its hot filled his head. She looks like such a nasty girl to him.

"Good afternoon, Pudgy Poo," Bee said. The greeting snapped him out of his sinful and lustful thoughts at the sound of his pet name that she calls him.

"What's up, girl?" He responded "Come on and walk with me into the store." Bee walked with Pudgy making small talk. She covertly put money in his uniform shirt pocket during the conversation before walking away to order a few items from the store. Pudgy handled his business in the store. Finishing the delivery, Pudgy walked out of the store with Bee trailing him. She hit her button remote to open the trunk of her car. Pudgy opened up the lift gate to put the hand cart inside of the truck, which gave Bee the opportunity to toss the boxes inside of the truck easy as pie. What they didn't know is that the exchange was being videotaped by an undercover State Trooper that conducted his surveillance with Paul Powers, who remained parked across the street in his car making his own video recording of the transaction. Bee drove her car out into Edison Highway, going southbound from the parking lot of 7-Eleven. She turned right onto Federal Street. After driving a few blocks, Bee saw police lights flashing in her mirrors, along with hearing the sound of a siren. She pulled over to the right side of the street, followed by an unmarked police cruiser. Bee sat confused trying to figure out what traffic laws she could have possibly violated. She reached for her license out of her purse and got the registration from the visor once she saw other police cars pulling up alongside of her in a police van. The van is used to transport the newly arrested. The undercover tapped onto Bee's window for her to roll it down.

"Hello, ma'am, are you Belinda Berry?" The officer asked.

"Yes, I am. What's the problem?" Bee asked, nervous and confused.

"You are under arrest, Ms. Berry. We'll tell you more

at the station. Can you please put your hands on the steering wheel where I can see them?" The officer instructed her. It sounded more like an order than a request. Bee got a little scared because she had a feeling that it is over for her and her Queens. *They'd been found out!* She couldn't do anything but comply with the officer.

Pudgy was able to drive onto Baltimore City Detention Center property before the authorities pounced upon him. Major Parker controlled everything from Bee's arrest to Pudgy's arrest. He didn't want a full scale investigation for the fear of whom else and how many of his officers were involved. He knows that this is an elaborate operation and had to have been put together by veteran employees and not the dumb young female and male officers trying to make a quick buck. Major Parker also figured that Mrs. Butler, the commissary officer, just had to be involved. So, that morning he went to her and informed her that she had to put in an immediate transfer or be arrested when the delivery truck arrives. The only reason that he spared her the humiliation is because they'd known one another for over 25 years and had a brief affair just as many years ago. They both maintained a very good friendship and he didn't want to see her suffer in that way. That, on top of the fact that the climate concerning so many rouge correctional officers in the news caught up in federal investigations and being fired for bringing in contraband made him want to keep this one as low key as possible. He would have found a way to keep Bee out of jail but that damn Paul Powers really had it in for her. The Major couldn't afford to let him go to someone else with all of the pictures and information that he gathered. He refused to allow this spot be blown. It just didn't look right. Bee will be hurt in all of this but, better Bee get pinched than to blow up something major on his watch. He's about to retire. Who needs this! That is the logic of his thinking.

Bee's bail was 75 thousand dollars. She and Pudgy had been charged with possession with intent to distribute heroin and marijuana. They were also charged with the delivery and smuggling of contraband into a correctional facility for the tobacco and cell phones. Major Parker paid Bee's bail after getting the phone call from his contact over the Central Bookings Intake Center very soon after the commissioner set the bail. Pudgy's bail was 100 thousand and by this time Gibson knew everything. She was surprised to know that Bee's bail had been posted before she had the chance to pay both of their bonds. This is a major blow to the operation. Recovering will be almost impossible. Bee's arrest and the loss of her job hurt everyone in more ways than one.

Hope made Landon promise not to tell anyone of their shopping expedition. However, Landon, knowing that her friend met someone that made her feel like bringing out her beautiful feminine qualities, stood looking at her friend. She is going to hook her girl up for sure. Not only are they going shopping, Landon also made an appointment with her beautician for Hope so that she will be styled to perfection. Hope's hair and nails must get done, as well as her eyebrows and make-up. She worked hard at convincing Hope to get some of her hair cut and styled. She is so use to the Allan Iverson look until she dreaded having anybody touch her braids. The shopping date also gave the women a chance to discuss their dismay at the hustle being shut down indefinitely and Bee paying such a great price for what happened. They all felt guilty about her going to jail and losing her job. The dark cloud around them grew thick again, like when Blackwell lost her job. Only Bee's situation is *much* worse.

Landon chose a navy blue Christian Dior two piece suite, with a waist length blazer. She picked out a pair of Louis Vuitton shoes and belt to match. The clothes were fitted to perfection. Landon and Hope had a nice time dressing Hope for Max's court date. They talked the entire time about Max, and although Landon was delighted about Hope finding an interest in this man, she gave her a stern warning about putting her faith and all her trust in a man. Especially one of the inmates. She went on to share with Hope the episode concerning Jay. Gibson and the other women already filled Hope in on Landon shooting Jay in the ass. The women had an uproariously laughing good time in the boutique while they shopped and Landon replayed the event. The conversation changed while on the way to Macy's for the purchase of a suit for Max.

"Hope," Landon began, "We can still do some things at the job to get paid if you want to."

"How? I'm not going to take any chances bringing *anything* in that jail right now, girl!" She squealed.

"Come on, now. You know we don't get down like that. It's this guy that Jay gave his phone to. His name is Samuel Jones, but they call him Chicken," she said.

"Oh, yeah! I've seen him a couple of times and I also can tell that he has a lot of influence in the jail. Max tells me that the BGF has a lot of respect for him and that he's one of the rare few that they would never push up on about whatever business that he conducts," Hope added, telling Landon that she is familiar with the guy that everyone calls Chicken.

"That's exactly right," Landon confirmed.

"Won't that cause a conflict between how you're operation with BGF and doing your thing with Chicken?" Hope wondered, knowing a conflict like that could be bloody.

"Nope. Not at all, because, as it stands, the BGF outlet, meaning us, is finished, but Chicken wants to continue on with the same system of how everything gets done. I already talked to Ochie, who took over for Uncle Twin, and he don't have a problem with it. He told me that he and Chicken are very cool and that they have a mutual respect already," Landon explained.

"Well how are they gonna get the shit in, anyway?"

"When the sheets and towels get picked up or delivered. Chicken's people drive the truck that delivers the laundry. Do you know Tameka Clear, you know the one who runs the laundry? Well, she delivers it to the inmates on laundry day so, she can be put on the team, too," Landon continued to give the details of the plan to her friend. She told Hope that Gibson already knew of her plan, but Gibson expressed her reluctance about being a part of it. She just wanted to chill out for a while and put in for a three week vacation that is to begin on the day of Elliot's first court date. Landon and Hope talked, plotted, and planned while they shopped. Hope purchased a suit tailored to the sizes that Max gave to her and a pair of shoes. Landon joked about Max's shoe size, which is a size 10. She started joking about the size of his manhood. Hope admitted that she really didn't know. Landon pleaded to be the first one that Hope shares that information with.

"*Damnnn!* Y'all are making too much out of me and Max! He's just a person that I'm really fond of and I admire his knowledge, plus the respect that he has for me! Ya'll know that I don't want a man! I prefer women!" Hope emphatically protested.

The two women went on to buy some things for their other men. Landon for her teenage son and Hope for Lamar. Landon made it a point to let Hope know, before they departed, that she did not mention Puddin' the entire time that they were together but, talked about Max the very same way that she use to talk about Puddin' when the two of them first met. After the shopping trip, they parted.

Steel-side went off the hook and more out of control than it has ever been since the major source of bringing in contraband stopped. The violence is on the rise and the M.S.C stayed in effect. Every time that you get lulled into believing that things calmed down and when the inmates were allowed to come out of their cells and resume normal operations, someone gets stabbed. Violence by the gangs increased dramatically. They started robbing the older guys on commissary days. Anybody that didn't have a connection in any organization got tested. Some assault victims had in their mind to make their robbers murder victims when they see them on the streets.

The protocol is now in disarray concerning the jailhouse politics and the chief of security didn't know what to make of what's going on. The straw that broke the camel's back is when an inmate came up missing from the count. No one could figure out where to locate him. But, just before they were officially about to alert the news media and put out an APB on the inmate thinking that he escaped, an officer found his dead body in the dumpster outside of the kitchen.

Ochie became furious about his opportunity to run things getting cut short before it ever got started. This brought the worst out of him so he let his boys run wild. Twin worked hard to get a little control, order, and diplomacy among the wolves and the bands of thieves. As long as he got 10% of the spoils, Ochie didn't care how his comrades got it. He controlled finances! He found out that Paul Powers is the cause of everything that went wrong for him. Every time he laid eyes on Paul he conjured up various ways to bring the wrath to him. He made a deal to get him some pussy, finally, from   Bee and that nigga fucked it up for him. Paul blew his shot at the money and his red honey.

Officer Landon advised Ochie to be patient because she has another move coming through. Ochie only had about two months before he went to court. How much more patient can he be? He almost messed up his dealings with Officer Landon by offering her some money for sex. She rocked out on him! Ochie didn't think he went too far because of the rumors that she gave Chicken some pussy. So, Ochie remained on his snake bullshit. One thing He believed in is that might makes right. He allowed the extorting of people and loved setting up those he extorted to be robbed. Then he stepped in to mediate the shit he started. He became so blinded by getting sex from Bee that if he'd only calmed down, he would have discovered that there are other C.O.'s that would have hit him off but, now the females are too afraid of Ochie to give him some. He led the pack of wolves viciously.

The suit of clothes that Hope put into the court package, along with the shoes, were very impressive. The alterations that she had tailored were perfect and Max couldn't have done a better job than if he'd gotten the suit of clothes for himself. Max looked rather tasteful for the morning court appearance. His life is on the line today, but, it didn't feel like doomsday. He put the outcome of his fate in Allah's hands and let the worry dissipate and replace it with thoughts of Glorious Hope. What a wonderful name she has. It describes the feelings he have that fuels his faith into believing that whatever happens to him, it will be by Allah's permission. He also understood that Glorious Hope is a woman created exclusively for him and that if he's released from the belly of the beast, he will love her until the end of time.

Max took a deep breath as the transportation officer put the waist chains and cuff box around his midsection, then on his arms. They put the leg shackles on Max and secured each ankle before sending Max into the line of men with court appointments for the day.

Hope couldn't refrain from her nervousness. She prayed that Max will be ok. A person like him doesn't deserve to be in a prison at all. He needs to be free and to make a difference in people's lives. He truly is a blessing to her. After completing her dress, she stared at herself in the mirror. The person looking back frightened her. She froze!

"WOW!" The young voice yelled from behind, snapping her out of the daze. She turned quickly to face Lamar in his pajamas and getting ready for school. "Glo, is 'dat you! You look great! I mean, you look like an angel!"

"Stop playing, boy! No, I don't," was her shy response.

242

"The hell you don't!" Lamar said, boldly.

"All right, now! Watch your mouth, Lamar!" She scolded.

"I just can't believe 'dat you look so good. All I ever see you wear are thug clothes. Girls ain't supposed to dress like that all the time. Ain't nothing wrong with dressing like a girl sometimes if it'll make you look beautiful like you are right now, Glo. Wait till I tell Puddin' this!"

"No, Lamar! Please don't tell her that I dressed like this," she pleaded defensively.

"OK. I won't. But, I don't know why you want to keep it a secret because you are a dime-piece. What man you're gonna see?" Lamar asked. Hope was taken aback by the question coming from Lamar. She didn't say a word. She walked over to the dresser and grabbed her keys and hand purse off of the bed. Before leaving, she kissed Lamar on his cheek and cupped his face into her hands.

"Have a good day at school, Lamar," She said before leaving.

Hope walked into the courtroom, suddenly, things happened as if time stopped and she moved while everyone stood still. Her beauty radiated and everyone's attention attracted to her what seemed like the same time. The court's bailiff asked that all counselors representing defendants to sit in the jury box until their client is called. He walked over to Hope and reached for her hand to escort her, thinking that she's someone's lawyer. Landon came through for her girl.

Hope sat silent listening to case after case. She tried to make out Max's family but, she just couldn't with all of the onlookers present in the courtroom. Then Max entered, escorted by a very familiar co-worker of Hope's. She now distinguished his family from the other spectators once they waved at Max. There sat an older distinguished looking woman along with a middle aged man and woman. Hope thought that the woman might be his mother. She moved closer to where they were sitting and waved to Max, also. Max halted in his tracks with is mouth wide open! He couldn't believe his eyes. He noticed Hope when he entered the courtroom among the sea of people, but he never would have guessed that she would be who she is until she came to sit by his aunt and his sister with her husband. He watched as she introduced herself to his family members. He hadn't expected her to be this gorgeous. He smiled before being interrupted by the officer with an aggressive tug on the chains urging Max to sit.

As the proceedings continued, the escorting CO continuously admonish Max about turning around in his seat. He and several other prisoners could not keep their eyes off of Glorious Hope. This appearance of her is a far cry from the correctional officer that he see on a daily basis. Max's case got called, so he stood while the CO removed the handcuffs for him to take his place at the defendants table. Max's lawyer stood by his side and the state's prosecutor read the charges against Maximillian Muhammad. The next thing that happened surprised everyone in the courtroom. The state moved to nolle prosequie all charges on the grounds of lack of evidence. Max didn't believe his ears. It came to the attention of the court that the only witness to the crime in question committed suicide on the eve of this court date at an undisclosed location. Max jumped into the air and Hope and is family jumped for joy like children at a party. They all began hugging one another. After he settled down, he turned to face Hope. He looked into her eyes and inside of her soul. She returned his gaze with a complete look of hunger. Max mouthed three short words to her.

"I'm coming home," he said.

"I'm going to be waiting for you," she said in return. Max's court case happened early in the morning, before the lunch hour. It's the policy of the courts in Baltimore that a defendant can be released from the courts if the proceedings ended before the lunch recess. Hope waited, along with Max's family, in front of the Clarence B. Mitchell Courthouse until they spotted Max walking down Calvert Street from around the corner where the sheriff released him from. The family ran up to him on busy Calvert Street and jumped into his arms filled with happiness. Max's life hung in the balance for over a year in the trenches with the wolves, snakes, and devils until the scale of justice tipped his way. After his family had their moment, he reached out to Hope and pulled her into his embrace for their first touch. They hugged for such a long time and reciprocated feelings of knowing that this is where they belonged. They belonged with one another.

"Did you do what I asked you, sis?" Max asked his sister in a commanding but endearing tone. She didn't say a word and handed him a small box. He opened the box to reveal a 1-1/2 ct. diamond ring and dropped to one knee on Calvert Street and said, "I know all about what I need and I know that my life's sacrifices are with you, for you, and to you; for us to live in heaven... Will you marry me, Glorious Hope?"

The Aftermath

All of the queens met at the Icon later on in the evening with the exception of Hope. She and Max married that very same day at the courthouse. His family was there to witness the event and Max promised Hope that they will have a bigger ceremony later, if that's what she wants. They then went to dinner at the McCormick and Schmidt restaurant at Pier Five in Baltimore's own Inner Harbor, where they spent the rest of the evening. Hope received a call from Gibson letting her know that she must be at the Icon Inn at the usual time because she need to see her. Hope figured that it would be a good time to share her own news. This one is a doooozy for them all! She and Max are Newlyweds. Puddin', Rashon, and Yolanda also waited at the Icon for Hope to arrive because Lamar just couldn't contain what he witnessed. He had to tell his mother. She did not hesitate to call Hope, either. Hope figured that she might as well get Puddin' at the bar, too, when she shares the news, with the consent of her husband.

Everyone were glad to see Bee, who hadn't surfaced since the arrest. She was in great spirits, and, in spite of what went down, she missed her job and her girlfriends. She was accompanied by Major Parker. Bridgette Blackwell also attended the gathering and the ladies were at the bar having a good time. Landon and Simms talked among themselves about the business. Landon is very close to making it all go down, with a stamp of approval from Gibson. Gibson let her know that she will do everything and anything to help them but, she don't want to be involved as a player anymore. Eyes and ears, cool. But, nothing more.

Simms planned to be in her new home soon and waiting for Pimp, who is scheduled to be released in a matter of days now. She's a little unsure about involving herself in with the new scheme so, she informed Landon that she needs a little more time to consider. They all know now that Paul Powers is the reason behind the downfall but, things happen for a reason and reasons develop all of the time.

Hope and Max walked into the bar looking stylish. Everyone continued to stare at the dressed couple without recognizing who they are. Then Gibson, Simms, and Bee recognized Max. That's when Landon yelled.

"Hope!" Everyone looked for a long three seconds before reality set in. Then all of the girls rushed to her, fawning over their friend. She looked amazing! Landon began to brag, telling everyone who listened that Hope's look is her work. She didn't lie, either. Then Puddin' pushed through the crowd rudely.

"Glo! What the fuck is this? Yo, you look so fine! My baby boy wasn't lying to me," she said, with her voice trailing off. The tears began to fall. Hope grabbed Max's arm and pulled him forward.

"Everybody, I want y'all to know that my name is no longer Glorious Hope... I am now Mrs. Maximillian Muhammad!" No one believed what they heard; let alone what they are seeing. Everyone began to order double and triple shots of whatever.

"You're married, Glo?" Puddin' asked, letting her tears flow.

"I sure am. I want you to be happy for me," she answered.

"But, I love you," Puddin' confessed.

"And I love you, too, but not in that way anymore. I want you to do the best for yourself, and if you take a step in the right direction, you'll find that you have a lot of good inside of you and you can do things that you never imagine you can do. Just understand that I have faith that Max can make me happy," Hope said. Puddin' called for Rashon and Yolanda, then ran out of the bar in a fit of tears. The unbelievably joyous and shocking celebration continued on.

Gibson noticed that Elliot came into the Icon. He spotted her and several of the COs from Steel-side. He even saw Max Muhammad, who slept in the dormitory downstairs from him. They both greeted one another and asked how long each other had been home. Elliot filled Max in on what's going on and telling Max about his new case. Max gave him encouraging words so that he don't beat himself up like so many men do when they pile their plate with the consequences of actions that are detrimental to a healthy life. Max introduced his wife to Elliot and once he figured out who she is, he ran to Gibson and whispered in her ear. She in turn whispered back to him. There were whispers going on all night about Max and Hope.

Now that Elliot is there, Gibson hit the glasses together for everyone's attention.

"I know that everybody is wondering why I called y'all, and I'm about to drop it on you. However, I don't believe that my shit is anywhere near the shit that Hope done smacked us with. I mean, the bitch dropped it on us. Didn't see it coming!" Gibson said among murmurs of confirmation and laughter. "I mean that shit is a doozy... Now for my news.

"I'm going on a vacation for three weeks, and once I return," she said, looking at Elliot, "I'm going on maternity leave because, I'm pregnant!" The women jumped all over Gibson. She yelled for them to hold it a minute because she's not finished. "Now, wait," she said, growing emotional. She poured her last drink and began, "I'd like to make a toast to my girl, Landon, who's been my partner in crime forever. Also, I would like to toast my girl Bee and her red hot ass. Bitch, keep your damn drawers up! Blackwell, who stays on her save the brothers shit; and she's right, they are our hidden treasures and I will be glad when Black men really get it together and force us to get different jobs...

"Hope, bitch, you got me fucked up! I hope you took my advice about the sausage tand banana. We need to give you a toast for finally getting yourself a real dick, too!" Everyone laughed at Gibson, but she didn't laugh one bit. She is serious.

"Last, but not least; to our baby Simms... Life is tough, boo. Don't be so hard on yourself because, you have many lessons to learn. We all do! With that, I say, I LOVE *MY STEEL-SIDE QUEENS!!!*" They all tapped glasses and drank up.

Meanwhile, today Ochie got the word that Paul Powers worked the three to eleven shift. On top of that, his post just happened to be on Ochie's old tier, N-Section. Ochie found himself a trash bag and ran over to that side of the jail. He waited on O-Section until a comrade called him on his phone instructing him to come on over to N-Section. Officer Powers left his desk and began to patrol the top tier and looking in the cells for rule violations or contraband. Ochie came over to the section fast. He made the occupants of the last cell on the bottom tier leave to join the inmates that were out of their cells and join everyone else for recreation. He then sent for Mu'Kmin and Nasir and gave them instructions. Mu'Kmin rolled out like a dutiful solider and went up the stairs to alert Powers of an inmate in the very last cell on the bottom tier in his cell that is very sick and needs medical attention. Powers grew frustrated at being disturbed from looking for something wrong and being an asshole. He looked over Mu'kmin and figured that it's probably one of his Muslim brothers, so he has no reason to doubt the validity of what is being relayed to him. The Iman is very humble and somewhat trustworthy. He never gave Paul any problems. Paul didn't know that the muslims' money is also suffering because of his bullshit. Mu'kmin is the Iman, it's true, but he is also a father, husband, and convict over Steel-side waiting to go to trial for conspiracy to commit murder. His family needs help, too!

CO Powers walked down the tier alongside Mu'kmin. Once they got to the cell, they saw an inmate balled up under the covers in a fetal position.

"What's wrong with you?!" Paul Powers asked the inmate. The inmate moaned but didn't respond. Paul moved closer to the inmate and inside of the cell. He yelled again, "What's wrong, I said?!" By this time Mu'kmin slid off without Powers detecting him.

Suddenly, Nasir's huge ass arms grabbed Powers into a head lock. Nasir carried him by the neck, choking. Paul grabbed and clawed at Nasir's massive arms to no avail. The huge man is just too powerful. Ochie acted! He sprang from underneath the covers with a black bandana tied over his face and a trash bag covering his clothes so that he won't get blood all over himself. He went to work with two twin six inch street blades that had sharp serrated edges. Ochie chopped Paul Powers up severely. He disregarded his gurgling and muffled cries. After being poked 27 times, Nasir let Powers go slumping to the floor. Ochie moved out quickly into the cell next to where Paul's limp body fell. He passed the blades to one of his comrades, who instantly disappeared. Ochie took the plastic bag off of himself, along with the bandana. He wrapped it all in a sheet and then passed that off as well. Ochie put his Inmate Advisory Council pass back around his neck and strolled away with a feeling of satisfaction and a smile.

The End!

Made in the USA
Columbia, SC
11 June 2024

36475142R00139